The Lady and the Dragon

Shayla Black

Writing as
Shelley Bradley

The Lady and the Dragon
Published by Shelley Bradley LLC
Copyright ©1999 Shelley Bradley LLC

Couple Image Copyright: Jenn LeBlanc/Illustrated Romance
see: http://jennleblanc.photoshelter.com/page2 (3.8)

Print ISBN 978-1-936596-32-4

Chapter One

1813

"What do you mean, blackmailing Manchester is out of the question? The old bastard doesn't have a *single* vice?" Drexell Cain demanded, fists clenched as he leaned across the warped surface of the pub's battered table.

Within the seedy inn's common room, raucous laughter exploded and drunken singing abounded. The smell of old liquor lingered. His friend, Gregory Bryce, Viscount Monroe, dressed in a fine coat of Devonshire brown, looked as out of place rubbing elbows with the dockside scum as the Prince Regent would.

Greg shook his head. "Not one sin, my friend."

"Damn!" Drex pounded a fist into the table. "I'd hoped he was following Melville's lead and using the Admiralty's money to speculate for his own profit."

"Why should he? Manchester is nearly as wealthy as the Admiralty's treasury."

"The old bugger can't be perfect," Drex insisted. "Isn't he sampling the goods in any bedroom but his own? What about gambling debts?" He raked a tense hand through his hair. "Did you check at White's and Watier's?"

"I've come as close to the man as I can without moving in like some spinster aunt. He doesn't indulge in tête-à-têtes or drink. He even runs with the tediously dull crowd at Boodle's."

"Sounds like a damned saint." Drex swore.

"Indeed, our Lord of the Admiralty appears the utmost in devoted family men. He is deeply involved in his granddaughter's life and attends services at Mayfair Chapel every Sunday."

"No man is without at least one weakness. He must have a flaw of some sort…" Drex pressed on, his voice urgent.

"I found nothing, nor did the detective we hired," Greg insisted. "Drex, you must try to free Ryan in other ways or you will get yourself killed. How do you know he is still alive? It's been four years. The conditions in the Royal Navy—"

"Are deplorable. I know." Drex grimaced. "But damn it, Ryan is my twin, my only family and *my* responsibility."

"He chose a life at sea."

"He didn't choose life in the Royal Navy," Drex bit out. "True, he wouldn't be at the whim of the Admiralty if he hadn't run off to seek adventure. I fully intend to make Ryan see that he has obligations, a wife and son who need him. I won't make excuses for him, but he deserves his freedom."

Greg sighed. "Very well. What other brilliant suggestions do you have? Blackmail is out of the question."

Drex swallowed a lump of anger and thumped his fingers against the table. "What about the signet ring I showed you? Were you able to find out who my scoundrel of a father is?"

Greg nodded, then paused. "The Earl of Ashmont."

"He sounds like a man of consequence, then." Even if he only used his position to impregnate his upstairs maid and cast her into the squalor of London's streets. But Ryan's plight insisted he ignore the fury and resentment pounding in Drex's veins. "Perhaps he can work with Manchester's office to—"

"Drex, he is not well. He's spent the last twenty years holed up in his country house in Devonshire and does not have the political connections needed. But I spoke with him—"

"He knows someone who can help?"

"Damnation, Drex, no. I am telling you that he has been searching for you and Ryan for fifteen years. He knew nothing about you until he received your mother's diary by post shortly before she died."

Drex spotted a man with a ragged beard on his mean face staring intently two tables down and lowered his voice. "You told him my name, my identity?"

"No, of course not. But the man wants you in his life."

Drex suppressed a surge of icy rage. "I've had no use for him in twenty-eight years. If he can't help me with Ryan's release, I have no use for him now."

"If that is truly your sentiment, the only other suggestion I have is diplomacy. Perhaps it will prove fruitful if you try again."

"Like hell." Drex gripped his mug of ale in white-knuckled fingers. "President Madison spares little concern for Ryan and the other Americans the Royal Navy has impressed. He's more intent on creating peace, even if it's false. Besides, the British Admiralty simply thinks they've reclaimed their own."

Greg winced. "Technically, Drex, you and Ryan are their own, being London born. The Admiralty doesn't care how long you've lived in America. To them, you're English citizens."

Drex took a sip of flat ale. "Another reason Madison's administration was reluctant to get involved."

"Indeed, but what other options do you have?" Greg leaned in, his voice dropping. "You haven't found Ryan by traipsing the seas in the guise of the Black Dragon, as you'd hoped."

Drex nodded gravely before adopting a rueful grin. "But more than a few of His Majesty's ships have met a watery grave. A sunken warship is one that can't impress more Americans."

Greg raised a pale brow. "With that outlook, it's no wonder you have a huge bounty on your head. God, for five thousand pounds, I might be tempted to turn you in myself." Greg laughed. "Then again, if you were caught and hung, Chantal would murder me for allowing that to happen."

With a hollow laugh overshadowed by drunken revelry, Drex scanned the crowded room absently, trying to erase the guilt that stung from his failure. He hadn't returned Ryan to his wife, Chantal, as he'd promised. Closing his eyes, Drex rubbed his aching forehead, mentally scrutinizing other solutions. Surrender was unthinkable, defeat unacceptable. He would find Ryan, *alive*, and force his brother to learn responsibility. Or he'd die trying.

Shaking the dismal thought away, he glanced across the poorly lit tavern. A burly hunk of a man slid his beefy arm around a serving wench. The slender girl swatted him and danced away. Watching the two, an outrageous idea jolted Drex.

He tossed it around, examining it from every angle. It was easy, almost flawless—and too good to pass up.

"What is his granddaughter's name?" he asked suddenly.

Greg swallowed from his cup, prolonging Drex's suspense. "Lady Christina Delafield."

"What do you know of her?" Drex prompted impatiently.

Greg grinned. "Manchester may control the Admiralty with an iron fist, but that hoyden has proven unruly since her nursery days. Impulsive through and through. Haughty as only a woman born to extreme privilege can be. A beauty, yes, but her grandparents, who have raised the chit, can scarcely control her. Why do you ask?"

Through the smoky air, Drex leaned closer, his voice dropping to a whisper. "Because if I can't hold a scandal over his head, I can hold his granddaughter hostage. When he releases my brother, I'll let the girl go."

"Have you gone mad?" Greg's brown eyes grew impossibly wide. "You cannot mean to add abduction to your crimes. You're wanted for espionage, thievery, illegal trade, and if they catch you, you can tack on treason, too. Perhaps it's time to quit."

"*Quit?* Not yet. This is my last chance to make the Admiralty meet my demands. All I have to do is exploit Manchester's weakness, his granddaughter." Sitting back, Drex sipped his ale. "After that, I'll gladly retire the Black Dragon and leave my criminal life."

"That is absurd!" Greg insisted, tossing his hands up in emphasis. "You cannot kidnap the girl."

Drex smiled, his grin deceptively pleasant. "Of course I can...with your help."

"Oh, no." Greg shook his head adamantly. "Absolutely not. You saved my life once, and though we've been friends for ten years, I am not willing to dig myself a grave for you. I've already arranged for you to meet an arms dealer and secured papers for you to dock here in London. Nor did I mind spying on Manchester, but I won't assist you in anything this devious. You'll ruin her for polite society and any sort of marriage."

"If I don't, and Ryan is still alive, he will die and Rory will grow up without a father, as Ryan and I did. I can't break my promise to Chantal." Dragging in a deep breath, Drex reached for his mug and offered, "Look, I'll make it easy for you. You know her, right?"

"Yes, through Manchester, of course. And were she to disappear, she could—"

"I'll make certain she can't point the finger at you," Drex assured. "Can you think of a social event where you plan to see her?"

"Manchester has decided to cut her season short, which can only mean she has done something beyond the pale, and will send her to a ladies' school in Switzerland."

"A ladies' school?"

Greg smiled. "I told you, she is quite a hellion. Circumspect is the last word anyone would use to describe her behavior."

Drex clenched his fists anxiously. "When does she leave?"

"Next week."

"Does Manchester have any upcoming social engagements she might attend?"

Greg paused. "Tomorrow night. His political crony, Lord Hartford, will host a ball. But—"

"Perfect. Tomorrow night it is."

"Drex, no. You will undoubtedly scare the poor girl. Lady Christina is high-spirited, I grant you, but far too sheltered for your—"

"I promise, I'll be gentle." Drex smiled mischievously.

Greg snorted in disbelief. "And I'm Henry the Eighth."

"I won't touch the girl."

"That is irrelevant. Everyone will believe you did."

"Lady Christina and whichever husband Manchester chooses for her will know the truth."

A long sigh signaled Greg's defeat. "I let you talk me into the most outrageous things." He turned and shouted, "Another ale!"

* * * *

The short, gruff man tossed a scowl over his shoulder. "When did ye say you made this appointment with the cap'n?"

"Several days ago," Christina answered, calling on the acting skills she'd last used two nights past when she made her bow on the London stage. Beneath her cloak, she adjusted the tight collar of her carriage dress and pulled on the bishop sleeves clutching her wrists.

"And it's personal, ye say?" the man prompted, frowning.

"Quite."

He shrugged. "Watch yer step," he advised from the dark bowels of the companionway. "It's hard to see these here footholds when the sun's goin' down."

Christina held in a sigh of frustration. Clearly, this man did not understand the urgency of her situation. In his defense, no one had ever threatened him with Swiss finishing school, where girls literally disappeared from polite society for years. She shuddered. He, a free-roaming sailor, had never been denied the opportunity to experience life. And she would not allow her grandparents to prevent her from experiencing hers. Aunt Mary awaited in the Bahamas and had offered to teach Christina all about her business.

The odd little man glanced over his shoulder. Anxiously, she gestured for him to go ahead. "Go on. I'm following."

He trudged on, mumbling incoherently.

She continued to trail the narrow-backed man down the cramped companionway, her nose wrinkling from the stench of the Thames that permeated the ship's damp wood.

As she'd paid a lad working the docks to discover, this ship was the only one leaving for Grand Bahama. She'd hidden since last night in a longboat beneath a greasy tarp slathered in animal fat and vowed to sail with this tub. Although Grandfather would probably never think to search for her among London's seedy docks aboard a merchant ship bound for the Bahamas, she knew better than to underestimate him by waiting for a more optimal means of escape.

Christina's shipboard guide halted at the end of a hallway, bringing her out of her reverie and back to the present. He knocked on the door before him.

"Who is it?" a deep voice, sharp with impatience, barked from behind the closed door.

His tone pierced Christina with a needle of doubt. Would he refuse her? Pulling the collar of her cloak up to cover cold ears, she lifted her chin. She couldn't let him turn her away. Her future depended on convincing the captain to accept her as a passenger. Otherwise, years of a cold Swiss castle's walls awaited. All because she'd spent a few trifling hours acting on a London stage!

"Cap'n, it's me, Hancock."

"I figured as much. What is it?"

"There's a woman here. Says she's got business with ye."

"If I'd wanted a woman's business, I would have had one last night."

Christina gasped. The man had intimated she was a—

"Not that type of woman, Cap'n." Hancock cleared his throat. "A *lady*."

"That variety of female I have no use for," he said in a hard-edged tone. "Get her ashore now. We sail within the hour."

His words plummeted to the bottom of her stomach, along with her heart. She had to persuade him, had to stay on board. If she failed, her grandfather would ensure she surrendered her freedom indefinitely and never saw Aunt Mary again.

Hancock nodded. "Aye, aye, Cap'n."

He faced her, his back pushed against the door, as if looking to add mettle to his spine. His puffy, wind-worn face clearly bore reluctance. "Ye heard the cap'n, miss."

Reining in her panic, Christina stole a glance at the warped wooden door. He didn't have time for her? Well, she'd insist that he make time.

A plan forming, Christina nodded tragically, eyes cast downward. "I understand."

Hancock frowned suspiciously.

Ignoring that, Christina stepped aside. "Please, lead the way. It's so dark, I shall certainly trip without your help."

Hancock shrugged, then took the lead. "Follow me."

She smiled before he turned to the ladder-like stairs.

Hancock stepped forward; Christina drew in a quick breath and whirled to face the captain's door, white-gloved fingers clutching her valise. She clasped the cold latch and lifted. The door opened with a quiet click. She dashed inside.

The captain's naked back, golden and muscle-hardened, filled her vision. She stifled a gasp at the snarling black and green dragon tattoo dominating one shoulder blade. Its open mouth breathed fire across the width of his back, to his other shoulder. The curling tail wound around a powerful biceps.

She couldn't move, could not tear her eyes away. *A tattoo?* Dear God, what kind of a barbarian would have that arrogant monster permanently embedded into his flesh?

One without the worries or scruples of a gentleman.

Uncertainty assailed her. This man was the antithesis of all she'd known, spawned from an opposite end of the Earth. She knew nothing about his less-than-civilized world. Would she survive long enough to see Aunt Mary in Grand Bahama? Trembling, she shoved the dismal thought aside and glanced about his cabin.

An exotic, Oriental aura dominated the space, which looked half the size of her dressing room. A burning taper filled the room with a pungent musk. Her shocked gaze fixed on the dramatic austerity of the black decor, relieved only by the pale wooden walls. An ebony and emerald silk coverlet on his bunk boasted the same scaled symbol of fire and power as his shoulder.

He reached for his shirt and pulled it on, concealing the intimidating dragon from her view. She swallowed in relief.

Feet planted apart, broad shoulders filling his black shirt, he tucked the cotton garment into skin-tight, biscuit-colored breeches. "I told you I didn't want to see you."

Startled by his acknowledgment, she stammered, "But I must speak with you. Please. Five minutes."

He whirled to face her. The sight rooted her in place.

A scrap of black silk stretched along the upper part of his square face, from brows to the bridge of his nose. She shivered. Only one type of man wore a mask: the dangerous kind.

The sight of his hard, bearded jaw arrested her next. A wall of power surged toward her as he stepped closer. Christina could not decide if she should attribute the feeling to the foreboding impression he made with black shirt, black mask, black beard, black eyes…or the displeasure thundering across the hard angles of his face. Then again, perhaps the sleek ebony length of his hair grazing his mammoth shoulders and the golden ring dangling from his left ear roused her unease. Either way, he was no one to trifle with; he'd made that abundantly clear without a word.

"W—why do you wear the…mask?" she stammered. "Oh, my… You hide your identity."

"Hmm. Perceptive." His low quip cut and didn't invite further conversation. But she could not give up and return home. Life in Switzerland was much more abhorrent. And cold.

Hancock burst through the door. "Cap'n, I'm sorry. The vixen tricked me." He turned to her, his look less than friendly. "Come on. The cap'n wants ye gone."

A crooked smile curved the captain's mouth as he waved the man away. Christina did not find his expression comforting.

"No need," he assured, his gaze shifting to regard her. "I'll handle her. Dismissed."

The little man glanced from her to the captain, then back again, smiling now. "Aye."

Hancock closed the door behind them, leaving them alone. In the ensuing silence of the small cabin, the captain scanned her with a thorough gaze.

She crossed protective arms across her chest and buried her apprehension. "I came to make you a proposition, Captain."

"A proposition?" His already suggestive tone dropped to a purr that set her instincts on full alarm. He leaned his hip indolently against the small cherry-wood desk bolted into the cabin's wooden floor. "Well, now you do have my attention."

Christina gasped. The cur actually had the nerve to smile! She trembled, and he grinned like a well-fed cat.

They stood on opposite ends of the minuscule cabin—three steps from each other. The captain pushed away from the desk; his stride ate up one of the precious steps separating them. With her back at the door, Christina had nowhere to retreat.

She struggled for her next breath. The scents of salt, incense and man filled her nose. She forced herself to hold his stare, even as a tingling awareness of the captain rose inside her.

"I am talking about a business proposal," she corrected. "And I will thank you to stop leering at me."

An infuriatingly insolent grin lifted the corners of his mouth. "Don't thank me; it won't happen."

He stepped closer. Closer still—only a breath away, a breath nearly shared. His gaze touched her face. The massive breadth of his chest rose a mere inch from hers. His presence swirled around her like a gust of hot wind. She found her gaze trapped deep in the intensity of his dark eyes.

"If you don't wish to be leered at, don't wander where you aren't welcome." His breath fanned across her cheek as he lifted a hand toward her.

Dear Lord, was he going to touch her? Christina's gaze ricocheted around the cabin, looking for somewhere to shift out of his path.

His hand neared her waist. Her breath caught in her chest. Closer, closer his outstretched fingers came…until he nudged her aside and opened the door.

"I expect you to be gone when I return," he said, then turned his back on her without another glance.

"Wait!" she demanded before he could leave. "What about my proposal?"

"I'm not interested."

"Please listen," she implored, clutching his sleeve. "You have not heard my idea."

He turned to her with a scowl. "I don't need to."

"Please, I'm desperate. Do you think I would have come here, suffered you calling me a light skirt and virtually risked my life to barge into your cabin if I was not?"

After a weighty pause, he replied, "Not unless you're a half-wit. Are you?"

Christina swallowed her anger and forced herself to meet his stare. "I will not leave until you listen."

His dark eyes behind the ebony mask gleamed as they scanned her up and down, heightening her anxiety—and awareness. She bit her lip in worry, wondering how to shift the conversation back to her purpose— hoping the warm, foreign vibration plaguing the pit of her stomach would cease.

"Perhaps we could do business…for the right price." A provocative note inched back into his voice. "What do you seek?"

His aim was to intimidate her, and blast the man, he'd hit his target. Her heart thudded; she felt hot and cold all over. Christina took a deep breath and forged ahead. "I require transport to Grand Bahama. My— my…husband is awaiting me there."

The man quirked a jet brow in speculation. "Husband? How long has it been since you last saw him?"

"T—two years."

The captain turned and stepped toward her, closing half of the much-too-close distance between them. His presence was looming, capable of more powerful impact on her beating heart than either his voice or his frightful, colorful tattoo.

He grasped her chin between firm fingers. She bit her lip, feeling shaky and hot as his gaze probed her face.

"You can't possibly have been married for ten minutes, much less two years. What is it you truly want?"

"I—I'm telling the truth."

"Princess, two years ago, you were still in the schoolroom. And if you're married, why are you uncomfortable with a man's eyes on your body? Why do you blush at the sight of a man without his shirt?"

She cursed his power of perception—and the guilty flush creeping up her cheeks. "You are *not* my husband. I am prepared to pay you two hundred pounds for transport to Grand Bahama. Why should you need to know my reasons for traveling?"

Instantly, his lazy manner disappeared. His hands encircled her arms, pulling her disconcertingly close to his muscled, half-covered chest. She released the valise. It hit the wooden floor with a deafening thud.

"Because I am the captain here, not a servant hired to do your bidding. I give the orders and I make the decisions." He released her, retreating to his desk. "The answer is no."

"But I offered you two hundred pounds!"

"It would not have mattered if you'd offered me two thousand," he growled. "This is not a passenger ship, I'm not a nursemaid, and I don't need you tempting my crew to mutiny."

"Tempting? I assure you I am no light skirt!"

A roguish smile tilted the sensual slant of his mouth and lit up his dark gaze. "That hardly makes you less tempting."

Christina gasped. "How dare you?"

He raised a wolfish brow. "Just like this…"

The captain whipped his arms around her and crushed her against the hard width of his chest. Standing frozen in shock, she felt his palms glide down the length of her spine in a commanding sweep and stop at the small of her waist. He pressed her closer, flush against his body. Christina was too shocked by his behavior—and the maelstrom of tingles screaming along the surface of her skin—to do more than gape.

Without pause, he claimed her lips by covering them with his own. He possessed them. His kiss was not like the tender, tentative brush of lips she'd received from an over-eager beau. No, this was much different. The bold exploration of his lips…and then, oh God, his tongue, exploded inside her, lashing her with a stunning blast of heat. He pulled her to return the kiss, tongue and all.

The man tasted of coffee and sin. His hands pressed her deeper into his body before he slanted his lips across hers again as if he had every right to. His soft beard rasped against her chin as he penetrated the seam of her lips with his tongue once more. A shocking liquid honey flowed through her veins. Knees weak, she melted against him, encircling her arms about him to touch the warm skin beneath his collar. He groaned in answer.

My God, what am I doing?

Kissing a masked criminal, came her answer before she wrenched from his embrace with a gasp and stepped away.

Heat crawled up her cheeks and shock slid through her system. He'd proved his point. She didn't belong on this ship, not with a man like him at the helm. Adventure often lured her into less than exemplary situations, but she hadn't planned on suicide.

Still, she could not risk waiting for another ship and a more civilized captain.

Angered by his presumption—and her own response—she hissed, "Take your bloody hands off me!"

"I'll touch you if I want. This isn't your kingdom, princess. You can't waltz in here and make demands. On this ship, I am master of everything...and everyone. Right now, that includes you."

Clearly, his bullying ways weren't any different from Grandfather's. Her determination rose another notch. "You will not ever maul me in that fashion again."

He met her stare with a chilly smile. "I can agree to that easily, since you won't be on this voyage."

The captain whirled about. "Hancock!" A moment later, the small crewman reappeared, and the captain said, "Have someone escort this *lady* off my ship and get your ass back here."

"But...but—" she blurted, realizing she'd ruined her chances of escape with her defiance. "Yours is the only ship leaving for the Bahamas this evening. I must be on it!"

"That's not my problem, princess."

"But you must understand—"

"No, I mustn't. Nor do I want to."

Hancock came toward her, awkwardly taking hold of her arm.

Desperation fired Christina as she tossed him an entreating glance. "Captain..."

Arms crossed, jaw tight, he looked away.

With chin lifted and hopes sinking, Christina grabbed her valise and exited. After scrambling up the ladder to the brig's deck, she eyed the silhouette of London's dingy, gray docks through the evening's golden mist, inhaled the putrid scent of the Thames in the heavy, humid air. Was Grandfather searching for her even now, ready to sweep her away to a remote Swiss hell?

Her gaze drifted down the passageway, in the direction of the ship's arrogant, handsome captain. Her choices were clear: Her grandfather's machinations for the rest of her life, or the captain and his insolence for a few weeks?

No choice, really.

Hancock called to a sallow youth named Randy, who raced to their side. The young man stared at her with pale blue-gray eyes in a malnourished face. Adolescent peach fuzz dusted his chin.

"Since this is yer first voyage with the cap'n, I'm going to start ye off easy."

Randy swallowed, his Adam's apple bobbing in his thin throat. "Yes, sir. Thank ye, sir."

"Take this lady ashore. We're castin' off soon."

"Aye, aye, sir."

Hancock nodded and turned away, fixing his attention on another sailor and his sloppy rigging.

"Well, miss... Ah, step this way." The boy pointed to the gangplank off the port side of the massive brig.

Studying his threadbare shirt, Christina said, "Randy; is that your name?"

"Yes, ma'am."

Poor thing. He looked terrified. "Do you have any family?"

He nodded. "A wife and a wee lad."

Her eyes widened, not completely with feigned shock. "And you're here at sea instead of with them on shore?"

Dropping his head, Randy shuffled his worn boots on the immaculate deck. "Times are tough. Got to take wot work I can."

"Well then, Randy, I have a job for you." Again, Christina studied him from his ill-cut hair to his faded breeches, and knew he would jump at her offer for much less money. With a satisfied sigh, she decided she would consider her upcoming offer a donation to the needy. "How would you like to make two hundred pounds?"

* * * *

Half an hour later, Drex stood on deck, watching the sun and its golden brilliance descend below the horizon.

Her hair had been that color, he decided before banishing the thought. She was... He didn't know exactly who she was, but he knew what she was: Trouble. Anyone could see that. He'd done well to send her packing.

So why were thoughts of her lingering about him like a sultry perfume?

She'd been desperate. Completely. He had recognized his own emotion in her exotic green eyes. Had his circumstances been different... But they weren't. How could he possibly cart the hoyden to Grand Bahama while holding Manchester's granddaughter captive and running a shipment of Brown Bess rifles for the American Army? Impossible.

Kissing her had been a big mistake. He'd meant only to intimidate her, but the moment he'd begun devouring her mouth, their contact had exploded into a hell of a kiss. Drex had not expected to enjoy it. He had. Too much.

"There you arc!"

Whirling at the shout, Drex found Gregory crawling up the ladder to deck, then running toward him.

"What are you doing here?" he asked in disbelief. "You're supposed to be leading Lady Christina into our trap."

"Drex," Greg panted. "Must...leave. Go."

"We will be casting off as soon as Lattimer arrives with the girl. What—"

"Lady Christina...gone."

"Gone? Where? How?" He studied Greg's flushed face for answers. "What the hell is going on?"

"Not the problem. Manchester."

"What?" Drex snapped. "You're not making sense."

Greg gulped air, then said, "To coin a phrase, the British are coming. This time"—he paused for breath—"to arrest you."

Chapter Two

A cold flash of fear washed through Drex as Greg's words sank in. "Arrest me?" He raked a hand though his too-long hair. "How? I've been so careful."

"A bloody anonymous note. Less than an hour ago," Greg panted. "I was with Manchester when a messenger delivered it. He hasn't had much time to prepare."

Another chill coursed through Drex. He lifted his fingers to his mask. "And my identity? Does he know that, too?"

Greg shook his head. "The note didn't disclose your name, thank God. But you cannot breathe easy yet. Your escapades on the high seas are practically legend." Greg scoured the dock with a worried gaze. "You're an embarrassment the Admiralty wants eliminated. Make no mistake, Manchester will go to any lengths to see you hang."

"Damn it!" Drex scanned the docks of the East India Company, panic gnawing at his gut. "I've got to get out of the harbor. Manchester can trap me too easily here."

Greg held out his hand. Drex shook it, then pulled his friend into a brotherly hug.

"Godspeed, and be careful." Face tense, Greg stepped away.

Drex clasped his friend's shoulder in reassurance. "Thank you for everything. I'll be in touch."

After a nod, Greg sprinted down the gangplank. Drex watched him go with a curse. All his plans were ruined now. The Admiralty knew of his presence and Lady Christina had disappeared. What else could go wrong?

Drex turned and shouted, "All hands! Up anchor, ahoy!"

Men of all sizes and ages sprang to his bidding in seconds. Some turned the heavy capstan, raising the anchor. Others climbed rigging and unfurled the headsails against the breeze. A few trimmed the remainder of the sails, while more experienced hands swung the foreyards about to their sailing positions.

"Hurry!" he whispered to the stationary ship seconds later. "Move your wooden ass out of here."

Finally, the vessel succumbed to the pressure of the breeze and the bow tipped into the water. *The Dragon's Lair* was away.

The frigate gained by mere feet, at a pace even a snail would be ashamed of. The mouth of the East India harbor yawned before him, the far-reaching chasm wide open. Beyond that lay the Thames and freedom. But other vessels, schooners, barks, brigantines floated in the still water, scattered around him. Few flew an identifying flag. Drex prayed none were the Royal Navy, lying in wait to surround him and his crew.

He glanced up at the gray, cloudless sky. Where had this morning's stiff breeze disappeared to?

Minutes ticked away; *The Dragon's Lair* crawled through the water. Drex paced the deck, observing the still around him with trepidation. Where were the boys in blue hiding?

From the aft crow's nest, his crewman Davie boomed, "Look, Captain! Behind us. Limeys!"

Drex whirled to find a sea of blue-jacketed sailors marching double-time past a warehouse—and up the docks toward him. From his spyglass, Drex saw their stern captain in a stiff-backed stride leading soldiers who carried Brown Bess rifles, exactly like those in his hold. Drex knew what the lethal weapons could do in the hands of men trained to use them.

His friend and first mate, Hancock, stood beside him on the quarterdeck. "What'll we do, Cap'n? Shoot 'em?"

Drex paused, watching the Navy men swarm aboard dinghy after dinghy, then push from the dock. They rowed in unison, each dip of their oars bringing them toward *The Dragon's Lair*.

"Not yet." He shouted to the crew, "Ready your rifles, but hold your fire. Load the cannons and listen for my call. Start a starboard tack into that breeze and keep at it!"

"Aye," the men shouted as one.

"We'll outrun those limey bastards," cried another.

Hancock turned away. The British continued their advance.

Sweat broke out across Drex's back as he stood stock still, fists clenched, while *The Dragon's Lair* inched across the water in a right-facing glide. Off the larboard side, the British sailors rowed toward him, each strong arm in synchronicity.

He could see the fear in one sailor's wide eyes, the awe in another's gaping mouth, as they confronted a notorious adversary.

None of those faces belonged to Ryan.

On the Navy captain's square countenance, Drex read confidence in his smile of anticipation. The man sensed victory, and, as the half dozen small boats pitched and glided closer, Drex feared the captain's instincts were correct.

The first dinghy bumped the frigate's side. Then another. Uniformed men from each small boat reached for a rope and hook. Once thrown, the sailors would board *The Dragon's Lair* and fight. If victorious, they would capture every man aboard. Drex had no illusion about their punishment; he and all his crew would die. His heart banged against his chest when he thought of the grisly manner in which the British killed men they considered traitors.

He shouted to his crew, "Take aim at any man in a blue coat."

The rag-tag bunch of men rushed to the rail, rifles poised for battle. Drex hesitated, then raised his own rifle. "Fire!"

The kick of the weapon set him back a step while explosion after explosion rent the air. A British sailor fell back into the boat, clutching his arm. Another, with a ball though his head, fell into the water with a final splash. Drex swore.

The Navy captain, chest heaving, screamed orders at his men, who scrambled for their weapons. Drex noted with grim satisfaction the efficiency with which his own crew reloaded.

Hearing the clink of a metal hook against the rail above the bow, Drex spun. As a sailor swung over the side, he raised his weapon and pointed it at the intruder. When the man hopped on deck, the barrel of Drex's rifle greeted him.

Another volley of explosions sounded. The scents of gunpowder and blood mixed with salt in the pungent sea air.

"Do you want to die?" Drex asked the young sailor.

The man swallowed. "N—no, sir."

A blessed gust of wind seized the air, filling the *Lair's* sails. The frigate surged forward. Drex saw the Navy's dinghies struggle against the gale. Relief slid through him.

The wind showered Drex with cold sea spray. "Dive over the side and tell them I pushed you."

The wide-eyed boy hesitated an instant before leaping over the railing and into the harbor.

Drex lowered his gun with a sigh and kicked the hook into the water. He was getting too damn sentimental for life at sea.

The wind kicked up again in a reassuring gust. Drex whooped in triumph as relief slid through him like hot syrup. By damn, they were going to outrun the British.

"Cap'n!"

Fighting the gust carrying the *Lair* even farther from the Navy boys, Drex whirled to find Hancock striding his way. His friend wore a giant grin. "We made it! And only three men hurt. Don't worry none; ain't more than scratches."

Eyeing the British dinghies, now looking much smaller as his frigate coasted forward, he asked, "How many of theirs dead? Two?"

"Four, I think."

Drex grunted, his lips pursed with regret. "Another offense Manchester will hang me for if he catches me."

Hancock nodded silently.

With a wave and a "Carry on," Drex strode to the quarterdeck to take the helm and scan the horizon for more surprises. As if this day hadn't hurled enough surprises at him already.

Damn! Who could have written Manchester an anonymous note? No one else but Greg knew of his recent activities in London. Had he been followed? Perhaps, but why an anonymous note? Did he have a traitor in his midst?

Drex shook his head tiredly. This facade of the Black Dragon was becoming increasingly complicated. It had started simply; he chased and boarded British warships by catching them off-guard at night. After searching the crew and not finding Ryan, he set the men in dinghies with food and fresh water, then burned the ship. Tidy and effective, with no loss of life.

The Crown had put forth a bounty for him, dead or alive, for his slow assault on their fighting force. Slowly but surely, every heinous act committed on the seas thereafter was attributed to his name. The bounty had doubled in four months.

The gun running was an added complication he didn't need. But Ryan's wife and son were Drex's responsibility to feed, clothe and house. He'd taken a loan in order to buy the *Lair*, and after that, funds had run low. Louisiana's Governor Clayborne had mentioned the American Army paid top dollar for new weapons to aid the war effort. Drex hadn't had much choice.

And now, if he made it back into London safely, he'd have to search for the mysteriously missing Lady Christina. He sighed.

The Dragon's Lair approached the mouth of the harbor, revealing mercifully light traffic on the malodorous Thames. God, he'd love to put London and his bad memories of the city behind. But the Royal Navy had Ryan imprisoned out there...somewhere.

And Lady Christina Delafield, wherever she was, held the key to Ryan's freedom.

* * * *

Fighting a cry of despair, Christina hugged herself tightly and drew her legs beneath her. She stared at red-eyed rodents through the black shadows of the ship's hold. The little beasts *eeked* in warning as they scurried toward her biscuits.

She hated rats, almost as much as she hated the dark. They had been constant, clawing fears in the countless hours since stowing aboard this rocking tub of a ship.

As if facing her two worst terrors hadn't been enough, gunfire had started, accompanied by a chorus of screams. She feared she'd been doomed to drown before leaving London's shore.

Something with spindly feet darted across her fingers. She smothered a shriek with her hand. The scents of dust and rotting wood exacerbated the feel of grit and salt coating her skin. Sleep had been impossible with a splintered, unforgiving plank against her back. Exhaustion seeped into her.

Yet the frights and discomforts seemed no more horrible than the captain's displeasure once he discovered her on board. His demand that she leave had been clear; he was articulate like Grandfather. And just like her elder, she didn't imagine the captain would be delighted she had disobeyed him.

21

Just how angry would he be? Enough to make her walk the plank? Or maybe he'd choose a good whipping with a cat-o'-nine-tails. She shuddered. Perhaps stowing on board hadn't been the most brilliant idea after all.

Christina stood. Whatever punishment he chose, she would endure. Aunt Mary had always preached that the truly independent woman found strength in handling life's unpleasantries. She would simply have to slot the captain into the category of perturbing, in more ways than one.

What if he subjected her to another wicked kiss?

She shoved the rebellious thought from her mind and fought the rise of sensation that possibility evoked. Perhaps she had only imagined the experience pleasant because she'd been overwrought. Over the course of the voyage, surely she would come to find the masked captain no more entrancing than the latest opera.

The thought gave her strength as she scrambled up the rope ladder toward the hatch. As she reached the top, a sliver of muted light leaked through the cracks, indicating afternoon had faded to twilight. Taking a deep breath, she shoved the door open, elated to be free of darkness and rodents. Yet she prayed neither death nor ravishment awaited her at the captain's hands.

Fresh air filled her lungs as she drew in a salty breath. Milky stars winked above in a sterling-shaded dance. The cool evening breeze brushed her cheeks, filtering her limp hair. She felt somehow better prepared to face her fate. Now, if she could just find the captain before anyone else found her…

"Holy cripes!" a young man yelled. "Cap'n, it's a woman!"

Whirling to the sound, an anxious jolt shot clear to her stomach. So much for finding the captain first. She held her breath. What now? Smile and try to justify her reason for stowing away? Or simply lie?

Trying to maintain an appearance of calm, she stepped from the hatch and closed it behind her. "Hello."

The tow-headed man swallowed, a nervous twitch plaguing his wide, pale eyes as he stared for an agonizing moment.

Christina stepped closer. "I'm sorry if I frightened you."

He retreated a stumbling step, his eyes riveted to her as if she were a ghost. "Cap'n!"

A moment later, Christina heard heavy footsteps behind her. Slow footsteps. Methodical. Reminiscent of controlled anger.

The captain.

Shoulders stiff, chin lifted, she turned to face him slowly. The sight of his massive chest, half-covered by a flowing white shirt, filled her vision. A wide expanse of golden muscle bisected the front of the shirt as it blew in the breeze. Her gaze made a surreptitious journey over wide shoulders and a strong, bronzed neck. She tried hard to bypass his lips, but her eyes had other ideas. For a moment, she succumbed to a foolish urge to study the mouth that had dominated hers so thoroughly.

Realizing the turn of her thoughts, she thrust her gaze up to his. A mistake. His black eyes, surrounded by that mysterious, silky mask, gleamed with displeasure. Her nausea returned in an inundating rush.

Christina shifted her gaze to more comfortable surroundings and discovered a crowd of motley sailors scattered about. From young to old, their expressions ranged from suspicion to awe.

"Get back to your posts, men," the captain directed, his stare never wavering from her face.

With nary a glance or raised syllable, the men scrambled to do his bidding. Images of her grandfather and the power he wielded over his own entourage detonated warnings within.

"I ordered you taken ashore." The captain's voice was calm but menacing.

Christina stood tall, straightening her spine, praying for courage. "I...stayed."

"Clearly. Your presence here explains my young crewman's disappearance, I suppose. You paid him for his perfidy?"

Again, his tone was placid, but Christina detected a calm before the storm. "The two hundred pounds you refused. I apologize, but I'm desperate—"

"I gathered that the first time." He stepped closer. His size alone intimidated her, but she would not retreat. "I also recall informing you that this isn't a passenger ship."

She resisted the urge to flinch as his voice rose. "You simply must understand..."

Mercy, what was she going to tell him? *Hello, I'm Christina Delafield. My grandfather is the Duke of Manchester. Though he probably has a reward out for my return as large as a king's ransom, would you take me to Grand Bahama instead?* Yes, that would motivate him to rescue her from Swiss finishing school and see her safely to Aunt Mary.

"Understand what?" he demanded. "You've already pleaded a deprived husband. What next, a dying mother?"

Sarcasm edged his tone, multiplying her anxiety. She needed to concoct a story—fast.

"Actually, yes," she blurted, stalling for time by searching her reticule for a handkerchief. Certainly now she couldn't tell him her mother had been in the grave for ten years.

With a glare, the captain unknotted the knotted kerchief tied about his biceps and thrust it at her. "Go on."

After a moment's hesitation disguised as a delicate sniffle, she answered, "My mother is dying of a weakening sickness. The physician says she has less than three months."

"Then why aren't you with her instead of plaguing me?"

Why, indeed? "Well, Mama's last wish is to see her sister, my Aunt Mary, again. So I promised my mother I would fetch her."

He shot her a skeptical glance. "And what does the rest of your family think of this journey? I doubt they approved of you, a young, unmarried woman, traveling alone."

She cast her gaze down, hoping to look forlorn instead of frantic. "The only other member of my family is my younger sister, Helen. She stayed home to care for my mother." A sister named Helen? Her imagination was indeed fertile today.

"Where is your father?"

"Poor Papa. He was such a happy little merchant," she lied as fast as her tongue would speak the words. "He died of the same weakening sickness Mama has."

He cocked a considering brow. "And I'm to understand your Aunt Mary lives in Grand Bahama?"

Christina smiled in a way she hoped the captain found grateful. "Exactly."

"If you're on such a saintly errand of mercy, why didn't you tell me that to begin with, instead of inventing a husband?"

"Well…" Christina hesitated, her mind frighteningly blank.

Well what? The captain's suspicious stare told her he was already skeptical of her latest tale. The crew hovered nearby, pretending involvement in their chores.

"You thought you'd be safer from lascivious attentions if the crew and I believed you were married?"

The excuse seemed so believable that she overlooked his mocking tone. "You are clever to have figured me out so easily."

The captain stepped closer still, until only a whisper of wind passed between their bodies. Christina was cognizant of a tingling pull, the oddest urge to touch the vital, solid breadth of him. The intermingled zip of fear somehow added to her excitement.

Blast it all, she was fighting for her freedom, her life! She did not want to grovel for it, especially in front of dozens of prying eyes, especially to *him*. In a couple of weeks, she would be a scrap of a memory to him. For her, he would bridge the way from a life controlled by Grandfather to the shore of independence and women's rights.

"Your reason for stowing away makes no difference. Either way, you've made a big mistake."

He looked so sure of himself that Christina felt a surge of apprehension. "Have I?"

For a long moment, he studied her, a furrow creasing his dark brow. Christina's anxiety multiplied.

"Do you know the name of the ship you're on?" he finally asked.

"No, I chose the first one bound for the Bahamas." At the time, it had hardly mattered which.

His deprecating laugh sounded between them, further rousing her unease. "Welcome, princess, to *The Dragon's Lair*."

In an instant, his stowaway lost all color in her beautiful countenance. Clearly, she'd heard of his exploits. And while Drex was glad he'd finally penetrated her bravado, he needed no great genius to see she was terrified.

After a series of rapid blinks, she swallowed hard. "Does that mean... Are you...?"

He flashed her a shark's smile. "The Black Dragon."

"Oh, dear God."

If possible, she paled another shade. Part of him was angry as hell she'd defied him, since her presence didn't fit well with his plans. He had to punish her, he thought with a disgusted sigh. Order and equality had to be maintained with the crew. He couldn't afford to tolerate stowaways. But he saw no purpose in frightening her further, especially if she had told the truth about fulfilling her mother's last wish, something he had not had the opportunity to do, to his deep regret.

"What is your name?" he asked.

Mutely, she retreated two unsteady steps, then a third. Frowning, Drex pursued. Damn it, was she going to faint?

When her back hit the mainmast, she gasped, jumping with fright. Drex reached out to steady her. The minx whirled about and scrambled away until he grabbed her arm.

As he turned her to face him again, her rigid body trembled. On her pale face, he read a struggle for courage as she lifted her chin and asked, "What are you going to do to me?"

Drex suppressed a laugh. Whatever lies she'd heard about him must have been greatly exaggerated. "At the moment, ask your name again."

"My—my name?"

He raised a challenging brow. "I assume your mother named you before her illness."

She pulled on her arm discreetly. He let her go without a word. She paused, then choked, "Lillianne. Are you going to throw me overboard?"

"Can you swim from here to Grand Bahama?"

Around her, some of his men chuckled. She cast desperate glances in their direction. "I cannot swim at all."

"Then we'll have to think of something else."

She stepped back. "Oh God, you're going to whip me."

He shook his head. "That's really my least favorite method of punishment. Too messy."

"That only leaves…" Lifting her chin another degree, she met his gaze directly. "Please, if you're going to ravish me, don't do it in front of the other men."

Another chorus of guffaws sounded from his crew. Drex stifled a groan. "Hancock!"

Within moments, his diminutive first mate appeared. "Take our…guest to my quarters." He addressed her again with a brief glance. "I'll be below shortly."

* * * *

Christina hovered in a corner of the captain's cabin, recalling the last time she'd been here. The dragons—sewn on his bunk, tattooed on his back—now made sense. What a terrible tangle! From the unpleasant prospect of a Swiss prison to the savage master of the seas, the Black Dragon. If her situation deteriorated any further, she'd soon be meeting the Grim Reaper.

Mercy, she was exhausted. She had slept mere minutes both of the nights she'd spent below. She glanced again at the captain's precisely made bunk. It looked inviting, as if she could rest on that soft surface in sweet slumber for hours.

But the captain was coming for her, probably sooner than later, and she needed her wits about her to stay alive and out of his bed. She only thanked God she'd had the presence of mind not to blurt out her real name when he told her his identity as her grandfather's number one nemesis. Now she'd have to remember to answer to her middle name for the rest of the voyage.

The short man, Hancock, entered and tossed her a blanket, along with a suspicious scowl. "Are ye hungry or thirsty?"

Christina grabbed the soft, woolen cover and wrapped it about her. "Both, and I require a change of clean clothing. My valise is below, in the hold."

"I'll find ye something for your stomach. You can fetch yer clothes later." A smirk shaped his mouth. "After the cap'n is finished with ye."

On that ominous note, Hancock exited, shutting—then locking—the door behind him. Dread plunged her stomach somewhere between her feet. She was trapped here, at the mercy of a vicious privateer who ate small women like her for snacks. And soon, he would descend to his cabin, ravish her and do God knew what else.

Her voyage to the Grand Bahamas seemed doomed to be less adventuresome, and more hellish, than she'd ever imagined.

She fought surging panic at the thought that the dark, dangerous stranger would ruin her, of the pain his defilement would bring. Or would ruination at his hands be as enjoyable as their kiss?

No. Notorious privateers weren't noted for their gentle natures, and she wouldn't play whore to one. Why, she'd heard Grandfather say the Black Dragon had once executed an entire boatload of nuns, after ravishing them, of course. Not the kind of lover she'd imagined having someday. But if Grandfather's tale was true, why hadn't the captain harmed her yet?

She shrugged the question away. Whatever the outlaw had in store for her, she would face with strength and dignity. She would persevere—especially if she had a weapon.

Upon cursory inspection of his small cabin, she found nothing but charts, nautical books and a compass. Not a single personal effect lay visible, and somehow that failed to surprise her. The captain could not be described as a personable man.

The key jangled in the lock. Christina whirled to the sound and watched with frozen horror as the door opened. The Black Dragon dominated the portal an instant later, assessing her with a long, expressionless stare behind that imposing black mask.

With a whispered oath, he turned away to his desk and removed the thong restraining the inky length of his hair. As it fell around his shoulders, Christina peered closer, studying his stiff, bearded profile as he paused and placed wide palms on the desk. He closed his eyes, bowed his head and heaved a wide sigh.

"You shouldn't be here," he said. "You should be in London with your mother and sister, or wherever you truly belong."

She squared her shoulders in defense. "I had to leave. If you believe anything, believe that."

He speared her with a glance. "I have trouble doing so, knowing you lied to me."

Christina said nothing.

With a disgruntled nod, he swung his gaze to her. "Stowing away isn't without consequence."

She swallowed in apprehension. "Can we discuss what—"

"No." His single syllable cut her short. "I make the rules and mete out the punishments."

Autocratic and implacable, just like her grandfather. And although her elder was more given to fits of shouting, Christina found the Black Dragon's hushed threats more powerful.

He raised his brown fingers to the top button of his shirt. Her gaze riveted on the captain in terrified fascination, she watched as he unfastened that and the other three below it, one by one, baring a wide expanse of satin bronze muscle.

Christina backed away until her back collided with a wall. "Dear God, your plan *is* to ravish me."

The captain cast her a sidelong glance, brow arched above his mask. "Ravish?" He mulled over the word, then added, "No. I have no intention of touching you."

Surprise lashed her. "You don't?"

His deep stare lasted an endless moment. "I learned my mistake the first time."

Even though she sensed an insult somewhere in his comment, Christina let out a sigh of relief as the captain doffed his vest. "I—I'm pleased to hear that."

The captain peeled his shirt up his torso, exposing the sculpted width of his chest. Christina couldn't stop the hungry slide of her gaze as he revealed his golden body. He slid the garment down the hard ridges of his arms, and images of clinging arms and impassioned kisses arose in her mind. She shifted uncomfortably.

"I don't suppose you enjoyed your two days in the hold?"

Ripping her gaze from his bare torso, she shivered at the memory of the rodents and the thick darkness. "Heavens, no. Terrible place!"

He crossed the room and opened the door. "Hancock!"

Within moments, the small man appeared, his mouth twitching with amusement. "Aye, Cap'n?"

"See that Lillianne has all the blankets, food and water she needs."

"Aye, Cap'n."

"And see that they're put down in the hold she emerged from. She's going to spend more time down there."

The moment he shut the door, Christina whirled on him. "What? You cannot mean that!"

"I do," he assured before he looked away.

The thought of being trapped in that perdition again sent Christina into a panic. "I beg of you, do not make me spend another night with your rats. Please."

Hands braced on his hips, he shot her a questioning stare. "Are you saying you would rather spend the night with me?"

She stole a quick glance at his bed, easily wide enough for one...but a cozy squeeze for two. "Neither idea appeals."

"So it makes no difference whether you bed down in the hold or my bunk with me?"

Christina glared at him. "You said you weren't going to touch me."

In two steps, he closed the distance between them and grabbed her arms. "I said I didn't *intend* to touch you. I'm not making any promises."

Christina glimpsed heat beneath the thunder and dark control in his silk-surrounded eyes. Did he, deep down, want her?

A shiver of thrill feathered down her spine, intensified by the sight of his fierce, muscled shoulders. The feeling made no sense, she knew. Yet she had the premonition that his touch might be one of the most exciting experiences of her life.

No. These runaway thoughts had to stop. The captain wasn't

exciting. He was boorish and rude and destined to make this journey miserable and painful.

But if that were true, why didn't he simply beat or rape her? She was at his mercy, his stowaway to punish as he pleased. If ravishing or hurting her would please him, why didn't he simply be done with it?

Whispering an oath that would have made her grandmother faint, he pulled away from her. He jerked the door open and yelled, "Now, Hancock!"

The first mate's uneven footsteps alerted Christina to his presence moments before he appeared in the doorway. The man took her arm in his blunt, brown fingers.

Christina dragged her feet, looking back at the captain, whose dark, unfathomable gaze clung to her.

"We'll talk about the rules governing the rest of this voyage when you come up again."

"Do not do this!" she shouted from the door. "If you have any mercy—"

"Mercy is a luxury I cannot afford."

He turned away and reached for a clean shirt, his movements slow, almost somber. Then he addressed Hancock. "Take her down. Bring her back to me at sundown on Thursday."

* * * *

Journal,

The old earl has lost his mind. Viscount Monroe showed him a signet ring and explained to Ashmont he has not one son but two. It does not bear thinking, the ruination of all my carefully laid plans! To validate the tale, I had my footman follow the viscount. He next met with none other than the Black Dragon, and in a seedy tavern! My man overheard much of their conversation. Wouldn't Ashmont be a proud papa if he knew his long-lost son was a notorious criminal? Maybe then he would be less eager to name the boy his heir.

I took action, just in case the Black Dragon is actually Ashmont's son, as Monroe claims. I tried to eliminate him and do my country a great service at once. Damn the Admiralty for botching the privateer's capture. That scourge of the seas has fled to God knows where. But if he stands in my way, I will find and destroy him.

* * * *

The wind blew like a cool sheet across his bearded cheeks as Drex stood on deck, hands clasped behind his back, and stared at the late-afternoon sun. Thursday afternoon, to be exact. He tapped his foot impatiently on the wooden deck beneath him.

Damn it, he should be angry. The girl had barged onto his ship and refused to take no for an answer. Then when he'd ordered her removed, did she leave? No, she *paid* a member of his own crew to disregard his authority and abandon ship. Two days in the hold she hated seemed a fitting punishment.

But he wasn't angry as much as he was worried. The terror on her face at the mention of the hold was too acute to miss. And her soft hands and well-made clothing told him eloquently that Lillianne wasn't accustomed to rodents and dark corners. Her desperate pleas reverberated in his head, warring with the knowledge that if he didn't punish her, trouble with Talbot or any of the others could be just around the corner.

Adding to his foul mood was the fact he'd had to threaten twenty lashes to the first man who laid a finger on her dewy alabaster skin, worsening morale.

Hell, he'd known from the first moment he'd seen Lilli, all anxious green eyes and sunshiny, wind-tousled hair, that she could only be trouble. More trouble he didn't need. And when she emerged from that hold, he had to make damn sure she didn't interfere—or distract him with her saucy allure again.

Ryan's rescue was too important to succumb to this perturbing case of lust now.

Drex heard shuffled footsteps behind him, heralding Hancock's arrival. "It's almost sundown, Cap'n."

He replied with a solemn nod.

"What are ye gonna do with her, friend? Put her off?"

A long pause ensued before Drex said, "I can't risk stopping anytime soon with the British at my back. Besides, to save Ryan, I have to sail to Grand Bahama, re-rig the ship, contact Greg for new false docking papers, then sail back to London. I won't waste precious time docking at another port."

Once back in London, he had to execute his plan, whatever that might be, to find and abduct Christina Delafield without a flaw, then

31

negotiate her ransom. Drex didn't delude himself, the process would take months, a period during which anything could go wrong—and Ryan could die.

"The men are restless with her on board. Don't think they can rightly decide whether to give in to lust or superstition."

"I suspected as much." He sighed, wondering just what he would do with his beautiful nuisance of a stowaway. "Put her in your cabin for the rest of the voyage, Hancock, and move to the infirmary. I'll watch her closely to keep her out of trouble."

"I've no doubt ye'll do just that." Hancock laughed. "Ye've been staring at the door to that hold all day."

He turned to his friend with a frown. "Have I?"

Hancock nodded. "And fidgeting, too. I've known ye for ten years, and I've never seen a woman distract ye so much."

Drex cast a warning glance at the other man. "Go to hell."

"Aye, Cap'n." But the laughter didn't leave his voice.

Turning away, Drex focused on the setting sun again. Another twenty minutes, then he could confront the girl, establish his absolute authority. He sighed. Be sure she was all right.

Then what would he do with her?

That question had plagued Drex for two days, during which he'd tried to put her—and their kiss—out of his mind. But his mind had been rebellious, filling instead with images of damp, naked skin and hungry sighs as her flesh filled his hands…while his cock filled her body. Worse, for her safety and the even keel of his crew, he'd have to declare Lilli his. His to kiss, to undress, to touch at will. His to take whenever and however he wanted. A disturbingly heady thought.

She was a pretty piece, damn it, with a graceful slope to her neck and a ripe curve to her breast. When sailors had invented the lore of mermaids and muses, they'd had a woman like Lillianne in mind. Drex wasn't immune.

"I've moved my belongings below." Hancock's voice sounded from behind him minutes later. "Want me to bring her to ye now?"

Staring at the sun, Drex shook his head. "It's not time yet. I suspect Talbot is looking for any partiality to use against me. Until we can put him ashore in Grand Bahama, I don't want to give the man any reason to grumble to those who are still angry we cut their leave in London short." He paused, irritated and edgy. "I have to be exact with her punishment."

"Aye. Maybe it would be best if ye waited. I can fetch her in ten minutes, when the sun's fully down."

Drex glanced again at the deepening pink and orange shadows of the sky transforming the puffy clouds to molten. Impatience cut into him like an arctic wind. He restrained it. "I'll be below. Bring her to me then."

Chapter Three

Taking a deep breath, Christina struggled to put one foot in front of the other as she descended the stairs into the companionway. She barely noticed Hancock behind her. Giving the Black Dragon a tongue-lashing was uppermost in her mind. She didn't care if the captain threw her overboard for it. After four sleepless nights, she already felt half-dead.

When they reached the final door, Hancock stepped around her. Through heavy, scratchy eyes, Christina watched him knock.

"Come in."

The Black Dragon's curt reply navigated a chill down her spine. He was a criminal who behaved like a dictator, the latter of which he had in common with her grandfather. It both annoyed and unnerved her that she'd escaped one autocrat only to fall into the hands of another.

Just a few more weeks, she vowed as Hancock opened the captain's door and prodded her forward. Then she would be with Aunt Mary, enjoying the independence of a modern woman.

Christina swayed tiredly before shuffling toward the captain, who sat on the edge of his bunk. The weary fog of her mind deciphered his fathomless expression, a furrow between his dark brows, made more forbidding by that dratted black mask.

"That will be all, Hancock. Show yourself out."

As if from a distance, Christina heard the click of the door that signaled the first mate's departure. The Black Dragon's gaze zeroed in on her, and she almost wished she could have followed the older man.

Almost. She still had a few words for the captain.

"I hope over the last two days you've had time to decide to be reasonable," he said without preamble.

Reasonable? She stood here, exhausted and paradoxically thrumming with an anger consuming enough to keep her upright, and he assumed she was willing to be reasonable? It was just like a tyrant to assume everyone else would agree to his demands.

Fury gave her a needed burst of strength. "Captain, I realize I stowed away on your ship. However, I am not a child and do not require your direction."

"Only children are oblivious enough to barge in where they are not welcome. What does that make you, then?"

"A desperate woman on a mission. Can you not understand that?" She flung her arms wide. "Your mission is to destroy the Royal Navy. My mission is simply more…noble." Even with her lie, that was true. Escaping a tyrant to seek freedom was far more righteous than destroying a fighting force, regardless of the losses of life and limb inflicted.

He bolted from his bunk and grabbed her arms. "You have no idea what I'm about. You were foolish enough to sneak onto a ship with men who make war. This is dangerous business, not an afternoon of tea in the parlor. Most of these men haven't seen a woman in months, much less a specimen like you, princess. Before you flounced on board, did you consider that there could be consequences to stowing away with a hundred randy men?"

She hadn't, not in those terms, but why confess that? "I put my purpose above my safety."

He turned away with a disgusted grunt. "Clearly. You're an even bigger fool than I thought."

"I do not appreciate your implication."

"I don't appreciate your reckless intrusion. I have a ship with a restless crew and business to attend to. Your uninvited presence here puts both in jeopardy."

Swaying slightly with fatigue, she steadied herself and shot him a narrow-eyed glare. "And locking me in the dark with rats helps you to keep control?"

He ground his teeth together. "No more pranks. Follow a few simple rules. That way, we all have a good voyage, and you reach your aunt in one piece."

His words made sense, and his request didn't sound too difficult. It didn't sound very exciting, either. Then again, her stint on a pirate ship had not been nearly as thrilling as she'd hoped. At least he'd finally agreed to take her to Aunt Mary. Perhaps she should agree to his terms, but she was too tired to think clearly. "What kind of cooperation?"

"One, report at six every morning and six every evening for duty in the galley. Two—"

"Six in the morning?" Christina groaned. "Is the sun even up at that hour?"

He laughed. "The discipline will do you good."

She rolled her eyes. "I've had my share of discipline. I find its value overrated."

A scowl turned his full mouth down at the corners. "But if you want to stay on my ship in one piece, you will obey. Rule number two, don't go on deck without me."

"I cannot breathe fresh air without your permission?"

He cocked a brow above that black mask. "Three, don't disobey me again. That doesn't sound too hard, does it, Lilli?"

Christina tried to meet his gaze. A wave of exhaustion engulfed her and she found herself groping for the support of his desk, instead.

At her silence, he turned his watchful eyes to her. In mute apprehension, she observed his approach and unwavering dark gaze, bracketed by the implacable black of his mask. He came closer, too close. Christina, confronted by his raw power, stepped back.

Her retreat wasn't fast enough. The Black Dragon reached for her chin and lifted her face to his gaze. He studied her for a long, suspended moment. Christina wished she could read his thoughts. Did he want to kiss her again, or just kill her?

"You look ready to collapse."

Piqued, Christina jerked her chin from his grasp. "Your concern is a tad belated, Captain."

He ignored her sarcasm. "When did you last sleep, Lilli?"

His gentle whisper soaked into Christina's senses. Closing aching lids over gritty eyes, she struggled to open them again. "The night before I came on board."

"Four days ago?"

His astonishment was audible, thrilling Christina with a shot of satisfaction, even as her heavy eyes slid shut again.

"Damn it," he swore as he reached for her. Before Christina could protest, he swept her up in his arms, against his chest, and strode to the door opposite his bed. With a dazed sense of unreality, she noted it opened to another smaller, less colorful cabin.

In two strides, he set her on her feet and turned her about. Before Christina knew his intent, he'd dispensed with the fastenings of her dress with the deftness of a lady's maid.

The garment slid off her shoulders, whispered down her body, to pool in a heap of stained pink twill at her feet. She looked from her dress to the captain over the ridge of her near-naked shoulder. He stared back wordlessly. The muscles in his jaw flexed as his fingers encircled her waist.

His touch was firm and hot. He nearly encircled her middle with his huge hands. Apprehension and excitement crashed through her. Maybe he had cast aside his intent and decided to ravish her. She should blast him and send him away, a fuzzy part of her mind realized. Instead, she stared.

Behind her, he stood. Memory reminded her of his shoulders, wide and taut. And, peering over her shoulder, she couldn't miss his chest, inch after inch defined by hard labor and half-exposed by the black vest he wore. His skin rippled like molten gold stretched tautly over muscle and sinew. She swallowed.

"Turn around," he demanded.

"Unhand me." She struggled in his grip. Why couldn't she yell, tell him she would not be manhandled? Blast her weariness!

The captain ignored her. His hands worked at her petticoats next. She tried stepping away to avoid this invasion of her person, but he pulled her back to him with the ties.

Her back collided with his chest, searing and unyielding. He raised his hands to clasp her bare shoulders and steady her, igniting a head-to-toe spark. His fingers were gentle as he drew her closer. His warm exhalations on her neck sent a shiver through her. She struggled for her next breath. How could he make her feel so shaky and hot at once?

"Stay still." His whisper sounded oddly choked.

As soon as the petticoats puddled about her feet, he lent his fingers to her corset. This had to stop. The hot, fluttering sensations swirling through her resembled those her married cousins had tittered about. She refused to believe she could feel so wantonly about a pirate who, according to rumor, ravished nuns. She could not want a man who ordered her about like a child. She was simply tired.

With the last of her energy, she turned to face him, arms crossed protectively over her breasts. "I can finish the rest."

Heat blazed across his taut face, lighting his black eyes. He drew in a deep breath. "Maybe it's better that you do."

* * * *

The following morning, Drex lingered around the kitchen, waiting for Lilli to appear. He didn't *want* to see her, of course, just make certain she followed orders.

Who was he fooling? Visions of Lilli's naked shoulders, the narrow curve of her waist, the downy skin at the nape of her neck, tortured him all night long. He still hadn't quite forgotten the catchy little gasps she made when he kissed her. His imagination fueled fantasies about the sounds she'd make during climax.

If he was smart, he would avoid touching her again. Hell, he should avoid even thinking about touching her. She was too willful, too mischievous. If he wasn't careful, Lilli could work her way into his head and distract him from his goals.

Six thirty arrived; Lilli didn't. He wasn't surprised.

With long strides, he made his way to his cabin, wondering if the woman could do anything she was told. Subservience clearly wasn't one of her virtues.

He paused before her door and heard...humming? Temper cresting like a tidal wave, he flung the door open.

With a gasp, she snapped her gaze up to meet his and stood half-naked, frozen in open-mouthed shock. The room seemed to shrink around them, slowly squeezing the air from Drex's lungs.

In a single glance, he took in the view he had avoided last night: Lilli's long legs bare below filmy linen. The silhouette of her small waist curving beneath the snowy, oblong chemise. The tips of her breasts outlined beneath the translucent fabric and accentuated by a plethora of pink embroidery that drew a man's attention.

She definitely had attention...from every part of his body. He leaned against the door for support, fisting his hands. It was either that or strip the damn chemise away with a long, well-placed rip.

With a shriek, she reached for a blanket and draped it across her front. Unfortunately, Drex couldn't tear his gaze from the delicate slope of her shoulders...or his imagination from what he could do to the rest of her.

"What are you doing here?" she demanded. "Did no one teach you to knock?"

"I'm not accustomed to having a woman on board." He told himself to look away. But after he blinked, he found himself still staring.

"What do you want, Captain?"

Dangerous question. What he wanted from her, she wouldn't give and he shouldn't fantasize about. Besides, her kind usually exchanged vows for a tumble, and a wedded life with Princess Lilli would be a disaster of epic proportions. She was too much a child, trapped in too womanly a body. They'd kill each other in a week...after spending six days in bed.

He sighed. Damn, this voyage was doomed to be a frustrating one.

"I thought I made myself clear yesterday when I told you to report to the galley at six this morning," he said.

She lifted her creamy shoulders in a shrug. "I'm going."

"When?" he barked. "It's six thirty."

"I shall go as soon as I finish dressing." She clutched the blanket closer to her chest. "For that to happen, you must first leave. And stop staring at me!"

She had a real talent for making his temper soar. Unfortunately, his desire to strip her, fill her and feel her dainty nails clawing his back wasn't far behind.

He crossed the floor and curled his fingers around her arm. "Listen, princess. I said six, not six thirty. Not when the mood strikes you. You have five minutes to dress in privacy. Five minutes," he stressed. "After that, I'm coming in, and I haven't decided if I'll dress you myself...or undress you."

Drex closed the door on her sputtering with a smile. Ah, he did enjoy irking her. *Don't think I've ever seen a woman distract you this much,* Hancock's assertion came back to him. She did distract him. And he needed to divert his mind from the spirited minx and refocus it on saving Ryan.

Regardless, he pressed his ear to the door. He heard grumbling, picked up "brute" and "tyrant" among her mutterings. Then came the whispered rustling of cloth. His imagination burst with images of sheer fabric brushing the silk of her skin and puddling at the floor, leaving her a naked Venus.

In three seconds, Drex felt his cock harden. Adjusting himself, he leaned against their adjoining door with a groan, wondering how he was going to keep himself from storming through it some night when his body craved the pleasure a tempting morsel like her had been created to give.

Perhaps Greg had been right; maybe he should have found a willing wench in London to satisfy him. Too late now. He was stuck on *The Dragon's Lair*, just him and Princess Lillianne—and a small door without a lock separating them.

Heaven help him. Images of a nearly naked Lilli assailed his heated brain, and his restraint was already hanging on by a thin thread.

A long minute later, Lilli emerged with golden hair demurely pinned atop her head, revealing her soft nape. Restraining an urge to kiss her there, Drex studied the rest of her. She sported a blue round dress frothed with lace—and a snug, square-necked bodice that did nothing to hide the creamy swells of her breasts.

Drex clenched his teeth. "Don't you have something else to wear?"

"I packed in a hurry." When he tossed her a suspicious glare, she added, "My mother's condition was worsening. I couldn't concentrate on something so trivial."

He eyed her with pure pleasure, knowing his crew would, too. "You didn't pack *anything* more…modest?"

"This dress is perfectly fashionable," she protested. "Besides, I only brought two others with me, and they're much more revealing."

And he'd get to see them in the days to come. Not a comforting thought.

"If you're going to wear that, don't even speak to the crew."

She glared at him. "Are you always surly?"

"Are you always willful?"

She glared at him, saying nothing.

Drex led her out the door, and they made a silent journey to the galley. He walked behind her, giving directions…and eyeing the alluring sway of her hips.

When they reached the small sunlit kitchen, a mess of ten men inhabited the room. A chorus of spoons clinking against clay bowls echoed against the wooden walls. No one said a word. In the stiff silence, his crew stared hard at his gorgeous stowaway.

Drex cleared his throat. "Men, Miss Lillianne will help in the galley. She will not help you with *anything* else. Understood?"

A hodge-podge of nods answered him. "No one is to touch her. Am

I making myself clear?"

With that, he slipped a possessive arm about her waist. He felt her turn as stiff as a hurricane gale as she whirled to face him, incredulity widening her emerald eyes.

When she opened her mouth to protest, he knew he had to shut her up. Fast.

Drex covered her lips with his own. She gasped into his mouth, her small hands making fists against his chest. Aware they had to be convincing, he clutched her to him and took possession of her soft pink lips again. His insides sizzled and blazed like the sun at the equator. He drew back for a ragged breath, saw her stunned expression, then devoured her again a man starved.

She tasted good, like a sweet mint. He explored deeper, thrusting into her mouth. His blood felt as if she'd replaced it with boiling brandy. The thick liquid sluiced through his veins to collect just beneath the buttons of his now-tight breeches. He pressed his erection against the lush heaven of her curves.

Lilli squirmed and gasped. He redoubled his effort so she wouldn't give the game away, stroking her back with needy hands and coaxing her tongue to mate with his.

The vision of her half-naked in that sheer chemise suddenly stormed his memory, shooting an erotic jolt through his body.

He inhaled the sultry scents of sea air and the flowered perfume of her skin. She'd probably never soften in his embrace, but for some damn reason, he ached for her to. In a last wishful effort, his tongue swept around hers, even as he filtered his fingers through the tendrils of hair lying in loose gold curls around her face. His thumbs traced tiny circles on her neck.

Amazingly, her body lost its starch, swaying against him like a wind-puffed sail. Her fists uncurled, flattened against his chest…then slowly curled around his shoulders. In a heartbeat, he pulled her right against his cock, not giving a damn how much of his arousal she felt.

Drex swallowed a groan, but he heard one from their audience. What he'd planned as a warning had suddenly become entertainment. Not a wise idea.

With effort and reluctance and a lot of regret, he broke the kiss.

Staring down into his stowaway's wide-eyed, swollen-lipped face, he tried to convey a warning to hold her tantrum. Instead, her expression held a blank stare, as if she were…dazed. Interesting possibility for a pleasure-filled voyage since he had never believed she would respond to him as a woman. But no, she would not assent to sharing mutual pleasure for its own sake, and he certainly didn't need to lose sight of his priorities because he was busy seducing her. Everything about her signaled trouble.

Holding Lillianne to him, he bellowed, "Any questions?"

Not a breath broke the silence.

He smiled icily. "Splendid." At that moment, bells chimed, ringing seven o'clock. "Get to your posts, men."

With gazes carefully averted, the ragtag bunch filed out, one by one. Knowing Lilli's explosion was imminent, he gestured Pauly, the cook, to follow the crew.

She shattered the three seconds of blissful silence with a huffy gasp. "How dare you? Why on earth—"

"To protect your pretty hide, Lilli."

Flashing green eyes widened with incredulity. "Protect me? By ravishing me while your crew watches?"

Drex gripped her shoulders. "First of all, I kissed you to brand you mine. Now you have less chance of being, as you so quaintly put it, ravished by another crew member." He pulled her closer and growled, "Second, if I had been trying to ravish you, you'd already be naked, on your back, and screaming my name."

Her expressive face displayed a booty chest full of panic—and a sailor's ration of curiosity. But that minuscule amount of intrigue almost proved too much for his control.

What was it about this hoyden that made him so hot?

Abruptly, he released her with wide-spread hands and retreated a step. "I'll send Pauly back in to instruct you on the finer points of shipboard cooking."

Drex brushed past her but felt her curious gaze burning his back. Inside, he sizzled. Damn it, he had to get her dewy mouth and tentative response out of his head. Her tangy-floral scent, her clenched fingers, her erratic breathing when they kissed, all raised hell with his self-control.

Glancing over his shoulder, he warned, "If you want to keep your bed a solitary one, don't kiss me back again."

* * * *

Christina spent the day in a daze. Her brain registered the sound of the cook's voice as he instructed her about the various instruments in the galley. But her concentration wandered elsewhere. As he spoke of the Friday diet consisting of oatmeal, cheese and dried peas, she could only think about the captain.

My God, she'd allowed the Black Dragon to kiss her, not once but twice. And instead of revulsion, she'd felt…tingles. Heat. A slow-burning desire firing her blood for more. Definitely not anything her grandmother would approve of. Nonetheless, the memory of his firm yet gentle lips on hers prompted her to consider kissing him again, as he'd warned against, just to feel his reaction.

Part of her was strangely giddy when she should have been repelled. Absolutely horrified to have such a heathen touching her. Something was wrong with her. Only that explained why she found such a dangerous man so intriguing. Yet it was more than his looks. She knew a bevy of dashing blades, all respectable peers, eager to win her favor. They bored her.

With a flash of insight, she knew why: The masked, tattooed captain possessed something all the *ton's* fops lacked—a passion for life. She saw it in his intent expression, heard it in the bark of his orders, tasted it in the flavor of his kiss. And she responded to him on a level so elemental it vibrated within her.

Dear Lord, was she a candidate for Bedlam? Maybe exhaustion was simply taking its toll on her thoughts.

As the morning shadows lengthened into afternoon, Pauly gave her small chores. The first, fetching ingredients about the galley for the meal, proved easy, if tedious. The second, slicing rations of cheese, became more difficult and less appealing. In an effort to keep her nose away from the smelly cheese, she winced and looked away—and sliced right into her finger. She tried to ignore the wound and finish her task, but bled on most of the meal instead.

Pauly was not pleased. Nor did she imagine the captain would be.

Mumbling something beneath his breath, the crusty cook sent her away—without a reminder to come back for the evening mess. Christina couldn't decide if she should be relieved or insulted.

Upon leaving the galley, she tiptoed her way about the maze of the ship, trying to find her cabin again. She passed one sailor, a tall man in a blue vest, shockingly minus a shirt.

Averting her gaze from his exposed flesh, she began, "Excuse me, can you…"

The ill-dressed man walked past, gaze trained down as if she didn't exist. The fear on his craggy face bespoke the captain's warnings. The Black Dragon had to be the most dreadful kind of ogre to inspire such fear. The overbearing, over-handsome lout!

Sweet heaven, the man was too much like her grandfather. Dictatorial, unbending, unhearing, unfeeling. Oh, his tactics were different. Grandfather claimed his ironclad decisions stemmed from his care and concern for her. The Black Dragon used her uncertainty of her tenuous position here, of him, as a means of control. Well, just as she had thwarted Grandfather, she would not allow the captain to get the better of her.

A difficult task, however. The man seemed to know her every thought. He awakened her senses and confused her so easily.

When she passed the next sailor, a stocky red-haired giant, she again asked for assistance. He turned to her, the lust burning in his gaze rooting her in place.

"Come here, sugar. If you're lost, ol' Talbot will be mighty glad to help ye find yer way."

"A—actually, I just remembered how to find my cabin."

"C'mon, now. Don't be afraid." He grinned, showing the gaps where his missing teeth had been. "I'll be your friend if you'll be mine."

His leer told her friendship was the last thing on his mind. Restraining her panic, she mustered up her haughtiest expression. "We are not acquaintances, sir, much less friends."

"Come closer, and we'll get to know each other real well." He inched nearer and reached for her.

Christina jumped back and sprinted away, the sounds of Talbot's mocking laughter ringing in her ears.

With an uneasy sigh, Christina continued, and to her relief, stumbled across the correct companionway a few minutes later. As she opened the door to her cabin, she heard a series of bells chime in the distance.

Even this motley bunch had some order, she thought sleepily, groping for her narrow bed. She lay down on the lumpy mattress and pulled the limp blanket up under her chin. She was used to far better, but at the moment, the bed felt like heaven.

Briefly, she worried about Talbot, but decided he wouldn't be bold enough to barge into the cabin adjoining the captain's.

The next sound she heard was a door slamming against a wall. She lifted a groggy eye, fearing she'd made an incorrect assessment of Talbot. Instead, the Black Dragon stood in her portal, wide chest rising with short, angry breaths, long, dark hair framing a taut, black-masked face.

"Now what?" she groaned.

"You're late. Again."

She stretched. "I overslept. I was tired."

He stared, his dark eyes following her every move. "The men are hungry. It's six thirty, the evening meal will begin soon, and I want you back in the galley."

Christina pulled one of her grandfather's favorite sayings out of memory. "And people in Hades want cold water."

With an oath, he stormed across the room to her bed. Christina tried to scramble away, but he snatched her into his grasp, holding her against his chest with a ferocity that made her tremble.

"Don't you understand? If you don't work, the crew will do everything possible to make your life complete hell."

"More than you've done?" she asked archly. At his warning glare, she smoothed her dress irritably. "All right. I'll go."

"Good. The men appreciate a female's cooking now and again," he said as he followed her out the cabin door and headed through the companionway.

Obviously, he hadn't talked to Pauly. "They will hardly appreciate mine."

"It can't be too bad," he argued.

Since she'd never cooked before, Christina knew better. But to admit she'd never stood before a stove would reveal too much about her identity. Instead, she mumbled, "We'll see."

They strode into the galley, currently devoid of anyone save the cook. "Ask Pauly for instruction."

After that brief command, the captain left. And Pauly gave her a job she knew she'd botch: cooking oatmeal.

After dumping a bucketful of the flakes into a tub of boiling salt water, he told her to watch it. For what, she wanted to ask, but didn't dare for fear they'd discover her ignorance and realize she was no impoverished merchant's daughter.

Pauly left to find an additional ration of peas and bring up another casket of ale.

A boring half hour later, the bearded cook peered over her shoulder at the slop of oatmeal.

"Good Lord! What'd ya do to it?"

Wide-eyed and aware she'd done something wrong, she answered, "Nothing. I—I watched it, just like you said."

"Ya didn't stir it?" He sounded shocked.

"You didn't say to stir it."

"Hell's bells, I didn't think I had to."

With that, he reached for a long, wooden spoon and stuck it in the mushy substance. The spoon stood straight up.

"I'm sorry," she said.

He waved her apology away with his usual bluster. "It won't be the worst the men have eaten. Go finish pourin' them mugs of ale."

Christina scurried about the kitchen, feeling three inches tall. Too bad no one here was going to ask her about the latest fashion or who sat where at *haut ton* dinners. Those facts she could recite in her sleep. But cooking? She knew nothing about that.

With a sigh, Christina began pouring ale. Behind her, she heard footsteps. That purposeful cadence could only belong to one person: the captain. As Pauly put it, hell's bells. Why was he here?

Jaw clenched, she turned to face him. Thrusting the pitcher on the counter to prepare for confrontation, she nudged it against an object on the edge of the counter.

The captain's eyes widened. He lunged toward her with a curse. She jumped out of his way.

A moment later, the sound of breaking glass resounded in her ears. Her eyes followed the clatter and found the lantern.

She watched with horror as the lamp rolled across the floor, saturating the wood beneath their feet with oil. It spun away from her and whirled toward the wood-burning stove.

Immediately, the captain barked at Pauly to grab towels. Even as the Black Dragon sprang into action, she lunged for the lantern, stopping it short of the stove's fire.

With short, urgent strokes, Pauly threw the wet cloths down and began mopping up the liquid. The captain tore off his shirt, disregarding its flying buttons, and added it to the towels. The Black Dragon joined Pauly's attack on the wooden floor.

"Help us mop this up!" he snapped.

Christina knelt to assist, but a spark from the stove arced into the oil. An instant flame ignited, tearing across the floor in an orange-red line. The captain shoved her away.

Both he and Pauly backed away from the line of fire zipping between them, but the cook was not fast enough. The blaze swept across Pauly's hand, scorching his skin. The cook screamed, and the captain cursed, his ripe oaths hanging in the air, along with the ghostly, cloying smoke. He reached inside a cabinet and snatched a canister, then dumped its snowy contents on the fire.

Flour, she realized as she watched blaze smother and die. With chagrin, she cast a wary gaze to the Black Dragon. She hadn't meant to start a fire. But as he returned her stare with a killing glare, she knew she'd made a giant mistake.

"How bad is it?" The Black Dragon approached Pauly with concern masking his fury.

"It's nothin'."

But that was a lie. His waxy skin proved the cost he paid to restrain his moan. His forehead beaded with rivulets of sweat as he pressed white lips together.

The captain turned to her. "Why is it that, wherever you go, trouble follows? Damn it, go to your room and stay there. I'll be down to deal with you."

Christina sent a remorse-filled gaze to the cook, who cradled his injured hand. "I really am sorry."

As he nodded, she followed the captain out of the galley and made her way to the back of the ship and her cabin. Dejection pulled her shoulders down. She hadn't meant to hurt Pauly—or anyone. He'd been the most likeable person she'd met on board, largely because he didn't say a word more than necessary. His expression told her he didn't judge her or her reasons for stowing on board.

Sinking onto her bunk, she dreaded the captain's arrival and their inevitable confrontation. She didn't have to wait long.

He pushed the door between their cabins wide open and hovered in the doorway. Inhaling a deep breath, he stood too still, except for the rise of his broad, naked chest. Wishing he had donned another shirt, Christina tried to look away. But her gaze lingered on the sculpted angles of his hard, golden torso and the tattoo of the dragon's tail encircling his arm. His skin resembled polished bronze. Her mouth went dry.

She'd never seen anyone like him in her eighteen years, not even on the few shipyards she'd toured with Grandfather as a child. With a shiver, she admitted he was magnificent.

Realizing she'd been staring like a dimwit, pride nudged her to meet his glare.

"What were you thinking?" he demanded. "That you'd torch the whole ship just to spite me?"

His growl raised her hackles. "Of course not."

"Lilli, you can't play with fire on a wooden ship!" He stepped into the cabin. Its tiny space shrunk around her. "You'll kill everyone. Did that occur to you?"

He clearly thought her dim. She was guilty of being startled by his approach. So she would use more caution in the future. But, in typical tyrant fashion, the Black Dragon shouted, just like Grandfather.

"The fire was an accident," she defended.

He considered her for a terribly silent moment before he lifted a dark, cynical brow. "Was it?"

"Of course! If you hadn't sneaked up behind me, I—"

"I didn't sneak," he corrected. "I came to check on you when Pauly told me you'd cut yourself. How is your finger?"

She spun away, feeling chagrined and wondering why he cared. "I shall heal."

He made no reply, and silence hung in the thick air, tinged with salt and damp heat. Christina felt the captain's eyes on her back, his stare single-minded. Part of her wanted to apologize, but she knew he'd only fling it back in her face.

"Let me look at it."

He grabbed her hand, engulfing it in his, and turned her to face him. Half-naked, he stood too close for comfort. She edged away as the captain inspected the slice on her finger.

She stared at their joined hands. Calluses lined his large palm and sun-darkened fingers; tender white skin, nursed by her idle days, covered hers. His hand looked capable with sturdy, long fingers. Her own seemed ridiculously frail in comparison.

Long moments slid past before Christina realized the captain's gaze had focused on her face. She raised her eyes to his, drawn by the probe of his dark stare behind his mask. For a moment, her memory lingered on his kiss in the galley this morning. The persuasive pressure of his lips, the swirl of his tongue around her own, igniting her internal fires.

"Who are you, Lilli? Really? Is that even your name?"

Not for anything could she afford to answer his questions. "Who are you behind that mask? Why are you hiding?"

He paused, as if deciding whether to answer. "When you've become as infamous as I have, you protect yourself in every way possible, especially your identity. I've no wish to end up dangling from the end of a rope after I've retired."

"Pirates retire?" He answered with a glower. Brow wrinkled, she asked, "But why wear a mask around your own crew? They must know—"

"Only Hancock knows," he cut in. "I don't trust anyone else." He settled closer to her with a tight smile. "Now that I've answered all your questions, princess, I want answers to mine. Is Lilli your real name?"

Christina dropped her gaze. "I told you it was."

He cupped her chin. "You also told me your father was a poor merchant. But your dresses are well made, Lilli. Your hands are very soft." His palm slid across her fingers as if to make his point, and she shivered. "You're educated and you can't cook. None of that fits with an impoverished merchant's daughter."

"My father didn't want us to work," she said softly.

He grunted softly, clearly disappointed, then trailed his thumb over her cut once more. "Be more careful from now on."

He released her hands and turned away.

Without thought, Christina touched his bare arm to stay him. "It *was* an accident," she reiterated. "I promise."

"Lilli," came his exasperated sigh. "If you're not careful, people get hurt. And sometimes, damn it, they die."

Christina flinched, realizing that if not for the valiant efforts of Pauly and the captain, the fire might have spread, destroying the ship, killing the crew, even the captain himself.

"The sea is exacting." His voice dropped gravely. "So I have to be the same."

"You believe it was an accident, don't you?"

"Stay out of trouble, Lilli. I'm not your nursemaid."

"I don't need a nursemaid," she said stiffly.

"In less than twenty-four hours, you've managed to agitate the crew and nearly set the ship on fire. I mean business, Lilli," he grated out. "Think next time. Otherwise, I might not be around when you need saving."

Chapter Four

Thoughts of the captain whirled in her head as she attempted to clean flour from the small but sooty floor in the galley. Dangerous described him all too well. Why did the most exciting man she'd ever met come in the unsuitable form of a masked, controlling privateer?

She also feared discovery. Each time he inquired about her identity, his questions probed closer to the truth. The Black Dragon could not learn her real name. Ever. Lord knew what he would do to her. Take her virtue for revenge? Ransom her back to her grandfather? As tired as she felt, despite a few hours' sleep, she'd have to watch herself and keep her tall tales straight.

The men shuffled into the galley for their meal. With wrinkled noses, they sniffed at the odor of charred wood blending with salty sea streaming through the open gun ports.

Christina retreated to the counter beside the wood-burning stove as the sailors ambled to the galley's lone table in silence. She set her rag aside, pressing wrinkles from her blue dress with a nervous brush of her hands.

The motley bunch wore greasy scarves about their necks and ill-fitting breeches below chests covered only by ropes, weapons or tattoos. One man, however, had donned what appeared to be a gentleman's brocade vest. Christina did not want to consider how the outlaw had acquired such a finely made garment. Coercion, the kind that included sharp knives and bared teeth.

Two more sailors straggled in. Her palms turned sweaty. What would her friends say if they saw her behaving in this manner with these cutthroats?

The crew's unfashionably long hair and coarse beards made her shudder. The assortment of gold jewelry and gems that dangled from shocking holes in their ears, just like the captain's, did little to ease her fear, either.

Christina sent them a stiff smile. The fact the crew gave her an equally wide berth lent her little comfort, given their quick but heated glances.

Then the last man ducked through the open doorway with a familiar swagger, and she almost groaned. Talbot, the brute who'd cornered her in the companionway as she'd asked for directions. As if the captain and his overbearing ways weren't torment enough, now she had to deal with Talbot. And judging from his obnoxious leer, the meal was going to be long.

Determined to look brave, she ignored him and met the stares of the others with arms crossed defiantly over her chest.

"Where's Pauly?" one man asked suspiciously.

Christina gathered her courage and answered, "There was an accident. He's resting."

She hoped her crisp reply was enough to deter further questions. But their narrow-eyed expressions didn't bode well. If they knew she had almost burned their cook alive, who knew what dreadful punishment they might see fit to mete out.

"See, I told ye she was dangerous," commented a stout, dark-haired giant, his tone righteous. "Bad luck, mates."

Another nodded, grumbling, "Only one thing a wench like her is good fer, and the cap'n ain't bloody likely to share."

The other sailors nodded in agreement. Their stares, a terrifying mixture of lust and distrust, added to the consensus.

To break the tension, Christina set out the food she and Pauly had prepared earlier. With shaking fingers, she circled the table, filling each plate, then tiptoed back with a sigh.

No one touched the food. Instead, the sailors stared at the meal, their faces a mixture of wrinkled brows and grimaces.

"What is this slop?" one asked, his eyes accusing.

"Pauly damn sure didna cook this mess," asserted the first dissenter in a thick brogue. "Are ye tryin' to poison us, lass?"

"I didn't try to poison anyone. This is my dinner, too."

"She don't belong on board," he called again. "Just like I said before, she's bad luck and she's dangerous!"

Hancock, the captain's surly first mate, considered her for a long moment. Biting her lip, she stared back.

"If ye ain't tryin' to poison us, ye vixen, why does the food look so bad?" he asked.

Christina thrust her hands on her hips and stopped just short of stomping her foot. "Can you do better?"

Hancock grinned. "Probably not."

Suddenly the others' expressions turned from scowls and leers to guffaws. Maybe they wouldn't throw her overboard after all.

She peered curiously at Hancock. He shot her an unexpected wink before turning his attention to the fare on his plate. He had intervened, but why?

All the others began eating—except Talbot. The barbarian merely pushed his plate aside with a sly curl to his lips and ogled her from his perch at the end of the table.

"She obviously wasn't made for cookin'. Look at them bosoms, all pretty and pink. Come here, sugar, and sit on Talbot's lap."

Nine pairs of eyes swerved across the room to rest on her. Their heavy gazes told her Talbot had been the only one cocky enough to speak their thoughts aloud. At that moment, Christina wished she'd had more time to pack adequately for this adventure. Her entire body burned with embarrassment and fear.

A skinny scrap of a man broke the long silence. "If we ain't allowed to touch her, neither are ye."

"Yeah," said a bald man beside him. "If I don't get no fancy piece like that, you don't."

Christina stared in shock, listening to the men haggle over her like she was a prime cut of meat.

"Quit whining, both of ye. There should be enough of her left after I'm through." Talbot leveled Christina a ribald smile.

Christina mimicked one of Grandfather's frostiest looks. "Find some tavern wench to sit on your lap. I will not."

Everyone in the room held their collective breath and turned their gazes on Talbot. Christina felt her hands begin to tremble as the lewd grin on Talbot's face slurred into a threatening scowl. His biceps bulged as he braced meaty hands on the end of the table and rose. "I told you to come sit on my lap, wench."

Swallowing the lump lodged in her throat, she squared her shoulders. "I would rather take my last breath."

In the next instant, Talbot unsheathed a knife at his thigh. The blade gleamed under the shaft of sunlight streaming through the gun port. Christina gasped.

Before she could move, Talbot hurled the knife at her. The blade flew end over end before burying itself in the counter just inches from her abdomen with a heart-stopping thud.

He smirked when she gasped. "Listen up, girl. If you spread yer legs for the likes of the captain, you can do the same fer me. Now get over here."

Christina's gaze flew from the knife, then back to Talbot's face. The ruffian's glare of conquest ignited her temper.

She collected her nerves, along with the last of the oatmeal, and strode to Talbot's side. The oaf sat back in his seat with a satisfied smile. "That's what a man likes, a warm woman and extra food."

"The cap'n'll slice your back open if you touch his woman," Hancock advised.

Talbot laughed. "Let 'im try."

"He'll do more than try, mate," Hancock warned.

Talbot's feral gaze monitored her approach as she listened to the exchange. Clutching the handles of the pot in her hands, she strode the length of the table and paused at Talbot's side.

"The captain will have no need to defend my honor, because I will not allow you to jeopardize it."

She turned the pot of oatmeal over—above Talbot's head. Giant lumps of the slop slurped downward, tangling in his hair, dribbling into his eyes.

With an outraged howl, Talbot bolted from his seat, swiped oatmeal from his eyes and reached for her. Christina danced away from him to the accompaniment of the others' wails of laughter.

Christina pressed her lips together to hold back her own chuckle. She should be terrified of the lout now that she'd embarrassed him. But she only felt triumph and a sense of relief.

Talbot shook his head to rid himself of more offending chunks of oatmeal. The masses splattered across the table, the floor. The others clutched their bellies, hopelessly doubled over with laughter. Hancock winked at her again.

Talbot muttered an oath. "Get over here, ye uppity bitch."

"That gives new meanin' to taking yer meals!" pointed out one sailor between convulsions of laughter.

"Shut yer bleedin' mouth," Talbot shouted. Then he shot Christina a glare brimming with fire and hate. She took a reflexive step away from that menacing glint in his eyes. Suddenly, Hancock stood at her side, a light hand on her elbow.

With pursed lips, Talbot backed away from the table. He lunged for her. Christina gasped, her heart racing. Seeing her fear, the bully stopped in mid-stride with a laugh.

"That's right, girl. Ye should be afraid. I'll find ye alone soon. After I'm done with ye, we'll see who's laughin'."

A silent moment later, Talbot stormed from the galley.

Hancock turned to her. "He's just talkin' mad. Don't worry. The cap'n won't let anything happen to ye."

Christina sent him a shaky nod, though she felt less than reassured. She didn't protest when he urged her to sit down.

As she sank down onto the bench, the sailor beside her shot her a wide grin. He was missing his front two teeth. "That's a brave lass! Talbot had it comin' to 'im, he did."

Hadn't this man called her dangerous five minutes ago?

Before she could reply, another called out, "Davie's right. Seein' a wee thing like you set Talbot straight puts me in a right good mood."

Listening to the last man's laugh, she turned to Hancock behind her with a questioning stare.

"He's made everyone's life hell. They've wanted to see him get his comeuppance for a long while."

Christina suspected she'd made an enemy who wasn't likely to forgive and forget, but she couldn't worry about that now. Not when the others appeared to be accepting her. She turned back and smiled tentatively at all the sailors. Watching them dig into the cold oatmeal on their plates, she hoped today's incident worked to her advantage. Without help, she didn't want to put Talbot's threats to the test.

* * * *

Drex ran to the galley, knowing he had missed most of the evening meal. And in his absence, any man who hadn't shown his stowaway the deference he'd demanded would know true punishment.

Down stairs and round corners he sprinted, hoping Lilli could handle the others as well as she had him. He took comfort in the fact Hancock had promised to help her if needed.

Still, a burning inside him urged him to learn if any of his mannerless bunch had harmed her. They were fine sailors, maybe even the best. But he didn't trust them around a beautiful woman like Lilli for an instant.

Hell, around her, he could barely trust himself.

As his eyes adjusted to the dim lighting of the galley, Drex looked over the small crowd. He'd been prepared for almost anything, screaming, even blood.

Never the shimmering brilliance of Lilli's smile.

She sat on one side of the table, just beneath the small window. The men had gathered all around her, like insects to their queen. The setting sun shone through the gun ports, illuminating Lilli's golden hair, her sunny smile. The men spoke over one another in a rush of conversation.

"I wrestled me an alligator once," one of them boasted.

"That's nothing," assured another. "I fought off two of the fancy English soldiers all by meself."

"Aye, ye did. And they be children next to the giants I fought on an island," a third bragged. "Scary buggers with one eye, they was. I killed 'em all."

Lilli threw her head back and laughed, the sound soft like trickling water from a spring. "Well, I do have some adventures ahead of me, then. How much more exciting than London!"

Drex stepped into the room, his footfall purposely heavy. As he expected, all conversation ceased.

The men jumped from their seats to attention. Lillianne stilled, her smile dying.

Why was it that every time he came within five feet of her, she welcomed him as warmly as a hangman? Though it was for the best, the fact she regarded him as the enemy irritated him.

"If you're finished eating, men, resume your posts," Drex commanded.

Nine men shuffled out immediately. Lilli tried to follow.

Drex grabbed her arm. "You stay here."

He turned to a departing Hancock. "Where's Talbot?"

His first mate burst into laughter. "Our little Lilli put 'im right in his place, and with no more than a bowl of oatmeal."

Our little Lilli? He cast her a questioning glance.

She swallowed, then offered up a stilted smile. "The man made some rather rude suggestions. I poured oatmeal over his head."

Drex bit back laughter. Talbot should be punished for whatever crude words he'd spewed to Lilli, but he doubted the man could be further humiliated. His beautiful stowaway was becoming a bigger handful all the time, but he couldn't suppress a flash of admiration.

"Don't be angry," she cajoled, batting her eyelashes like a practiced coquette. "He was behaving like a brute."

She was hopelessly mischievous, he decided, shaking his head. That probably accounted for the reason he couldn't decide whether he should seduce Lilli or spank her.

"Oh, you are angry," she observed, her red mouth turned down into a pout. "I'm sorry, but—"

"Not here." He released her and gestured to the galley's door. "My cabin. Now."

Lilli grimaced, waved good-bye to Hancock, then exited. He followed her down the companionway, focusing on her shoulder blades. But damn it if his gaze didn't keep drifting lower, fastening on the graceful curve of her hips and her derriere. He really had to take his mind off of her body and all the things he'd like to do to it if he was going to confront her.

Once they reached his cabin, he pulled out his desk chair and pointed to it. She hesitated, then sat. Unfortunately, standing above her provided him a disturbingly clear view down the front of her dress and the lush swell of her breasts.

He turned away. She was beautiful and spirited. As much as she created havoc on his ship, he couldn't deny he wanted her. Badly. More today than yesterday. Tenfold more than the day he'd first laid eyes on her. And not for just her beauty. Her resolve was equally captivating, calling to him like the challenge of taming a wild sea, despite the fact that, like Ryan, her antics inevitably caused trouble.

God, was this sickness something he shared with the insane?

"Don't be angry," Lilli said suddenly, bringing him back to the present. "I had to do *something*!"

"I'll discuss Talbot's lack of manners with him later. Right now, we're going to talk about your mission of…mercy."

A flash of fear raced through her green eyes. She quickly masked it and rose to her feet. Planting her hands on her hips, she said, "You may not care what that heathen said to me, but—"

"I will deal with him. Separately," he assured, lowering her to her chair with firm hands on her shoulders.

She responded to his words with a wary lift of her chin.

"Tell me more about your mother's illness," he began.

Her wary green gaze brushed his face before looking away. "She developed a very high fever and sleeps most of the day. She refuses to eat."

"You're very collected, Lilli," he observed. "You haven't wept once over the imminent loss of your mother."

She pursed her lips together and clasped her hands in her lap. "We're not very close, actually."

He paced to the bed and sat, meeting her gaze at eye level. "You're making a dangerous journey for a woman who doesn't mean much to you?"

Placing a hand on her chest, she had the presence of mind to look affronted. "I *am* a dutiful daughter. Only someone dreadfully callous wouldn't fulfill a dying mother's last wish."

"Naturally," he replied, not disagreeing. But in her case, that truth seemed more of a convenience. "What kind of merchant did you say your father was?"

She tried to wave a casual hand through the air. Her fingers shook. "You know, spices, tea, that sort of thing."

"He must have been a wealthy man, then."

"No."

He crossed his arms over his chest. "Where did you live?"

"I can hardly see that it matters."

With a finger crooked beneath her chin, he lifted her gaze to his face. How could such guileless eyes be so full of untruths? "Then you won't mind answering, will you?"

"As you wish. We lived in London," she said, face carefully blank.

"Where in London?"

Her gaze darted about the room. "Not too far from Fleet Street."

"Expensive neighborhood," he commented.

"Well, we ah…lived above our shop."

He feigned a confused frown. "I thought you said you lived not too far from Fleet, rather than on it."

"Our front door leads out the back, onto another street," she babbled. "Besides, father taught us to tell customers we lived elsewhere."

"And your sister, Ellen, lives with you?"

"Of course, Ellen lives with us. Where else would she live?" She smiled, looking as tense as a sailor on his first trip up the rigging in a storm. "What is this all about?"

Even so, she tempted Drex to touch her, possibly even believe her. But he knew better.

"I thought you said your sister's name was Helen?" he asked.

"Ah…" she faltered. "Isn't that what you said?"

"No. I said Ellen." He leaned forward, bracing his elbows against his knees. "So did you."

"I'm sure you heard wrong," she insisted.

"Where did this come from?" He tossed a brush set in pure silver in her direction.

She caught it, then glared back at him. "You took this from my valise! How dare you—"

"Because I don't know who you are, Lilli, and you're lying to me. Answer my question," he demanded softly. "Where did you get that?"

She bit her lip. "It was a gift from an admirer."

"Was this a gift from an admirer, too?" He tossed a delicate linen chemise in her direction, trimmed in blond lace, too expensive to belong to a poor merchant's daughter.

Drex waited, praying she'd say no. She'd have to be some man's mistress to receive undergarments from an admirer. Somehow the thought of Lilli willingly allowing another man to touch her, kiss the sweet lips he'd kissed, made him want to growl and bash in a head or two.

"I…ah, made that with scraps of material my father couldn't sell."

With a tight smile, he strode to a chest in the corner. He lifted the lid and tossed her a piece of black silk. "Since you're so talented with a needle and thread, you wouldn't mind making me a robe, would you?"

Her panic-widened eyes answered Drex with more eloquence than another of her stammered lies.

Lilli's mouth opened. No sound came out.

Drex leaned closer, pressing her against the back of her chair with his presence. "Why do you believe you cannot tell me the truth?"

Her green eyes widened. "You have hardly been forthcoming about your identity, either, strutting around while hiding beneath that beard and mask. Who are *you*?"

"It's not the same, Lilli. I could be executed if the Crown learns my identity. People I associate with could be implicated and punished to death," he bit out. "I don't enjoy hiding behind this bit of silk. But I must." He crouched down before her. "Unless you're wanted by Manchester and his men, too, I think you can trust me with your little secret."

The panic in her green eyes transformed to something near fear. "I can't tell you."

Her voice was a raspy, quiet thing that barely cleared the air between them. She bit her lower lip, looking like she'd had a vicious nightmare. For some reason, she roused Drex's protective instincts almost as much as his loins.

Damn it. He *was* getting too sentimental for life at sea.

"Why? Because you're running from someone?" he asked.

She nodded, the movement jerky. Her breathing sounded erratic as it clashed with the soft swish of the ocean against the wood of the ship.

He gentled his voice. "Do you think that someone wants to hurt you?"

"He—he doesn't think so, but he would." She cleared her voice and added, "He would destroy me."

"Who is he? Your father? A lover?"

Drex's gut tightened as he waited for her answer. The idea of Lilli with a lover disturbed him—and for reasons he didn't want to examine too closely.

Of course, his sentiment had nothing to do with the fact he looked forward each day to seeing Lilli, despite the mischief she seemed destined to create.

"I don't think I should say anything more." She lifted her chin and stood.

Drex reined in a grunt of frustration. Why wouldn't she trust him? If she was in danger, maybe he could help. If she had a cruel lover, he'd cheerfully volunteer to hang the man—by his testicles.

He stalked to the door and opened it. "We'll talk about this again later. For now, stay in your cabin."

"But Pauly… His injury is my fault. Shouldn't I help to care for him or something?"

Drex shook his head. "He's being taken care of. You need sleep for your morning mess. Besides, I don't have time to play your guardian in the event some of the men decide you're too tempting to resist."

"Oh, bother. I don't want to be cooped up in this stuffy cabin. I want to see the sun set over the—"

Drex grinned. "And people in Hades want cold water."

The slamming of the door behind the captain didn't hide Lilli's sigh of frustration. As he made his way to Pauly's cabin, he swore she had not heard the last of his quest for her true identity.

Chapter Five

"I will not stay in this cabin," Christina vowed once the Black
Dragon had gone. Arms planted on her hips, chest puffed out, she
mimicked, "Don't move without my permission. Don't breathe. Don't
think. Answer my questions." She rolled her eyes. "Not bloody likely."

Petulantly, she dropped her arms to her sides. It wasn't fair. Why
was she always expected to do as she was told while the men of the
world enjoyed the freedom to indulge their every whim? She had
dreams, too. A lifetime full of them.

Christina turned for the door. The captain's trunk, tucked
inconspicuously in the corner, drew her eye. Staying here had its merits.
After all, if he'd searched her valise, that gave her a right to search his
baggage as well.

Without pause, she stomped to the trunk and grabbed the gleaming
black lid. Just what would he keep in his chest? Weapons? Skulls?
Sunken treasure?

An anxious whirl wound about her stomach as she lifted the lid,
expecting the worst. Nothing in her imagination had prepared her for the
captain's simplicity.

Bolts of silks and fine linen lay on top in a rainbow of color. With a
puzzled frown, Christina set them on the floor. Below the cloth, she
found an extra pair of his boots and black leather gloves. She reached
again into the trunk, digging deeper. This time, her fingers grasped the
spine of a book.

A book? Who taught notorious privateers how to read?

With a scowl, she pulled the tome free from the trunk. *Romeo and*

Juliet by William Shakespeare, it read. The Black Dragon reading classics? And why something so tragically romantic? She would hardly call him the sentimental type.

She flipped open the hard red cover. Inside, the flowery, faded script of a woman's hand caught her gaze. *To my beloved Ryan, read this tale and weep, yet know our love burns too bright to end in sadness. Forever, Chantal.*

With numb fingers, Christina closed the book and set it back in the trunk. His name was Ryan. It fit him, she supposed, though the sound was somewhat softer than the man himself.

And his love was a woman named Chantal.

The thought rose like an ache inside, even as denial surged hard in her belly. Maybe Chantal was merely the captain's sister. She doubted it. The man would hardly keep the book with him if he did not treasure the tome.

Chantal. The name conjured up images of an exotic French girl with dark hair and cat-like ebony eyes. Christina sighed, irritated by an irrational surge of jealousy.

Or what if, dear God, Chantal was his wife?

She hardly cared. He was the worst sort of barbarian. Completely arrogant. She hoped he did have a lover.

Even as she thought the words, her shoulders sagged. True, he was a tyrant, and she *should* be happy he had a woman in his life.

She wasn't.

Thrusting her feelings aside, she rose and placed the items back in the trunk. She would not cry; there was no reason. The brute of a captain had a love, something she had never wanted. Independence was much more fascinating.

But the memory of the Black Dragon's lips—Ryan's lips—lingered. Closing her eyes, she relived the burn of his kiss. His possession of her mouth had felt so complete, so full of desire. Now she wondered if he'd been imagining Chantal while she'd been melting like butter in the summer sun.

After shoving the last of the material back into the trunk, she shut the lid and whirled for the door. Never mind the Black Dragon, or Ryan, and Chantal, his wife or mistress or whatever. She had some fresh air to breathe and her autonomy to maintain.

She certainly hadn't come on board to be ordered about like a child—or lose her heart.

* * * *

Christina awoke in the infirmary with a cramp in her neck and a damp rag dangling from her limp fingers. The wick on the lantern burned low, and she could barely make out Pauly's sleeping form. Rising with a stretch, she wondered how many hours she'd slept here. The ache in her back told her more than a few.

Quietly, Christina set the rag at the corner of Pauly's bed. She wanted to ask him how he felt, but didn't dare wake him after his painfully sleepless evening.

She crept to the door and exited. After ascending several ladders, Christina couldn't resist a peek at the night sky.

A breeze warmer than any she'd known on England's shores blew against her skin in a damp caress. She inhaled the scents of salt and wood and tang in the air.

Her mood was a restless one. Pauly would soon recover, so that no longer upset her. More important, she'd truly escaped Grandfather. And she had no illusions about her standing with the *ton*. If he ever found her and dragged her back to London, she would be a ruined woman no man of consequence would wed. No one would have to know that, other than a few kisses, she remained as virtuous as the day she'd been born. Grandfather certainly wouldn't stoop to marrying her to a commoner. He would have to let her live her life peacefully with Aunt Mary. She should be pleased.

Christina made her way to a corner of the deck and leaned against its rail, lulled by the gentle swish of the white-capped water below and crisp whip of the wind above. Stars twinkled in a display more brilliant than any chandelier. She felt awed by the serenity of nature, privileged to be wandering about its realm.

The wrinkle in her happiness could only be attributed to the captain. Why, given his autocratic ways, did she have a hard time driving him from her thoughts?

His kisses lingered in her memory. It was puzzling, really. To be so…curious about a man whose face she had never seen. He could be horribly deformed. But given the bronzed flesh rippling all over his body with silent power and those fathomless dark eyes that could make her shiver with just a glance, she didn't think so.

Even more odd, for a man of such vicious reputation, he had not

63

harmed her. Not really. The hold had been unpleasant in the extreme, and her banishment there still infuriated her. Her duties in the mess hall were no picnic. But she was alive. He had not whipped or raped her. He'd made no mention of walking the plank or sharing her with his crew, only manning a stove. While she'd never imagined she would do anything as menial as cooking, the chore had hurt only her pride—and the men's stomachs.

"You're supposed to be in your cabin," a familiar voice rang from behind her, ripe with displeasure.

She refused to turn his way. "I shouldn't think a moment of air is too much to ask."

He stepped up beside her and directed his next words to her profile. "You're not safe on this ship alone. My men are well trained, but men, just the same."

Christina shot him a sidelong glare. "Believe what you may, I can look after myself. I'm hardly a wilting flower."

His laughter echoed in the air, rich and deep. "A wilting flower is the very last description I would give of you."

"How would you describe me"—she paused, glancing askance for his expression—"Ryan?"

His laughter ebbed. His smile died, replaced by taut fury darkening his eyes beneath his mask. "What did you call me?"

Christina checked the urge to retreat a step. "Ryan. Is that not your name?"

"Searching my belongings, I see." He grabbed her arm and yanked her closer.

Christina tried to concentrate on the feel of rough fingers biting into her arm. The view of his golden flesh flexing beneath his half-buttoned shirt distracted her.

She whispered, "You searched mine."

"If you were trying to find evidence to hang me with, sorry to disappoint you. Ryan is not my name," he bit out.

"Then Chantal isn't—" She broke off in mortification, unable to believe she'd almost asked the Black Dragon about his private affairs.

"My wife? My lover? No. I don't have either." He paused, gaze probing her with a heat far from comfortable. "Why ask?"

"I was merely curious about…" *You.* But saying it aloud was too much of an admission. "About the kind of man who becomes a pirate."

"Privateer," he bit out. "I don't steal."

There was a distinction between the two? She smiled and wriggled her arm free. The captain released it, wearing a scowl.

"So what kind of man becomes a privateer?" she asked.

"Don't try to solve me, Lilli. I'm not a riddle devised for your amusement."

She rolled her eyes in response. "Where did you last sail to before London?"

He hesitated. "New Orleans, if you must know."

She drew in a quick gasp of surprise. "Do they really have swamps with scaly creatures?"

His compressed lips gave Christina the impression the captain was holding back a smile. "Outside New Orleans, yes."

"How exciting! I think I would like to go there someday."

"A swamp is hardly a place for a lady."

"It seems no place is any place for a lady." She frowned. "Life is extremely tedious when limited to needlepoint and drawing room gossip."

He cocked a brow. "So you stowed on board my ship simply for an adventure?"

"Oh, no," she protested. "I fled London."

"Why? I know you don't have a sick mama or a sister named Helen. You can't be a merchant's daughter if you spend your days over needlework. What is the truth? Is someone chasing you?"

Christina nodded, thoughts racing. She still could not risk revealing her identity. He would likely strangle her posthaste—or worse, ransom her back to her grandfather.

"Who are you running from, Lilli? A shade more of the truth this time, if you don't mind."

But she did mind, which meant she had to make up something—fast. Latching onto a tidbit of the latest scandal she'd overheard before leaving London, she said, "I—I ran from my lover. He's quite mad."

A lover. Drex absorbed her information in gut-churning silence. He wanted to deny her story but held his tongue. Lilli was young. Too young to be married, perhaps, but old enough to have an illicit lover. Still, she had lied to him before, more than once.

"Mad?" he queried.

"Yes. Jealous of any man who even casts his eye my way."

If her story were true, Drex could understand the man's emotions. He felt them himself just listening to Lilli say that someone else had

65

kissed her sweet berry lips and stroked the curves of her hips while sinking deep into her body, as he fantasized about during long nights, knowing that only a rickety door separated them.

"He's dangerous," she added.

Drex snapped his attention back to her. "Did he hurt you?"

Lilli merely looked away, leaving Drex to assume the worst. Yes, her tale could be yet another tall one, but something in her face, the pensive cast of her eyes, said she had been hurt. Besides, she had spoken before of a man who would destroy her once he found her. Maybe she told the truth this time.

A lump of fury settled in the pit of Drex's stomach. How could a man, any man, look at Lilli and want to hurt her?

Drex ached to comfort her but refrained.

Her story explained much: The haste with which she had fled, the expensive gifts stashed in her valise, the skittishness she exhibited around him, especially when he had been shirtless. Even now, her wide eyes bespoke anxiety.

Had some bastard beat or raped her? An urge to do violence rose up inside him. "How did he hurt you?"

She glanced up warily, her small white teeth worrying her bottom lip. "Let us not speak of it, please. It's past, and I will never see him again."

Clenching his fists, Drex held a frustrated sigh. He wanted to know the truth, learn the scoundrel's name and... What? Avenge her like some knight errant? Down that path lay dangerous thoughts and feelings. No matter what she said, Lilli was a lady, not the kind of woman who belonged on his ship. Not the kind who consorted with privateers born on the wrong side of the blanket.

Besides, he did not need Lilli and her penchant for trouble. Saving Ryan and keeping the British off his back were paramount. He needed to remember that fact when confronted with his stowaway's artless smiles and mouth-watering curves.

A gust of ocean breeze swirled the salty air about. Beside him, Lilli shivered, hugging herself.

Drex eyed her short, puffed sleeves. Even in the moon's buttery light, he could make out the goose pimples on her arms—as well as her hard nipples poking the light muslin fabric of her bodice.

He held in a groan as the tightening at the front of his breeches let Drex know his thoughts had wandered too far.

"Didn't you bring a wrap from your cabin?" He tried to sound annoyed, but all he wanted was to press Lilli against him and feel her soft curves melding into his body.

"I no longer have one. The cloak I wore aboard smelled dreadfully of animal fat, so I tossed it into the water."

He wanted to curse her for her impracticality, her lack of planning…and for being so damned tempting. Instead, he stepped in front of her to shield her from the wind.

"Go inside."

Drex's words came out more harshly than he intended. His inexplicable urge to protect her warred with his desire to have her in his bed. Either he was going to shout at her—or touch her.

God, what if her latest story was true? If one man had frightened her from all others, she would hardly be in search of a new lover. True, he would gladly volunteer for the position, in any position she desired, given other circumstances. But he could not succumb now. Taking a lover who had Ryan's aptitude for irresponsibility would be beyond foolish. He did not have the time for dalliance, no matter how much his body wished otherwise. Besides, if some man had hurt Lilli, he could not change the past, and she would hardly be likely to invite him into her bed or her body for a night of hard sex.

Instead of leaving, Lilli seemed to have her own agenda, as usual. She sidled closer to his back and shivered against him. Drex felt her breasts against his back, the wispy touch of her fingers on his arm. His cock tightened again in response.

"Damn it, Lilli. Stop shivering and go to your cabin."

"But I was enjoying the fresh ai—"

"Now you're finished."

He grabbed her by the arm and began hauling her below deck. Predictably, she struggled.

"I won't be ordered about like some naughty child."

He gripped her tighter. "On this ship, you will."

With that, he dragged her to her cabin and shut the door on her sputtering. In his own cabin, he could hear her muttering through the closed door separating them. Clearly, she wasn't happy with his behavior.

Neither was he. Continued rumination about whether Lilli's breasts would fill his hands perfectly and how tightly her sex would grip his cock had no place in his plans to save his brother.

Drex lay down on his bunk with a sigh and tried to concentrate on who might have written the anonymous note to Manchester back in London. The mystery needed solving.

The culprit certainly could not have been Greg. But had somebody overheard them talking at the tavern? Even so, how would that somebody know which club Manchester frequented?

And would Lilli's skin, damp from their exertion, taste as sweet as pure cane sugar?

His thoughts had to stop, even if the throbbing between his legs didn't. Her spirited unpredictability both fascinated and annoyed him, while her golden hair and smile drew him like a lighthouse in a storm. Damn it, how not to think of Lilli? He wanted her more each day. Denying that fact was like denying the tides of the ocean. Impossible in the face of such tangible proof.

Drex searched his trunk for the bottle of brandy he'd been saving for a sleepless night. Staring at Lilli's door, trying not to remember it had no lock, Drex took a swig from the bottle and vowed not to stop until he'd emptied it.

* * * *

Christina laughed into the crisp morning as she watched some of the men scramble about the ship's rigging. The farther they climbed, the more they looked like rats fleeing a cat's teeth. Oh, but the freedom. She could imagine the exhilaration of ascending into the heavens, witnessing the origins of the wind, feeling nature unencumbered against her skin.

Halfway to the sky, a sailor named Davie called down, "Aye, lass. If you think 'tis easy to climb up here, ye be wrong."

She stared up skeptically. "How hard can it be?"

"What could you know of a man's job?" called another.

"It looks no harder than climbing trees," she teased.

"Aye, is that so?" said Davie. "Yer welcome to prove yer skill, lass, anytime."

Knowing the captain still slept, Christina strode to the ropes with purpose. "All right, I shall prove it."

"You canna climb wearing that!" Davie exclaimed.

Christina glanced down at herself, frowning. "Why ever not?"

"It's not fit fer climbin'. Ye need...er, breeches."

Christina pondered his stammers. Where would she get breeches? In her cabin. Yes! She'd spied an old pair of Hancock's lingering in an abandoned trunk. But a shirt...

Besieged with a plan, she ran to her cabin and grabbed the breeches. Clutching the garment in hand, she tiptoed to the door separating her cabin from the captain's. As she opened the portal, it creaked. She winced and crept farther into the room.

She discovered that the captain slept naked.

In addition to the pile of discarded clothing at the foot of his bed, including yesterday's breeches and his mask, her gaze roved across the privateer.

She took in the strength of his sculpted back. Broad, bronzed shoulders dominated over half of his wide bed as he lay on his stomach, exposing the beguiling dragon tattoo on his back. Below that, a trim waist tapered to narrow hips...then firm buttocks shades paler than his back. Slightly spread legs gave her a glimpse of the heavy sac between.

His nudity evoked tingling, warm sensations in places her grandmother had never discussed with her. Very like the time the Black Dragon had kissed her. What would the rest of him look like?

Christina knew she should be shocked. Instead, excitement zinged through her. Sneaking these forbidden stares felt deliciously scandalous...but the view was even more appealing. Of course, she didn't have another man's backside with which to compare the captain's, but his enticed her.

The possibility of glimpsing his bare face gripped her next. She could not see his naked profile from where she stood, but if she tiptoed a few paces toward him, maybe she could get a glimpse of the countenance he took such pains to hide from the world.

One step. Then two. Getting close... A board creaked beneath her feet. She stood frozen to see if the sound had awakened him. Nothing.

She drew another step closer, restraining an oath when the floor beneath her creaked again. Christina held her breath as the Black Dragon stirred and rolled to his side, away from her. He grabbed at the blanket riding low on his hips and pulled up. The scintillating view of his buttocks disappeared.

Fearing he would wake at any second, Christina cursed beneath her breath and tiptoed in retreat.

Blast it all, anyway. Her curiosity about the man's face and anatomy would go unfulfilled. Why did the autocratic oaf rouse her interest?

Holding in a sigh, she bent and grabbed his discarded shirt from the floor, trying not to stare at the accusing eye of the captain's dragon tattoo. She could have found a clean shirt, she supposed, but none lay in sight. This one smelled of him, man, salt, sea. Her insides tightened. Part of her wanted to stay with him and simply stare, but she refused to miss out on this new adventure that he, no doubt, would not approve of.

Christina darted for her cabin and threw on her borrowed clothing. The breeches fit well enough, as Hancock was a small man, except for the waist. She snatched a ribbon off one of her dresses and belted it about her middle.

The captain's shirt presented another challenge, however. The shirttails hung to the middle of her thighs. One collar slid down to bare her shoulder.

Knowing there was no help for the shirt's size, Christina gathered up the loose ends in front of her and tied a knot about her waist. She glanced down at herself with a grin, refusing to contemplate her atrocious breach of fashion. Focusing on how displeased her grandfather would be if he could see her was much more gratifying.

Humming beneath her breath, she found her way to the deck again and spotted Davie, who had returned to solid ground. "Now I'm ready to climb."

The man's eyes could have left his head, for all they bugged out of their sockets. "You canna mean to wear that."

With an annoyed grunt, she picked up the dangling collar from her shoulder again and covered the exposed shoulder of her chemise. "You said I needed breeches. Now I have them."

"Aye, no mistake. But look around ye, lass. Yer gettin' more attention than a sea full of the Admiralty's schooners."

Christina glanced around to test his assertion. Indeed, all activity about her seemed to have stopped. Their gazes appeared all but sewn to her body. She stiffened her spine.

"Let them stare," she said coolly and reached for the ropes. "I intend to have fun."

"But—but..." Davie called.

Christina stepped up on the first rung of what Davie called the ratlines, which led to the rigging. Ascending the first few feet wasn't too difficult. She focused on the well-worn leather in her hands and maintaining the shifting footing beneath her.

"Don't go too high, lass," Davie warned.

"I shall climb to the top," she assured him, laughing.

He protested with all the vehemence of a scandalized matron. "You canna mean to go to the topgallant. 'Tis too dangerous."

She grinned. "This is fun!"

Scrambling up farther, Christina chuckled into the breeze that had steadily turned warmer as they'd sailed south over the past weeks. A fine mist dampened her hair, her skin as the sun breathed golden fire on her face. This was living!

How many other of the *ton's* misses could claim such adventure? Not a one. She laughed as she licked sea spray from her face.

The wind kicked up. Christina ignored the gales that whipped her tresses across her face. More gusts followed, harder ones, tearing away the bow holding her hair at her nape. Suddenly, the ratlines teetered beneath her. As she held on for balance and tried to grip the ropes beneath her with her hands and feet, her heart pumped with wild anxiety. Then, the ropes flipped, forcing her beneath the ratlines. Her feet left the leather, and she found herself dangling like a rag doll in the wind. She looked down and panicked. When had she climbed so high? Only the vise-grip of her hands on the ropes prevented her from crashing to the deck in a heap.

"Hold on, lass!" Davie called, his voice faint in the wind.

A glance down confirmed that the crew on deck all stared up at her like a spectacle from a traveling fair, yet no one climbed up to help her.

The wind stirred again, thrashing her about. Her fingers ached. Her stomach crunched in fear. If she fell…

Feet flailing, grip slipping, she kicked out, praying she could find some footing on the ropes in front of her again. Her feet caught—and slipped—through the damp rungs. Sweat beaded on her upper lip and broke out across her back. Her arms ached with a fierce burn. She looked down again. The flat deck stretched beneath her like vengeful stone, as if to remind her she did not belong on board.

Then came the worst vision of all: the captain.

Shirtless and scowling, he strode out on deck, casting his masked gaze up in the lines, along with everyone else.

She knew the instant the Black Dragon saw her. He tensed, then pushed the sailor aside.

The captain launched himself onto the ratlines and scrambled up with a speed and grace that astounded her. Even climbing beneath instead of above the ropes, he sped toward her. Once at her side, he looped an arm about her waist and drew her against him. Instinct guided her arms about his neck. He speared her with a furious glare, but she didn't care. The instant he wrapped his arms around her, Christina knew she was safe. He loosed a string of colorful curses over the sharp wind as they descended. Disquiet blended with her relief.

On the deck, he set her down with a grunt. "Are you hurt?"

Christina stared mutely at his disheveled dark mane and bare torso. The mask and beard obscured his face. At the moment, his disguise didn't matter. Her heart chugged in her chest for a reason that had nothing to do with fear. The dampness of her palms increased tenfold as she stared into the sharp, fathomless depths of his dark eyes.

"Are you?" He shook her shoulders.

She shook her head. "Ju—just my fingers."

The captain grabbed her wrists and turned her palms up to him. Christina stared at the red pressure stripes marring her skin. A moment later, he released her with a curse.

Shoulders tense, he pointed an accusing finger at Davie. "You should have bound and gagged her to keep her off those lines, damn it." Mouth taut with displeasure, he speared the man with a glare. "I'll deal with you later."

Christina wasn't allowed a word in Davie's defense before the captain wrapped his fingers about her arm and dragged her down to his cabin.

Slamming the door and enclosing them in privacy, he shouted, "Are you completely insane? Or do you simply want to die?"

"I just wanted to learn," she protested.

"Learn to be a corpse?" he shot back. "That's what you would have been had you fallen. Damn it, do you ever think before you act?"

"Of course."

He rubbed his forehead with a broad palm. "What if I hadn't come up? Davie's too small a lad to have taken you down the ropes with him. You would have both died."

Fury dripped in his voice, sparking Christina's pride. She thrust back her shoulders. His shirt fell off her shoulder, exposing fine linen and white skin. The rest of the damp garment clung to her breasts, riveting the captain's gaze to her. Quickly, she clutched the collar and yanked the garment back in place.

"And what the hell are you wearing, besides my shirt?"

"B—breeches. I was told I couldn't climb in a dress and—"

"And so you thought you'd do well to parade around in breeches before my sex-starved crew."

"I was hardly parading," she said through clenched teeth. "I just wanted to climb the ropes and feel the wind."

"Do you have any idea what those men would do to you with any encouragement on your part and any weakening on mine?"

"No one touched me," she returned. "Nothing happened."

"Nothing happened?" He curled his fingers around her arms in a tight grip. "It isn't over…"

An instant later, his mouth crashed down on hers. The uncompromising slant of his lips over her own stifled her protest. He wound his fingers into her damp tresses and pulled her head back to meet his punishing kiss.

Before she could think—could tell herself to fight—he deepened that kiss, stealing the air from her body. A dizzying wave swept through her until her head felt light, her thinking unclear.

He parted her lips with an insistent slide of his tongue. Once he thrust inside her, heat flooded her belly and pooled lower. A hot zip of thrill shot through her as he caressed down her back, to her hips. His fingers splayed against her, pressing her closer, into the hardness between his legs. She moaned. Of their own will, her hands slid up the satin of his muscled chest. She kissed him back, trembling with an ache she didn't understand but desperately wanted more of.

Instead, he released her with clenched fists, his chest heaving as he drew in shuddering breaths. Christina watched the rise and fall of his broad, bronze shoulders with a tingle of excitement igniting her body.

"What else could they have done to me?" she murmured.

He shook his head and growled, "Don't tempt me, Lilli."

"What else?" she insisted huskily.

The Black Dragon stood staring, unmoving, as if in indecision. Christina tossed her hair off her shoulders, sending his shirt dipping low again. "What else?"

At her taunt, he swore beneath his breath and stared at her bared skin. A muscle ticked in his jaw. Tense moments ticked by, and Christina measured them by the wild thud of her heart.

"This." The captain reached for the buttons of her shirt.

They seemed to unravel beneath his nimble fingers. He pushed it off her shoulders, baring her to the waist, except for a sheer, damp chemise. His gaze locked on her, fixed on the hard nipples pressed against the clinging garment. The heat of his body, of his stare, sizzled her.

"Kiss me again," she instructed.

He jerked his gaze up from her breasts to her face. She read a struggle in the downward slash of his brows, in the restraint in his frown.

She sidled closer and pressed her body against him. His breathing ceased for the briefest of moments.

Then he groaned and seized her lips again. His tongue wound its way into her mouth in an instant, as his hand trailed from her shoulder, down her aching breast. He cupped her, engulfing her sensitive flesh in the heat of his palm. His thumb brushed across her nipple. Tingles splashed across her skin in a hot drizzle. Christina hoped he would do it again, but he caressed his way to her hip. With a gentle pull, he gathered her thigh in his hand and held it around his body.

Christina felt him press the hard stalk of his sex to the joining between her legs. A new thrill shot from her chest, all the way to her fingers and toes.

"You make me crazy, Lilli. Sometimes I can't decide if I should throttle you or throw you in my bed."

Before she could reply, he bent to her and captured her chemise-clad breast in his mouth. A burst of lightning seemed to split her in half with pleasure. She arched toward him. The captain answered by taking her buttocks in his palms and fitting her closer against him.

His teeth and tongue played with the bud of her breast, teasing it to an aching stiffness. Pleasure skittered down to her belly…and lower. She cried out, fingers clasped about his shoulders.

"You're too damned sweet," he murmured before turning his attention to her other breast and, with a nudge, rocked his hips against her.

Molten heat spread throughout her body, singeing her with a need for more. Little cries slipped from her throat as she peppered his bearded face, his salty neck, with feverish kisses.

Seconds later, he yanked his shirt from her body and let the transparent garment slip to the floor. He untucked her chemise from her borrowed breeches and fitted his hands beneath. Christina felt his hot palms against the chilled skin of her abdomen.

Feeling his way up her torso, he skimmed his thumbs across her sensitive breasts. Christina gasped at the dizzying sensation. Then he lifted her undergarment above her head. It, too, joined his shirt on the floor.

He swallowed hard as his eyes roved over her bared flesh. "Dear

God," he breathed. "You are…perfect."

Before she could reply that she felt much the same about him, he lifted her against his chest and set her on his bunk.

He followed her down, covering her body with his. "Is this what you want, Lilli? Do you want me?"

She sighed. "Yes. Oh, yes. I've never felt like this, so alive. How wonderful and new!"

He backed away suddenly, withdrawing. Christina peered at him in confusion through the fog of her desire.

"You never felt like this with your lover?"

She shook her head, wishing suddenly she'd never told that lie, but she didn't want to spoil the moment with the truth, either. "This all feels new to me. So exciting."

"And you're willing to take another lover, just like that?" He snapped his fingers. "Even though the last one hurt you?"

"Well, I—yes. You're different. I trust you." She frowned. "I thought you understood."

"I do understand, Lilli. You've given absolutely no thought to the consequences and complications of letting me bed you. You were ready to jump into it, just like everything else in your life." He reached for a fresh shirt. "Me today. Who tomorrow?"

"That is unfair! I just told you I've never felt this way. It made me realize how much I have missed by not—" Marrying. But she couldn't say that. It was too revealing.

"Not taking another lover sooner?" He buttoned his shirt in a furious working of fingers. "I won't be one of your dalliances, Lilli." He shot her a scowl. "And stay away from my crew."

He stormed to the door. Christina rose from his bunk and grabbed her chemise, covering her breasts with the thin garment.

The captain turned back, anger narrowing his eyes. "Maybe your lover was jealous because you gave him reason to be, Lilli. I'm not about to play his replacement."

Chapter Six

Drex clapped the irons about Davie's ankles, trying to ignore the pounding of his head due to the excess drink he'd consumed last night. The pounding in his loins didn't improve his mood, either, since the discomfort only roused a vivid vision of Lilli, half-naked and flushed, in his bed.

"I'll come back for you tomorrow," he told Davie. "After that, I expect you to stay away from Lilli. Is that clear?"

"Ye—yes, Cap'n."

Turning away, Drex inhaled a deep breath of sea air. Davie assisting Lilli in her recklessness didn't anger him as much as his own regrets. He should have bedded Lilli when she had given him the chance and purged himself of his obsession with her. If he had given in to what she'd wanted, what they both wanted, maybe he wouldn't still be thinking about the honey perfection of her skin and the tight clasp of her wet sex.

But he had walked away. Drex couldn't decide whether he should crown himself this century's biggest fool or accept a medal for sainthood.

He shouldn't touch her. More each day, he realized the scope of her ability to create trouble wherever she went. She, like Ryan, thought of nothing but the present, of the pleasurable moment in their grasp. Never of responsibility or consequences. Drex wondered if they could not comprehend them or simply didn't care.

Undoubtedly, if he had become Lilli's latest lover, there would be repercussions he could only begin to guess at, even if she didn't realize it. He'd done right to simply walk away.

Too bad his body didn't understand that.

Worse, he had no illusions. If she laid herself out on his bed again and invited him to take his fill, Drex knew he would not have the strength to resist.

* * * *

Hours ago, Christina had finished her evening mess early, though her thoughts lingered on the captain all day. Her cooking had improved, not to Pauly's level, but enough to make her smile. She knew now how Aunt Mary must feel, taking charge of her own business, seeing it function smoothly. She looked forward to being equally independent once on Grand Bahama.

Whistling a merry ditty some of the men had taught her, Christina strode into the night air, to the poop deck in search of the captain, and sighed at the thought of his kisses, of his hand on her breast. Even the thought made her tingle.

Independence was a fine thing, but his touch added a zing of spice. Since autonomy and pleasure matched like a fine pair of gloves, Christina saw no reason why she shouldn't take advantage of their proximity. Besides, having a lover seemed so daring and modern. And the captain, as long as he did not try to control her, would make a dashingly scandalous *amor*.

According to the crew, the ship should be docking in Grand Bahama within the week. She pushed away an odd notion that she might miss the captain after they separated.

Without warning, crushing fingers closed about her arm. She jerked from the grasp and turned, ready with a sharp tongue.

Talbot hovered over her, his blue eyes boiling with malevolence.

"Release me," she warned.

He merely laughed.

Wide-eyed, Christina jerked from his grip and backed away. Her back hit the rail. Talbot sent her a cruel smile, and her stomach plummeted to her toes.

Talbot advanced and a jarring shot pain up her spine. "Now that I've got ye all alone, bitch, I've a mind to teach ye how to treat a man."

Christina wriggled for freedom. "Leave me alone."

Talbot laughed. The eerie rumble sent slivers of fear slicing through her skin. "Ye ain't going anywhere, 'cept down on your knees, not until I say so. You can go after I've had a piece of yer uppity arse."

"I shall scream," she threatened.

His meaty hands manhandled her shoulders. "I hope so. The watches'll be changing soon. 'Tis doubtful the crew will hear. So those screams will all be for me."

Talbot's clammy palms left her shoulders. Christina leapt away from the rail to run. He grabbed the neckline of her dress and pulled her back. Then he turned her to face him. The tips of his fingers pressed into the swell of her breasts, and Christina struggled, but he yanked on her round dress.

She screamed as the sound of rending fabric snapped at her lacerated senses like a whip.

Talbot grabbed her chin between brutal fingers and shook. "Keep yer screams to yerself until I'm fuckin' ye. Then ye'll have something to scream about."

Warning shone in the feral glint of his eyes as he shoved her to the deck, despite her writhing and kicking. Her head struck wood with a painful thud. She felt dizzy, couldn't breathe. Panic rose.

Talbot laughed with evil glee as he pulled a knife from his boot and cut her petticoats away.

For the first time in her life, Christina begged. "Please don't do this. I didn't mean to pour oatmeal over your head."

He whisked the blade of his knife to her throat. "'Tweren't no accident, ye lying wench. Just like it ain't an accident I waited to find ye without the Black Dragon to protect you."

His knife glinted a sadistic silver in the moonlight. Christina's blood roared in her ears.

Talbot stared at her, his ugly face furious, as he held her down with one hand around her throat. With the other hand, he pulled away the remnants of her dress and petticoats. Christina wished fervently she had not sworn off corsets in the name of women's liberation and the ability to dress herself.

Other than her chemise, she lay naked to Talbot's mean gaze.

He pressed his blade to her throat, while his free hand dipped to her thigh. "Now I'm going to get me a piece of wot the cap'n's been keeping to himself."

* * * *

Cursing torn sails and unexpected winds, Drex rubbed a thumb and forefinger across sleep-weary eyes. Damn it, he'd spent most of the day seeing to endless details that made his massive headache all the more painful.

Worse, his thoughts had lingered on Lillianne, the feel of her body, the taste of her skin. His growing need to have her soft and wet and welcoming under him.

Drex trudged the last few steps to his cabin. He shrugged out of his vest and crossed the room to Lilli's cabin, as he did each night. The gentle rise and fall of the blankets over her body somehow soothed and aroused him at once. The sight had become a strange part of his evening ritual.

Tonight, he found her cabin empty.

He cursed. During the wee hours of the morning, where could she be? And why the hell couldn't she stay where he told her to?

With a sharp snap of his wrist, Drex donned his vest, then strode out into the companionway. Climbing the stairs two at a time, he swore the moment he got his hands on Lilli, he'd make her understand that he'd given her orders to stay in her cabin to protect her. Didn't she understand that his men weren't gentle or kind?

He stomped down the passageway. Blast her. What tangle had she wound herself in now?

Hot annoyance coiled through his veins, enough, he decided, that he might be able to forget her tempting curves once he found her. At least long enough to throttle her.

As he stepped onto the deck, he heard a muffled scream. High-pitched. Definitely female.

He tried running to the sound, but the wind distorted its direction. He ran anyway, praying he'd find her safe, unharmed.

A tight knot of dread filled Drex's chest as he traced the deck from the bow and the port side of the ship, working his way aft. Nothing.

He raked a stiff hand through his long hair and sprinted for the larboard. If anyone had touched her, Drex vowed he'd make the man wish to God he had not—ever.

One long stride after another ate up the deck beneath his feet, along with his hope of finding her unharmed. God, what if she really needed him and he failed to find her in time?

Forcing down the wild beat of panic in his heart, Drex retraced his steps and listened for the slightest sound.

He heard her scream again.

This call sounded desperate. Fearful. Her cry made his churning heart pump ice in his veins at double speed.

He ran faster, rounding the aft of the ship and darting up the larboard side again. In the dark, between a pair of longboats, he spotted two struggling forms, the larger one pinning the smaller one down—and a torn pink dress cast aside like seaweed littering a beach.

He ran like a man on fire. With a savage grunt, he pulled his blade free, grabbed her attacker by his hair and yanked the man to his feet, shoving the knife at her attacker's throat.

Talbot.

"Damn you!" Drex cursed.

Without retort, the crewman lunged back at Drex, knife in hand. He ducked and countered with a solid gut punch that had Talbot clutching his abdomen. The bastard's blade skittered to the deck. Drex leveled a kick to the man's face. Talbot fell to the deck, cursing and clutching his bleeding nose.

Drex threw Talbot's knife overboard, sheathed his own, and bent to Lillianne's shaking body.

He scooped her up in his arms and held her cold, delicate form against him. He thought of nothing, only felt a piece of his heart tear when she clutched at his neck and held on as if he were the only thread holding her between life and death.

He heard the odd rhythm of Hancock's shuffle and shouted for his first mate to summon the rest of his on-duty crew. Within moments, reinforcements arrived, taking in the discarded dress and naked stowaway with round eyes.

"Hancock," he instructed. "Lock Talbot up in the hold. I'll join you there shortly."

Drex watched with cold satisfaction as Hancock and three others yanked Talbot to his feet and dragged him away. For the first time ever, he could honestly say he looked forward to a man's whipping.

A sob sounded in his ear. Soft, almost silent, as if Lilli were trying to hold her feelings inside. The sound ate at his heart.

"Shh," he whispered, groping for the right words to calm her. He stroked her hair, which had fallen loose during her struggle. "I won't let him hurt you again."

He felt her jerky nod against his neck and held her tighter.

80

"Look at me," he instructed softly.

She didn't move at all, except to eke out another quiet sob.

"Lilli, honey," he whispered. "Look at me. Tell me if you're hurt."

Finally, slowly, she lifted her head to regard him with a wide gaze, eyes drenched in tears. The dark spikes of her lashes framed dilated emerald eyes that saw him...but didn't.

God, he had no idea what was wrong, what that bastard had done to her. Drex feared the worst, and the images running in his head damn near made him sick, but he had to find out.

On trembling legs, he carried her across the deck and down the ladder to his cabin. Once inside, he eased the door shut and set Lilli on his bed. She looked tiny and pale against the giant black dragon that dominated his coverlet.

The urge to protect her rose strong.

Lilli lay on her back, staring at the wooden ceiling with sightless eyes and drenched cheeks. He lowered himself to the bunk beside her and reached for her hand. Her skin was ice cold. He covered her, then wrapped her against his body.

"You're okay now, Lilli. Talbot's gone," he assured.

No response.

Trying to suppress panic, he maneuvered himself closer and pulled her into his arms. She stiffened momentarily, then after glancing at him, she relaxed again.

"What happened?" he asked in the darkness.

Lilli said nothing for a moment. He stroked her hair and held her tighter. A few moments later, she snuggled against his body and sighed.

"W—why did he...?" Her broken whisper stopped on a shudder.

Drex drew in a breath, looking for the words to explain man's savagery. "You humiliated him in front of his shipmates. He wanted to humiliate you in return."

She shuddered. "I tried to stop him. He only said he wanted to get a piece of what you had been keeping to yourself. When I told him you— you had not..."

She inhaled raggedly, slicing him with both fury and a fierce need to protect her. Drex held her tighter.

"He laughed," she choked. "And called me a lying slut."

"Did he force himself—"

"No," she interrupted, as if she couldn't bear to hear the rest of his question.

81

Thank God. Relief shook him, and he held Lilli a little tighter. Talbot would definitely pay, not just for disobeying a direct order but for shattering Lilli's peace of mind. But that could wait. Right now, his terrified stowaway needed him.

That thought warmed a dangerous place in his heart as he felt her curl up against him, body to body, like a kitten.

* * * *

Christina awoke to the feel of a strange pillow. Hard, like satin steel. A pillow that moved.

Jarred out of the last remnants of sleep, she opened her eyes. The sight of the captain in slumber, illuminated by thin morning light through a murky window, filled her vision. The man wore his mask in sleep tonight. She couldn't deny that his scrap of black silk, combined with the dark beard and golden earring he sported, added a dimension of power and mystery. The shimmering red vest half-covering his bronzed chest added to the image.

Last night, he'd come to her rescue just like a knight of old. Why?

Easing away so she wouldn't wake him, she rose and discovered she was clothed only in his shirt, which carried his scent. Once, she would have blushed hotly at the thought of the Black Dragon's eyes touching her near-naked form. Oh, she might still blush a little today, but adventure and adversity—and the memory of his comfort—made her see the event differently now.

Last night, she had gotten her first real taste of life on her own. An unpleasant one, to say the least. With a frown, she decided she had not handled herself well. Shouldn't a woman of the world have been able to escape Talbot?

Leaning on the captain afterward like a child… Another slip in her modern-woman mode of thought. She had actually allowed him to carry her. No, welcomed it. Such behavior when she wished to rely solely on herself would never do.

She took a deep breath. Very well. She would thank the Black Dragon for his timely intervention, then learn to be more self-reliant in the future.

"Did you sleep last night?" His question broke the silence.

Christina's gaze jumped up to his face. His gaze traveled the length of her body; his expression remained carefully blank.

She looked about for something—anything—with which to cover her bare legs. Her own clothes were in the adjoining room, and he lay on the only blanket in sight.

"Indeed. And you?" she returned nervously.

Without a word, he rose and tore his coverlet from the bed. On slow footsteps, he approached. The combination of tenderness and concern in his eyes shocked Christina. Could it be the Black Dragon might be more than just the scourge of the seas?

He disappeared a moment later, coming to stand behind her, and draped the blanket over her shoulders. Christina clutched it to her breast thankfully.

"I'll give you a minute alone."

Nodding, she turned. Funny, the visage she'd always regarded as daunting now appeared gallant. "Thank you. For everything."

He swallowed, looking as if he had something to say. But he remained silent.

A moment later, his hand rose to her shoulder. Christina felt the warmth of his fingers curl around her neck, sending little pinpoints of warmth and pleasure scattering about.

The Black Dragon nudged her closer. She went willingly. A moment later, she felt his lips gently brush hers.

"You're welcome, princess," he whispered, then left.

* * * *

Later that afternoon, Christina stood beneath the baking summer sun, watching with mixed emotions as two sailors strapped Talbot to the mainmast. Her attacker was stripped to the waist. The ample flesh of his middle hung over the waist of his breeches. His skin's darkened tone almost disguised the faded scars criss-crossing his back.

Today, he'd get fresh marks. She shuddered.

Talbot turned an angry glare on her, then shouted at the captain, "I tell ye, the bitch deserved wot I gave her and more."

"The same could be said of you," the captain returned. His voice sent chills through her body, despite the overly warm day.

Hancock approached the Black Dragon, whip in hand, then handed the coil of leather over. Revulsion turned her stomach.

Talbot would have hurt her had the captain not rescued her. Still, she couldn't celebrate this punishment.

"Wait," she whispered as the captain raised the whip.

He lowered his arm and shot her an angry glare. "Damn it, he deserves this, Lilli. If I let him go, the others will believe they can behave like Talbot without consequence."

She bit her lip, considering his words. "I know," she said. And she did, even if she did not like it. "Must I watch?"

A muscle worked in the side of his jaw. "Maybe if you do, you'll understand what happens when you step on deck without me."

"But if you—"

"No more, Lilli. This is my ship."

Without further hesitation, the captain raised his arm and lowered it with a snap. Talbot cried out. Christina looked away as a line of red oozed across his back.

He deserved his punishment. Christina knew it. But as usual, the captain wasn't interested in any opinion but his own.

As the Black Dragon raised his arm again, she tore away from his side. Christina heard him call her name as she ran the length of the poop deck. She didn't dare stop.

Gasping for air, she ran in rhythm to the thud of her heart for her cabin and slammed the door behind her. True, the captain would find her soon enough, and she had no doubt he'd give her a full dose of his displeasure. Too bad. If he could do with his ship as he pleased, she would do the same with her eyes.

Christina sank down on her bunk, cheeks in her palms. Blast him, why did they always argue? Couldn't they ever discuss anything but responsibility and truth? The man never listened to others. He always assumed she wanted his opinion and guidance. Just like Grandfather.

So why did all of her thoughts center around the boor? Yes, he possessed magnificent shoulders, and her remembrances of his backside were stimulating, indeed. But the man hardly ever smiled. She had only seen a grin crack his implacable expression once or twice. Did he even know how to have fun?

He wasn't completely awful, though. The tenderness he'd displayed after saving her from Talbot's attack had amazed her. She had never believed the captain capable of such gentle concern. And who had ever heard of a privateer who could read?

She sighed. The man was a paradox. He titillated and confused her, intrigued and annoyed her. And when they reached Grand Bahama, he would be gone from her life forever. She would miss the freedom of the wind in her hair, the sway of the ship rocking her to sleep. She feared, however, she would miss the captain most.

The sound of his door and footsteps in the adjoining cabin brought Christina out of her reverie. The captain had returned from Talbot's whipping and no doubt wanted a word with her.

She stood and smoothed the front of her dress. The click of his boots indicated that he approached the door. Perhaps she could distract him from his anger and indulge her desire for more of his kisses at once, persuade him to become her lover. Maybe then she would discover he was not nearly as fascinating as she fancied and would not lament their parting.

Maybe.

Christina inhaled deeply, her stomach aflutter, and waited for the Black Dragon to walk through her door.

* * * *

Drex stood at the door separating him from his stowaway, hand perched on the latch, exhaustion turning his eyes gritty. He paused. How could he chastise her for running from the brutality of Talbot's punishment? He would never have forced Chantal or any other gently bred woman to watch such an event. Although Lilli had more backbone, she was still a woman.

And therein lay his problem.

If he walked through her door, his anger wouldn't confront her. He'd spent all of that on Talbot. No, frustrated desire and confusion would talk instead, and say God only knew what. He might yell. More likely he would strip her bare and make love to her.

She was trouble personified. But between her lies and half truths, he'd formed dangerous feelings for her. He'd come to covet her. Why, he could not fathom. Lillianne went hand in hand with distraction. His brother needed him, damn it. His stiff cock could wait.

But he wanted her. Too much, too deeply to explain.

Lilli had gotten under his skin. Beneath his rhetoric, he feared that if he touched her, took her into his arms and into his bed, tasted her skin and her passion, that letting go two days hence when they reached Grand Bahama would tear out part of his heart.

Drex dropped his hand from the door's latch and turned away with a sigh.

Chapter Seven

From the deck of *The Dragon's Lair*, Christina stared at the lush, green land of Grand Bahama soaking in the afternoon sun. Pristine white sand met water such a clear shade of blue-green, she saw the brightly colored fish swimming beneath the surface.

The island's beauty was everything Aunt Mary had claimed in her letters, and freedom would be hers as soon as she found a way off the ship. So why hadn't she demanded a row to shore?

Christina glanced over her shoulder at the Black Dragon barking orders at his crew. His shoulders appeared impossibly broad in a dark blue vest—with nothing beneath.

As if aware of her gaze, he turned in her direction and sent her a stare that singed her insides. She whipped her gaze back to shore, pretending interest in the swirl of afternoon activity.

To her right, two sailors led a shackled Talbot off the ship. The red-haired giant glared at the captain and sneered, "You ain't seen the last o' me!"

"If you know what's good for you, I have," the captain said, then turned to her, concern reaching her from his dark eyes.

She looked away. Why did the thought of parting with the Black Dragon make her ache? He was domineering and stubborn...and tender and occasionally fair-minded, something Grandfather never was, even in his finest of moods.

"Lilli?" he whispered from behind her as she stood at the rail.

She turned, meeting his dark eyes that seemed heavy with unreadable emotions. Something within her leapt. Maybe he cared a little. She didn't want to examine why it mattered if he did.

"I know you're anxious to go ashore," he said. "As soon as I clear port, I'll take you."

Then again, maybe he just wanted to rid himself of her.

Heart heavy, she nodded. "Thank you."

"I have to meet with the port master, but I should be back within the hour. You can pack while I'm gone."

The captain stared for the barest of moments. For some reason, she couldn't tell him she had already packed her belongings that morning, when she'd heard the call of "land ho!" Instead, she memorized his dark eyes framed by the ebony spikes of lashes, his strong jaw evident beneath his close-cropped beard, his lips, thin in fury and full in passion.

Christina wished she could touch him or talk to him, something to clear up the emotions whirling inside her. But he nodded and disappeared down the gangplank, and perhaps for the better. She hated good-byes. They were so teary and sad...and final. Besides, the captain was probably glad to be rid of her, and she shouldn't make a fool of herself by hoping differently.

"Know where yer goin'?" Hancock asked as he approached.

She nodded. "My aunt's."

He chuckled. "So there's an aunt, after all?"

"Yes," she said with a smile. "I have not seen her in years, not since before my mother died."

"The cap'n'll see to ye when he returns from havin' a few ales with the port master. God be with ye."

Hancock turned away, and with him, her last chance for escaping the ship without the Black Dragon's assistance, as well as enduring an awkward and prolonged farewell.

"Wait!" she called to him. "Could you take me ashore now?"

The short man studied her from beneath bushy brows. "The cap'n'd have me hide if I did. He wants to take ye himself."

"It would be better if I left now. He's a busy man and I..." She bit her lip. "I think I should go."

Hancock paused, then nodded. "The cap'n's been distracted of late."

Christina yearned to ask Hancock a dozen questions about his statement, but did not. Leaving the captain would be easier if she knew less of the man's feelings.

"All the more reason for me to leave now."

He frowned. "Get yer bag, lass, and hurry."

She ran across the deck, winding through companionways that had seemed like a maze to her once. Inside her cabin, she lifted her valise and headed for the door.

At the sight of the captain's closed door, she paused.

Though Hancock waited for her, she strode to the portal and lifted the latch. A rush of memories assailed her: their first conversation, which had also become their first argument. Their first kiss. His first display of tenderness. The moments when he had almost become her first lover. All had taken place here.

Tears pricked her eyes. She swiped them away. A better life awaited her with her aunt. Under it all, the Black Dragon would always have a tyrannical, inflexible side. He would only act as a shackle, never giving her enough slack in the chain for independence.

Today, she would begin a new life of freedom. The Black Dragon and his meddling ways need not be a part, and without his constant proximity, she would forget him.

Grabbing her valise, she rushed out of the cabin and shut the door behind her. She ran up to the poop deck before she could change her mind. Hancock stood where she'd left him.

During the quick row to the shore, Christina studied her new surroundings beneath the cloudless sky. She focused on the smells of spice, sweat and damp air. Anything but the captain.

Upon reaching the shore, Hancock helped her from the small boat. She took a closer look at the dock's inhabitants. A rough crowd, with grimy clothing and probing stares. She looked away.

"I can obtain a hackney to my aunt's. You needn't trouble yourself further, Mr. Hancock."

He shot her a dubious stare. "I already rowed ye ashore. The cap'n'd string me up if I let ye wander this rough town alone. Tell me where yer aunt lives."

Christina recited the address. Hancock's eyes widened with incredulity. "Are ye sure, lass?"

She recoiled. "That is where I send her letters."

"And ye want to visit?"

Christina stared at the first mate, confusion wrinkling her brow. "Actually, I wish to live there."

Hancock's face became a tight-lipped mask. "I see."

What he saw, she didn't know. Shrugging, Christina followed the man through the narrow streets surrounded by straw huts and luxuriant fields of green. Wild flowers of purple, yellow and white grew hither and yon, their perfume pungent in the breeze. Living here would be a relief, a balm to her soul. Especially if she could banish the Black Dragon from her memory.

After ten minutes of winding streets and rich foliage, Hancock stopped before an elegant house. Its pale hues and large windows invited tropical drafts. A large veranda ran the length of the dwelling and swept about its side. Stained glass decorated the massive door, depicting a bare-breasted maiden on her horse.

The house was perfect, exactly as Aunt Mary described it. She would enjoy her life here, relish her freedom. All she had to do was say good-bye to Hancock and walk inside. Then she could start a new life and put the captain out of her thoughts.

"Yer sure you want to stay here?" Hancock asked.

"Of course," she answered, wide-eyed. "It's lovely."

He sighed. Frowning, Christina watched Hancock turn away and step out onto the deserted street.

"Hancock," she called out. "Tell the captain…" Tell him what? That she wondered if she would always regret their parting? "Tell him good-bye."

"Aye, lass. I will."

Christina held her valise, watching as, a few moments later, the small man disappeared around the corner, and along with him, her last tangible reminder of the Black Dragon.

* * * *

"I still cannot believe you've come," her aunt said twenty minutes later. "How exciting! We've years to catch up on."

Awed by her surroundings, Christina nodded absently and turned her gaze to the drawing room. Hues of blue and burgundy, accented by dark furnishings, dominated the room with an understated elegance. A Brussels carpet stretched across the floor, indicating her aunt's good fortune. Yet she couldn't take her eyes away from a Rubenesque nude that commanded the spot of honor above the fireplace, its gilt-edged frame lending elegance to an otherwise shocking painting. She smothered her surprise, since she'd always heard morals in the islands were somewhat lax.

"Is London as dreary as ever?" Mary asked.

"Indeed not. I saw interesting people during my season, but Grandfather would not allow me to converse with them."

Mary rolled her eyes. "So the old man is still controlling?"

"It's why I've come."

A black-skinned maid shuffled in moments later and left a tea service. Aunt Mary poured two cups and handed her one.

Christina took the cup and drank. "I'm certain you're terribly busy with your social club, but I had nowhere else to turn. And I had so hoped you could teach me what you know."

Aunt Mary sent her a long, measuring look as she sipped her tea. "Indeed, I think I can. But tomorrow is soon enough to start. You must be exhausted."

Her aunt was right. The past six weeks with the Black Dragon haunted her. Of all that she'd endured during their time together, leaving had been most difficult.

"You're right, of course," Christina answered finally.

Mary rose. "My…club will be open tonight. The boarders to whom I rent rooms will meet here with some of the local gentlemen. But you rest up. I vow I shall introduce you to everyone another time."

Standing, Christina nodded. Another time would be soon enough to delve into local society.

"Thank you," she murmured.

With a grand flourish, Aunt Mary waved her appreciation away. "Think nothing of it. Abebi will show you to your room."

A moment later, the African woman who delivered the tea service appeared, her expression solemn. She nodded to Christina and turned for the stairs.

"Sleep well, darling," Mary called out. "We shall begin on your future tomorrow."

* * * *

Drex tore through the door joining his cabin to Lilli's. Gone, along with her valise of belongings. Damn her!

He'd worried when she wasn't on deck, when he had not located her in the galley with Pauly or in the ratlines with Davie. Now, both his cabin and hers stood empty.

Why? He'd promised to row her ashore.

Yes, but had he intended to keep that promise?

This morning's docking had forced Drex to face some unpleasant truths, chief among them that he would miss Lilli. A part of him didn't want her to say good-bye and walk out of his life. Why, he didn't know. He didn't have time to tolerate her reckless behavior, which reminded him too much of his twin. Besides, finding and rescuing Ryan should be his focus.

But Lilli could have at least said farewell before fleeing.

Slamming the door behind him, Drex bounded up to the poop deck. When he learned who had taken Lilli ashore without his permission, he would string the bastard up. If he had harmed a hair on her golden head, the man should consider himself dead.

"Who took Lillianne ashore?" He enunciated each syllable in the modulated tones of controlled anger.

Hancock approached and muttered, "That be me, Cap'n. The girl was wanting to leave. I thought it best, so ye could focus on the ship and her crew again, like before. But—"

"You defied my wishes."

"Aye, but—"

"I had plans to see her ashore myself." He raked a hand through his long, disheveled hair. "I intended to see her safely to her destination."

"Which I did," Hancock said. "But I think ye should know something else."

At Hancock's pause, Drex shouted, "Get on with it, then."

The little man swallowed, increasing Drex's alarm. "Lilli had me deliver her to the door of St. Mary's."

Drex opened his mouth to deny Hancock's assertion, but no words came forth. *The* infamous St. Mary's? The brothel? Not possible. Not his Lilli.

But hadn't she been prepared to jump from the bed of her deranged lover and into his own?

No, she wasn't the kind of woman to sell her soul, or any part of herself, to a stranger—to anyone. Lilli was determined to make her own path, and he doubted she intended to make it on her back. Then what the hell was she doing there?

"And you *left* her there?" Drex exploded.

"The lass was eager to be inside but said to say good-bye."

"Did anyone greet her?"

91

Hancock shrugged. "I didn't stay to see."

Panic churned his gut. "Did she say what she intended to do at St. Mary's?"

"She said she'd come to live with 'er aunt."

Her aunt? Confusion and anxiety warred with anger. Had Lilli lost all her remaining faculties? He sighed, grasping for rational thought. Did a woman who believed she was going to live with a relative expect to employ herself in Grand Bahama's most expensive and dissolute bordello? Usually not, but with Lilli, anything was possible.

Still, what if she needed him?

His emotions thickened into a rock of determination. Lilli had proven time and again that she didn't think about her actions, that she needed guidance. He knew there existed a very real chance she didn't know what went on at St. Mary's. After all, if she had merely aspired to sell her body for a living, she could have done so in England, or on his ship even. Yes, she had admitted to having a lover, but that hardly made Lilli a whore.

Damn it, now what was he supposed to do?

* * * *

Christina set aside the tray on which Abebi had delivered her meal and left her appointed room. The scents of perfume and some earthier musk hung in the air, so thick even the tropical gales streaming through the open window couldn't disguise them. From behind the closed door down the hall, she heard a man groan. An unusual sound in the midst of the chatting revelry downstairs, to be sure. Perhaps he was ill.

Shrugging, she crept closer to the stairs and peered down into the press of bodies occupying her aunt's home. A bevy of beautiful women conversed with men of all ages. Nothing so unusual, she supposed, except the shocking attire of the ladies. Dresses cut scandalously low, exposing a dangerous amount of bosom. The island gentry certainly did observe lax standards.

She searched about for Aunt Mary. Instead, her gaze encountered a woman adorned in a vibrant shade of green. Her dress possessed a slit from ankle to knee, exposing most of her leg when she walked. In deference to the heat?

Men all around the room leered at her and the others. Little wonder, Christina supposed, given the way the local women attired themselves.

Still, if she had any hope of belonging to their free society, she must stop thinking like a London miss.

A man circulating within the crowd gained her attention. His back faced her. But those wide shoulders, that dark hair, bisected by a knot of black silk, could only belong to one man.

The Black Dragon.

A redhead in a copper-hued dress approached him, her bosom exposed like some of the fast women her grandmother had warned her to avoid. The woman spoke, leaning close to the captain. He said something in return, which the redhead answered by shaking her head and placing a hand on his shoulder.

Christina stared, mouth gaping open at the pair. If the woman exhaled, they'd be touching in a most scandalous way!

He dipped his head closer and spoke again. As the woman swayed yet closer and the conversation continued, Christina felt fury rise up within her. How dare he! The man had made her feel something for him. She clenched her fists at her sides. She had been prepared to make him her lover. How quickly he had cast her aside to flirt with a woman she would hardly call a lady.

Well, she would just let him know what she thought of him. The brute. The knave!

Lifting her skirts, Christina marched down the stairs and headed directly for the captain. Before she could reach him, she was waylaid by a paunch-bellied man with bleary eyes holding what couldn't possibly be his first glass of brandy.

"Well, m'dear. Don't believe I've seen you before."

"I've just come from London. If you'll excuse me—"

"Don't rush away. I couldn't bear to lose a tempting morsel like you tonight. Why don't we—"

"Why don't you leave her alone?" said a voice Christina recognized instantly.

"I saw her first," the man argued, then turned to look at the competition.

The instant fear on the older man's face was nearly comical.

And grew more frightful when the Black Dragon reached for the dagger at his side. "She belongs to me."

Immediately, the drunkard backed away quickly, stumbling over his own feet in his haste to get away. "O—of course."

"I would have dispatched him on my own, thank you," she said stiffly.

He stared at her a fathomless moment. His gaze told her he had a million thoughts to voice, yet he remained mute. Why had he come here? To say good-bye? Her chest ached with fresh hurt.

He grabbed her arm and led her toward the stairs. "We need to talk privately."

His tone sounded familiar—and forceful. Couldn't he once just be a man, instead of an autocrat? She twisted and jerked her arm, trying to free herself from his grasp. "I will not have you order me about like a child any longer. I am not on your ship and I no longer have to respond to your orders."

"Shut up, Lilli, and listen to me."

The urgency of his voice quieted Christina. He was obviously concerned about something.

"Do you want a new lover so badly that you would come here to find one?" he asked. "If you're that damned adamant about having one, why didn't you tell me?"

"What?" His question made no sense. How did they leap from his dictatorial order giving all the way to her contemplation of taking a lover? "I have no idea what you mean, and *if* finding a lover were foremost on my mind, you would be last on my list."

He drew in a deep breath. "Where do you think you are?"

"At my Aunt Mary's house."

"Mary is your aunt?" His astonishment was thick.

"Of course." Did he know her, too?

"And you've come to live here? On purpose?"

"And to learn her business, yes," Christina replied, frowning. "What is this about?"

"You *want* to be a whore?"

Christina's jaw dropped to her chest. "What a horrible thing to say! Just because my aunt is an independent woman with her own business does not make her a—a woman of loose morals."

"Damn it." The captain pulled on her arm and drew her closer. "Do you mean to tell me you have no idea that your aunt is the most notorious madam in the Caribbean?"

"That's ludicrous. She runs a social club."

"That happens to sell female companionship by the hour."

Christina jerked her arm from his grasp. "I will not listen to this another instant! I have no idea why you insist on feeding me these lies, but I will not be controlled by you or any man. I mean to make my own way in life, just as Aunt Mary does."

She turned away and mounted the first stair. The captain hooked an arm about her waist and drew her back. "Look around you. Do you see women dressed like this in London? They stand damn close and touch the men in a very familiar manner."

Christina closed her eyes stubbornly. "No, I won't look or listen anymore, either. I'm happy here and I refuse to let you spoil it."

He shook her. "Open your eyes, damn it."

She did, intent on expressing her displeasure. A woman with her arm wound through that of a well-dressed man passed them and mounted the stairs.

"Where do you think they're going?" he whispered furiously.

She drew herself up and squared her shoulders. "Just because you choose to give the most lascivious meaning to a simple stroll does not mean I must."

"They're going to her bedroom!" he insisted.

The man thought he knew everything! Infuriated, Christina tried her best to look down her nose at the captain. "I don't care. You are not welcome here any longer, and you certainly are not welcome to meddle in my life."

"Come, dear," her aunt's familiar voice chastised gently. "You are hardly being polite to our esteemed guest." She turned to the captain. "I'm honored to finally have the Black Dragon beneath my roof. You've met my niece?"

He nodded coolly. "I brought her here from England."

"My, what a noble gesture from such a feared man. Did she pay you properly for your trouble?"

Christina's eyes widened as she watched the captain's jaw flex tightly. "I declined."

Mary's expression conveyed intrigue. "Should you change your mind, I suggest you return in three days. Make yourself comfortable, if you care to...occupy yourself until then."

Before Christina could say a word, sputter her questions about the entire bizarre conversation, Mary took her arm and swept her up the stairs and into her room.

Chapter Eight

The next afternoon, Christina took her tea on the veranda, determined to enjoy the breeze. She peered down the hill to the docks. A collection of ships stood at anchor in the port's calm blue waters. Was *The Dragon's Lair* one of those ships?

It hardly mattered if he had left her behind. His suggestion last night had been insulting in the extreme. Her aunt, a madam? He insisted on taking the worst view of others. She was better rid of him, and soon her heart would know it, too.

Her aunt opened the door and stepped onto the veranda, looking much like a woman who had just awakened, despite the late hour. She rubbed her pale eyes.

"Good morning, or I suppose, afternoon." Mary chuckled. "Forgive my lateness. I'm not one for early hours."

Christina smiled. "I confess I was the same in London."

"Of course." She touched Christina's shoulder. "Why don't you come inside. I think we should discuss your future."

A bout of apprehension knotted her stomach as she followed Mary through the drawing room and passed the dining room. Now that her freedom had arrived, apprehension gripped her. Though Aunt Mary hid her fatigue well, the fact her club had not closed until the wee hours of the morning served as an indicator that her aunt worked hard. Could Christina be as successful?

They finally halted inside an enchanting room decorated in pale

96

blue and white. Flowered pillows rested at each corner of the sky-hued sofa. Tassels of gold added extra accents. Mary threw open the window, which overlooked a vast expanse of ocean. A salty breeze drifted in, contenting Christina.

Mary motioned her into a Queen Anne chair upholstered in a creamy shade of yellow, then sat behind a dainty writing desk.

"Have you given your future a great deal of thought?" her aunt asked.

"Oh, yes. I so want to be independent, to make my own choices, experience all that life has to offer."

"Of course you do," Mary quickly agreed. "But the reality is not an easy one. How do you expect to support yourself?"

Christina frowned, realizing she hadn't figured that out yet. "I suppose I hoped you might teach me about your vocation. I, too, could run a social club, I should think."

"You could, in time. It takes some…practice to learn how to please your guests. And you must have money for your own house, but I'm getting ahead of myself." She smiled and shifted in her chair. "I considered supporting you myself, to shield you from the reality of life's difficulties, but—"

"Oh, no. I truly want my own independence, which you said meant facing the good and bad, and overcoming them in spite."

Mary nodded thoughtfully. "Yes, I did say that." She sighed. "Well, since you feel that way, we must make plans."

Christina folded her hands in her lap to restrain her excitement. "What should I do?"

"First, I must tell you that the Black Dragon was correct in his claims last night, Christina."

She felt her stomach crash to her toes. Her eyes lost focus; her hearing faded. "*You* are a light—"

"I prefer to think of myself as a female companion," Mary cut in with a tight smile.

Her aunt's assertion brought Christina to shocked silence. The illusions she'd held these ten years shattered. Mary was a madam. No wonder Grandfather had forbid her to exchange letters with her aunt. He'd known the truth. As had the captain.

"Now," Mary prattled on, apparently interpreting her silence as acceptance. "I shouldn't like to make your first days as a companion unpleasant, so I've worked up something special. I'll need to know, love, have you been…intimate with a man? If not, the price you fetch will be much greater."

"I don't understand. I thought…" Christina frowned, struggling. "I envisioned you ran a club like Boodle's for the ladies of the island. That they came here for tea and gossip."

Her aunt's laugh trickled down Christina's spine like a frigid waterfall. "I'm not surprised my father hid the truth from you."

Why hadn't she thought much beyond her arrival in Grand Bahama? She had not considered her future in detailed terms.

Christina jerked her hands away. "I cannot possibly become what you're suggesting."

Mary scoffed. "Child, the ways in which a woman can make the kind of comfortable living to which we've become accustomed are two: She may marry and be leg-shackled to the same sorry gentleman for her lifetime or provide the services of a wife without the restraints of marriage. If you truly wish for independence, I should think you would prefer the latter. Your money, time and thoughts will be your own."

Christina grappled with her aunt's words. "But to allow a perfect stranger to know your most intimate secrets… How can you abide that?"

"It's a simple matter, really, once you learn to disconnect the mind from the body. Time will teach you to adjust. Now"—she cast Christina a demanding stare—"are you a virgin, dear?"

"I will not do this!" she replied. "I will not lie down and bare myself to a stranger."

Mary shrugged. "Of course I can put you on a ship back to London. But now that you're ruined in society's eyes, your grandfather will only marry you off to some brutish pauper who will use you in much the same manner as any man you take into your bed here. He will expect children and keep a mistress, use your money and give you little, if any, consideration. But if that's your wish…"

Rubbing her aching temples, Christina acknowledged the truth of her aunt's words. London was not a viable option. But neither was becoming a common trollop.

She thought briefly of the Black Dragon. Maybe if she could get a message to him, he would help. As soon as the thought materialized, she dismissed it. He would only give her his superior I-told-you-so expression before chastising her with the full force of his contempt. And running to him for help would hardly make her independent. Blast him, did he always have to be right? She sighed in frustration, vowing to escape this mess on her own. A self-reliant woman would do no less.

"I see this is something of a shock for you," her aunt murmured and snapped her fingers. "Abebi will show you to your room. I've many arrangements to make."

Christina stood at her dismissal. "Cancel your plans. I won't become any man's harlot."

Mary raised a thin brow. "What will you do? Live on the streets? Christina, as women, life offers us limited choices."

"I—I'll become someone's governess," she blurted.

"With no references but me?" Mary laughed. "How sweetly idealistic you are. You will make some man a handful of a mistress, for which he will adore you."

"I shall become a traveling companion, then."

Mary sighed. "Really, do stop dreaming. After spending a night here, you're ruined for respectable society. Now, tomorrow we shall cover the basics of what your duties to a protector will entail and ways to prevent pregnancy. I think it would be helpful if I explained the rudiments of sex. Yes, I will, later today."

Christina's stomach curled with revulsion. A moment later, Abebi's surprisingly strong grip wound about her arm. She resisted the woman's pull, but Abebi proved stronger.

Halfway to the door, Mary called, "Do rest well and think about what I've said. Soon, you will realize I'm helping you."

"I will not be any man's whore!" Christina shouted, trying to pull her arms from Abebi's grasp.

Mary stood, all pretenses gone. "Stop being so dramatic. You will learn, as all women do, to accept your place in life." She cast her stormy gaze to Abebi. "Lock her in her room."

* * * *

Drex dropped his forehead into his hand and swore. Haunting images of Lilli being pawed and raped by strangers in her aunt's high-class brothel chased themselves through his head, denying him a moment's peace. Why hadn't she seen reason when he had spoken with her on the stairs at St. Mary's? The evidence of her aunt's profession was irrefutable. Yet Lilli had insisted on arguing. She was rash, unthinking, lacking in genuine understanding of the world.

He was worried as hell about her.

99

Hancock knocked on his cabin door, echoing the pounding in Drex's head.

"Enter," he barked.

His first mate stepped in reluctantly. Drex sighed, knowing his demeanor had been that of a wounded bear for the past two days. Consciously, he softened his voice. "What is it?"

"The hull's been scraped and repairs are done. The ship be ready to sail," Hancock said. "We can leave with the next tide."

Drex nodded. Leaving this hellish island as soon as possible would get his plan back on track. He must return to London, abduct Manchester's granddaughter and ransom her off for Ryan's release. He shouldn't linger another moment here.

"Do we sail?" Hancock prompted.

"Damn it," Drex cursed. His answer should be yes. The journey back to London alone would eat up at least four precious weeks of Ryan's life. But now he had Lilli to consider, too. He couldn't just turn his back on her.

"I went back to St. Mary's last night," he muttered instead. "Lilli was nowhere in sight. I'm not convinced she's living there of her own free will anymore." His gut ached with the pain he feared Lilli was suffering. "God, what if her aunt has already put her to work?"

"She hasn't." Hancock handed him a scrap of paper with a sigh. "Read this."

Drex grabbed the paper. "What is it?"

His first mate shrugged. "Ye know I can't read much. But one of St. Mary's men delivered it. He was real insistent it reach ye, Cap'n."

Drex swallowed the cold fear clogging his throat. Clutching the paper in his hand, he read aloud:

"You are cordially invited to a special one-time offering of tempting English innocence. Refined yet abandoned, she will enchant all but leave with only one. Bidding commences precisely at ten this evening.
St. Mary"

Below, the infamous madam had inscribed a personal note:

"Perhaps, for the right price, you would care to enjoy what you once declined..."

Drex crushed the invitation in his fist, wishing it were St. Mary's neck.

"What are ye goin' to do, Cap'n?" Hancock asked.

Absent of a ready reply, Drex said nothing. An auction of the flesh? He'd never been to one, and not for lack of opportunity. He had refused to attend in the past. A woman up on an auction block, much like his own mother had been on the streets each night—the very thought left a bitter taste on his tongue. But to see proud Lilli there, bared to flesh-hungry debauchers ready to use her and cast her aside, as his cad of a father had done to his mother... He would not tolerate it.

* * * *

Nine thirty according to the clock on the table. Resolving not to panic, despite the fact her doom lay but half an hour away, Christina darted past the lush cream, red and gold decor of her bedroom prison to the door again. She lifted the latch, only to catch sight of the guard's icy glare.

For a moment, she considered running as fast as her slippered feet would move. But Aunt Mary's human imitation of a bloodhound was quicker without yards of petticoats to drag him down, and stronger, too. She had the bruises to prove that fact. Besides, how far would she get, clad only in undergarments?

Feeling tears sting the backs of her eyes, she shut the door and closed her eyes. Dear God, what was she going to do, a penniless woman without even a dress? If she didn't do something soon, she'd be sold off like a brood mare before night's end.

Whirling, she ran to the window, only to find it locked, as she had every other time she'd sought escape. Blast it all, she had to find a way to flee, to hide. But where? And how? She must think of escape.

A click of the door's latch was followed by the opening of the portal. Dread clenched her stomach as she watched Aunt Mary drift through, with a glaring red dress and an impersonal smile.

"You look lovely," she said. "Abebi did a fine job styling your hair. Don't forget, men love it loose and long like that."

"Please, Aunt Mary. Put a stop to this." Her voice trembled. "If you're trying to scare me, you've done it well."

Mary set the dress aside on the bed. "Christina, of course you're nervous. You don't know who your first lover will be, yet you will have one before the night is through. It's an intimidating thought. But you're a courageous girl." She smiled. "I've no doubt you'll flourish."

"Let me stay here," Christina offered desperately. "Let me cook for you. That's what I did for the Black Dragon."

Mary laughed. "You're a wasted asset in the kitchen, darling. I have a roomful of men downstairs dying to get a glimpse of you. I suspect even the Black Dragon would choose you as his lover, not his cook, if he could see you now." She sighed breezily. "But time will tell. I've invited him tonight. Somehow, I think he'll come."

Christina's heart leapt both in hope and fear. Would he save her? Or would he come to watch her downfall, witness the sale of her body and soul to another man?

"Now," Mary said, a scandalous red dress designed to cover virtually nothing in hand. "Let us put this on you."

Christina stood stock still, arms crossed over her chest. "I will not wear that!"

Her aunt dragged her gaze over Christina's body clad only in sheer undergarments, then back to the dress. She tossed the red abomination on the bed. "Perhaps you're right. What you have on is much more to the point."

Christina's eyes widened. Tears slid down her cheeks in a hot drizzle. Would this nightmare never end? "Give me the dress. I'll wear it."

"There's a good girl," Mary praised, delivering the garment into Christina's hands.

Reluctantly, she dragged the tight dress of red silk over her body. It clung like an extension of her own skin about her shoulders and waist. The décolletage dipped dangerously low, exposing the upper swells of her breasts. A slit up both sides of the dress exposed her from ankle to thigh.

Christina felt every inch a whore.

Her aunt fastened the back and smoothed the fabric in place. "You remember everything I told you about mating, don't you?"

Christina sent her aunt a pained frown, not wanting to revisit the gruesome discussion. She still shuddered at the knowledge her aunt intended her to touch, and even kiss, certain parts of a stranger's anatomy. Intercourse itself sounded suffocating and painful. She couldn't fathom that tonight she might be forced to allow an unknown man the same liberties.

No, she wouldn't allow it. Instead, she would encourage some unsuspecting older gentleman to purchase her, then run from him. Yes, that would be her plan.

Drawing in a deep breath, Christina let the measure of calm her plan created cascade over her distraught nerves. She wouldn't surrender her body on someone else's terms.

The clock struck ten. The deep gongs of the clock cracked the façade of Christina's fragile peace. She sent her aunt a questioning glance.

"Yes, dear heart. It's time to face your future."

Chapter Nine

The buzz of conversation died abruptly when Christina entered the large drawing room, led by two of Aunt Mary's henchmen, who each gripped one of her arms. She swallowed hard.

Her darting gaze took in the crowd of nearly fifty men scattered about in the refined dark green and burgundy room. Their lascivious stares made them look like depraved fiends, despite their gentlemanly modes of dress. She did not see the Black Dragon anywhere.

Cigar smoke hung thick and pungent in the air. Christina bit her lip to rein in a cough. She'd never had to endure this sharp smell in England. Smoking was socially prohibited in front of ladies. Clearly, the men in this room no longer considered her worthy enough to observe the social graces.

To them, she was a whore. Tears stung her eyes—and not just from the smoke.

A young man tossed his blond head roguishly as he whistled low and long. "You're a fine piece I plan to enjoy." His gaze scanned her up and down, insultingly thorough. "For a long, long time."

Christina turned away, feeling the burn of shame. She hated her red dress, hated these men.

God, how had her bid for freedom gone so horribly wrong? From a yearning for independence, she had become a veritable slave.

Fortifying anger surged. She clung to her plan, her gaze scouring the crowd for an old gentleman to encourage, one who couldn't run quickly enough to catch her. The smoky room made her quest a burning challenge on her eyes, until pointed fingers and whispers of awe drew her attention to the back.

Surprise clutched at her throat. Her heart began to pound in a quick thud.

She spotted the Black Dragon, leaning against the farthest wall. Hancock stood at his side.

She'd half expected to see him here, but his presence washed her with a mix of hope, fury and despair. Had he come tonight to save her? Or shake his head at her stupidity? His face gave nothing away. True, he had rescued her from Talbot, but probably because he'd needed to maintain discipline on his ship, not because he wanted her for himself.

Christina's gaze clung to him. His white shirt contrasted with tight black breeches that encased the length of his hard thighs. She took in the familiar shag of his shoulder-length hair, admitting that he looked massive and dangerous with strong arms crossed over his chest and a gun strapped to his thigh.

If he was worried in the least about the fact that soon she would be forced to bed a stranger, he didn't show it.

One of Mary's men ended her stare by pushing her toward a raised dais. The two workmen lifted her up into a plush chair of white velvet. She sat stiffly, shoulders squared to prevent displaying even more of her cleavage in this sieve of a dress.

She closed her eyes. This could not be happening! Maybe she could run for freedom now. If she could hide until she found a way off the island...

Christina jerked forward in her seat and lifted her skirt, preparing to run. Aunt Mary's man grabbed her arm in a vise grip and discreetly returned her to her chair. A warning glare and a display of the firearm concealed beneath his coat convinced her to remain seated.

Trembling, she raked the crowd with her gaze. On the left half of the sumptuous room, she spotted a thin man whose spectacles, thinning hair and shaking hands gave her hope her plan to ensnare a frail protector would succeed. She sent him a smile she prayed wasn't nearly as stiff as it felt.

Aunt Mary took the stage by her side, wearing a sapphire dress that hid her less-than-lean waist but displayed most of her ample bosom. Christina felt the collective awe of her guests.

"Gentlemen," she called, "feast your eyes on this lovely girl. Imagine, if you will, plucking the petals of her untouched flower and making her a woman."

Someone groaned. Christina saw the men's hungry gazes wrap around her tighter, squeezing the air from her lungs in a terrified rush.

She closed her eyes to block out the view.

"A genuine virgin, ripe for the picking," Mary said in a throaty voice. "For the right price. Because she is my niece, you are assured the bonus of passionate blood. Jonathan…"

The audience clapped as Mary gestured to a man in the corner, dressed to the nines in immaculate black and white.

This whole event seemed much like a nightmare. God, why couldn't she wake up tomorrow and discover that was all the last three hellish days had been?

Jonathan, the auctioneer, tossed her an impassive gaze before positioning himself at the front of the room. "Bidding begins at one hundred pounds, gentlemen."

"One hundred," called three men at once.

Christina's stomach threatened to revolt. She clenched her fingers into tight fists.

"One hundred fifty."

"Two hundred."

"Three hundred twenty-five!"

Her every pore burned with shame. In retrospect, not questioning her aunt's way of life, which Grandfather had always referred to as shocking, had been foolish. In fact, failing to plan details, ask questions and think her life through—all mistakes. Too late for regrets now. She spied the old man she'd smiled at earlier and gave him another encouraging grin.

He mopped his damp brow. "Four hundred pounds."

She let out a deep breath at this good development. Still, she wondered about the Black Dragon's presence. Had he come to witness her downfall? Worse to contemplate, maybe he had come for the same reason as every other man in this room. He had yet to say a word, give her a hint, to ease her anxiety. But she wasn't his responsibility, and Christina knew she could not expect him to intercede on her behalf.

She had to escape this mess without him.

Holding her breath, she prayed no one else would bid after the older gentleman.

"Five hundred," called the young man who had threatened to enjoy her for a long time.

"Five fifty," replied the older man again. The quiet, even tone of his voice set her at ease.

She cast a quick glance at the Black Dragon before she could stop herself. His stoic expression showed no emotion.

"Six hundred," came the young man again.

Christina batted her eyelashes at the older man. *Please, please bid again!*

Her target sighed. "Six seventy-five."

The reluctance in his voice didn't encourage her. The knot in her stomach tightened.

His young opponent laughed. "Give over, Smithers. I can outbid you any day. We all know that." He ogled her again. "Seven hundred fifty pounds."

A dense silence followed.

Christina's stomach careened in a sickening slide to her toes. She looked to the Black Dragon in panic. Yes, she wanted to be an independent woman, but sometimes life forced one to accept help. Like now.

The captain merely raised a brow.

"Seven hundred fifty pounds is the last bid, gentlemen," reminded Jonathan. He let a significant pause slide over the room. "Seven hundred fifty pounds going once." His gaze scanned the hushed crowd, then rested on Christina.

Wasn't the captain going to say anything?

"She's lovely goods, gentlemen," Jonathan added. "Are you planning to allow Mr. Caulfield to steal her from you all?"

No one breathed, it seemed. Not even the Black Dragon. Blast him! Panic surged. Her heart raced.

"Twice," Jonathan said.

She turned her expression of undisguised terror toward the captain and found his gaze focused on the auctioneer.

Her eyes slid shut with the knowledge that her future was nearly ruined and her humiliation just beginning.

"Well, then, the lady is—"

"One thousand pounds," another voice thundered into Jonathan's speech. "In gold."

The sound of the audience's gasp receded as Christina's eyes snapped open and followed the voice to the back of the room. But she'd know that voice anywhere.

The Black Dragon.

Relief swept over her. The edges of her vision turned fuzzy, her equilibrium tilted dizzily, whether from the tight dress or shock, she wasn't sure.

The captain pushed away from the burgundy-papered wall and strode between the aisles of chairs, his masculine grace shouting lethality. Around him, the room stopped.

The young bidder's face turned a mottled red. He whirled to find his new opponent. When the Black Dragon entered his line of vision, mask, weapons and half-concealed tattoo, the blond man's eyes widened as his complexion waxed white.

The captain approached Mr. Caulfield with a slow, purposeful gait. The man stood his ground.

In a seemingly casual pose, the Black Dragon shifted his hand closer to the gun at his thigh. "I'd be vastly disappointed if you were to outbid me," the captain said.

Surely everyone in the room saw the meaning of his veiled threat. She held her breath, waiting for his reply.

"She's not that beautiful," Caulfield said, then shrugged.

"I'd hoped you weren't stupid," said the captain. He followed the words with a chilly smile.

"Take her," the other man insisted with a gesture to Christina. "She's not worth what you paid."

She swallowed her tears at the crass exchange, wishing to God she were anywhere else. She glanced at the Black Dragon. His eyes were black with fury and another emotion she couldn't quite name.

"Sold!" shouted Jonathan. "For one thousand pounds."

The nightmare was over. Christina sagged into her chair, not certain whether to clap wildly or burst into heaving sobs.

As the grumbling guests stood, then made their way to Mary's waiting girls, her aunt bent to whisper in her ear. "I knew he would come for you."

Dazed, Christina turned to her aunt. Yes, the captain had come for her. He'd paid one thousand pounds for the privilege.

What exactly did he expect in return?

She lifted her gaze to him, waiting for him to do or say something. He merely returned her stare with a weighty one of his own that set the uncertainty in Christina's stomach whirling.

Then the Black Dragon strode toward her, his gait swift, his mien possessive. Too many emotions to name assailed her.

"Good luck, child," her aunt prattled on. "You may call upon me if you fall on hard times again."

Christina shot her aunt a disbelieving glare. After all the horror she'd endured, being locked in one room for two days, forced to listen to a revolting explanation of sex that involved men shoving hard flesh into her various orifices, being sold like a common slave, Christina would never come here again, no matter how desperate a twist her life took.

Without a word, she turned her back on her aunt.

She faced the Black Dragon, head held high. Anger rolled off of him in waves.

Her emotions brewed like acid in a boiling cauldron. She had a million questions, yet she could find no words. His ominous expression said that her situation was still tenuous.

Aunt Mary wore a polite but amused smile. "I believe there's a small matter of payment."

He opened a small sack he'd strapped around his hips and counted out a brimming handful of gold coins. He gave them over to her aunt without a word—without even looking at her.

Mary smiled. "You've made a wise choice. She'll need a firm hand, no doubt, but she'll serve you well."

Irritation piqued Christina. "I will not—"

The Black Dragon squeezed her hand tightly, ending her short-lived tirade in a fit of crushed fingers.

"I intend to give her a firm hand."

"Among other firm things, I'm sure." The trill of Mary's throaty laughter set Christina's nerves on edge, while her aunt's words reintroduced dread that the Black Dragon now expected a bedmate. "Thank you for the business, Captain."

He nodded at her aunt in dismissal, his stare still focused her way. "Hancock has gone to retrieve your luggage. Let's go."

Apprehension flooded Christina like a deluge. This was the same man who'd seen her safely to Grand Bahama, protected her from a ship of lusty men, held her after Talbot's attack. Yet tonight, he wasn't the same man at all.

The captain threaded a possessive arm about her waist, and they turned for the door. She bit her lip in worry as they descended the stairs.

On the moonlit veranda, Hancock stood, holding her valise. That sight, along with the warm night wind, struck Christina with one reality: She was leaving, escaping the inhuman barter of bodies and souls her aunt engaged in. She wanted to sag against the captain in relief.

But she didn't know if he'd saved her or planned to use her for his own pleasure.

He hurried her into a coach, then eased onto the seat beside her. Hancock jumped onto the box, and the team lurched forward at his command.

She turned to the captain. The tight jaw and pressed set of his lips bespoke fury, even beneath his beard. Finally, he turned to her and leveled her with a hard stare that began at her face and ended with her display of cleavage. He was *leering* at her, just like all the other men. How could he? He had to know she'd been through hell in the last three days.

Unless he'd bought her for the reason her aunt intended.

Her heart raced as she angled away and grasped the neckline of the hated dress and jerked upward, though with so little material wrapped so tightly around her breasts, it did no good. Beside her, the captain grabbed her wrist and swung her back around to face him.

"Did you expect me not to look?" His question sliced her with its razor-sharp tone.

No, she hadn't expected him to look. But she didn't say so. His tone told her she'd been a fool for thinking it.

He released her wrist and swept his palm up the length of her arm. His fingers ended at her neck and tangled in her tresses. His touch left a shocking trail of tingles and heat.

"Don't," she said.

"Don't what?" he shot back. "Don't touch you? Don't take what I just paid for?"

His free arm reached around her and brought her closer. Christina's breathing constricted in a mixture of fear and anticipation. The Black Dragon wanted to kiss her. His gaze focused on her mouth, shouting that fact. She held back. He seemed much angrier, more dangerous. Not at all like the same man she'd left mere days ago.

God knew she wasn't the same woman.

"You may have paid for me," she began, "but I cannot be bought."

He sidled closer, so close his face blocked everything else in her vision. "Think again. I *bought* you, all of you. Had someone else bid higher, he would have torn that red dress to shreds and had his way with you. Why should I be different?"

Christina covered her ears with her hands. "How can you say such horrible things to me after what I've endured?"

"As if I enjoyed myself worrying over what your aunt had

schemed," he growled. "Do you really think I relished handing over a thousand pounds in gold for you?"

"I will find a way to repay you. Perhaps if you had bothered to bid sooner, the price would have been lower," she shot back.

He shot her a withering glare. "I've been to enough auctions to know you let the others outbid themselves before you join in. Otherwise, you start a frenzy and drive up the price."

Though his assessment sounded shrewd, Christina couldn't dismiss the feeling there was an insult to her person somewhere in there. Was he insinuating she wasn't worth more?

"You scared the life out of me, waiting—"

"You know, Lilli, only you would complain about the manner in which someone rescued you. I haven't heard a single syllable of appreciation. My purse is a thousand pounds lighter, thanks to you. And what do I hear? Complaints. If you had taken the time to find out your aunt's vocation before you traveled all this way or thought for two minutes about your future before stowing aboard my ship—"

"That is enough!" Tears pricked her eyes. "I refuse to sit here another minute with you."

He laughed. "Should I leave you here for Mr. Caulfield to find? Or there's always your aunt."

She sent him a narrow-eyed glare. "That's beastly! But I am hardly surprised. Let me out!" she insisted. "I'll find my own way."

He tugged on her arm, hauling her nearly atop his chest. "To where? London?"

She cringed. Definitely not there. "To…" She raised her chin, conscious of the captain's withering glare. "To Louisiana. Yes. I'll visit swamps. It sounds very exciting."

"Princess, you wouldn't last five minutes in a swamp."

Fury and humiliation burned her. He was a brute without care for feelings but his own. What infuriated her more was the fact she'd actually missed the cad during their separation. But him, he waited to bid for her, then complained about the price.

"You're a terrible man. Mean. Autocratic!" she shouted, then drew in a ragged breath. "I've just spent the worst three days of my life and you give me a lecture. I won't have it. I shall happily leave you to your own devices!"

"I've known for some while that you are irresponsible and impulsive, but you're insane if you think you're leaving now."

The carriage lurched to a stop. She peered out and saw they were before a lonely white house. A pair of windows faced the beach like unblinking eyes searching the sea for someone's return.

She threw herself toward the door of the coach and thrust it open. Below, the damp earth beckoned, and Christina jumped, landing with a jarring thud that rattled her teeth.

"Get in the house." He didn't raise his voice. Then again, he didn't need to in order to convey his anger.

Follow him like a servant? No, a slave. A whore. He'd bought her, after all. But by God, he was a fool if he thought he owned her.

Retrieving another of Grandfather's more scandalous sayings from her memory, she yelled, "Bugger off!"

She whirled about and darted for the beach, anger enabling her to make ground-eating progress.

Behind her, the captain followed.

Faster she ran, sprinting down the narrow path to the deserted sandy surface below. The scent of salt in the breeze barely pierced the haze of her anger.

With a curse, the captain grabbed her wrist and turned her around to face him.

She collided with the solid breadth of his chest.

"You're not going anywhere," he snarled.

"You do not own me!" She tried to tug her hand away.

His nasty grin sent shivers down her spine. "Oh, I do. And I plan to prove it."

Christina tried to ignore the zing his nearness shot through her body, but his familiar scent made her senses blossom with awareness.

No! She wanted to stay angry with him. He was insulting, infuriating and—

Very good with his mouth, she realized as the Black Dragon bent his head to her neck. She felt his lips caress her skin in a velvet sweep. His teeth grazed her earlobe. Christina shivered as sensations rioted down her spine.

"What are you doing?"

"Not another word," he whispered against the shell of her ear. Goose pimples broke out across her arms at the vibration of his deep voice within her. "Kiss me."

With that, he thrust his hands into her wind-tangled hair and claimed her mouth.

Chapter Ten

Christina tore her lips away and scanned the beach for someone, anyone who could help her. Not because she was afraid he would hurt her. Because, despite how much he infuriated her at times, the captain roused dangerous yearnings inside her.

Only the surf and its gentle crash against the distant rocks surrounded her.

"Looking for help?" he mocked. "You won't find it here." He lowered his mouth gently, ever so slowly, daring her to resist, before he laid a blistering kiss on her lips. "This beach belongs with the house." He nodded to the white structure on the hill above. "Both very private."

"Hancock," she reminded him, breath shallow.

She knew she should find the strength to twist away—but she couldn't. Somehow, whenever the man touched her, common sense melted away and left only an ache, an odd need, for his touch.

He laughed against her mouth, his tones low. "He's no doubt had the presence of mind to occupy himself elsewhere."

The Black Dragon leaned forward, pulled her closer. Christina felt her will to resist ebbing away. He cinched her surrender with a drugging kiss. She tried to resist, to wield her anger to ward off desire's rush. But they both knew she wanted this.

At once, his kiss chastised and absolved her, persuaded, worshiped and demanded more. Her anger receded into the haze of memory under the insistent temptation of his mouth. She found herself straining toward him, eager for his touch. He burned fire against her lips, singeing her inside and out. Every muscle in his body grew taut, affirmed his want, from the clench of his arms about her waist to the heavy rasp of his breathing. And the unmistakable erection pressing into her belly.

Need shook her. She clung to him, shocked at the ache he evoked—low and between her legs. The want spiraled her into sighs and husky murmurs of urging between the sensual assaults on her mouth.

He drew his lips over hers again in a possessive kiss. Intimate. Explicit. No longer gentle or cautious or patient. He took, commanded that she give. For once in her life, Christina obeyed.

She opened for him. His unrelenting invasion robbed her of breath, of the ability to think. Clinging to him, she melted as his tongue made a full sweep through her mouth, his arms crushing against every inch of his work-hardened body, pressing his erection against her again.

Before she caught her breath, his lips descended in a blaze to the sensitive hollow of her neck. He breathed against her damp skin, sending shivers of pleasure racing across her skin. She answered with a ragged exhalation, clutching at his arms, his neck.

As he spread kisses down her shoulders, over the swells of her breasts, the fire within erupted to an inferno. Her fingers brushed the silk of his mask, then tangled into the soft length of his hair. The scents of salt, earth and man seduced her.

He reached for her breast, his fingers lifting her flesh from the snug confines of her dress. An instant later, he fit his mouth over the aching tip, sucking, licking, then giving her a shocking nip with his teeth. An arrow of need flashed straight down, converging between her thighs. She gasped and arched into him. If the end of the world felt this good, she'd follow him to its fiery finish.

"God, you taste so sweet," he rasped.

His tongue circled and teased her rigid nipple before he shoved the dress farther down, then devoured the tip of her other breast. Her breathing grew fast and harsh. She threaded her fingers into his hair and drew him closer to her.

"Yes… Touch me," she whispered before she could stop the words.

He inhaled quickly, the demand in his touch conveying his desire. His gaze raked her, lingering on her breasts, now bared to the moonlight.

Christina lifted her shaking fingers to the buttons of his shirt. One button slid free from its confines, followed by another. Finally, a third. She pulled the garment from his breeches and reached for its hem.

He jerked his shirt from her grasp. "God, this is insane. But I want you."

His whisper played like a confession. He closed his eyes. Her heart leapt as she reached out and caressed the rippling slab of his chest.

At her touch, he sucked in a breath. "I can't stop wanting you."

Before she could respond, the captain yanked his shirt over his head and tossed it into the sand below.

Without another word, he grabbed her face, bringing her mouth up to meet the onslaught of his ravenous kiss again. Desire flashed like lightning in her body. She reached for him, her fingers meeting the heat of his solid chest, so warm, so male, need evident in its rapid rise and fall, its pounding heart beneath. She matched the urgency of his kiss with the sweep of her tongue.

The captain slid his insistent fingers down the curve of her neck and shoulders, leaving a track of tingles. His hands met at the small of her back and pulled her into him. Suddenly, she had a firsthand feel of the unyielding staff as he pressed tight against her.

Christina knew exactly what he would do with that cock, as Aunt Mary had called it. But the thought of the Black Dragon parting her folds, filling her with his flesh and moving within her, didn't inspire revulsion, as her aunt's description had. Instead, the knowledge burned her, made her greedy, gleeful. She could scarcely wait for every touch he would give her. Every touch she could give him in return.

She moaned as he bent and stroked his erection directly between her legs, against that secret spot her aunt had called her quim and told her would grow damp as she desired a man. Damp didn't begin to describe the flood of need she felt.

Breathing harsh, he clutched at the waist of her dress with a desperate grip. Then he gave a single yank. Buttons flew, fabric ripped. The garment fell away, revealing the thin lawn chemise beneath.

Christina gasped and glanced up into the roughhewn angles of his face, anticipation dancing in her veins. Heat ten times the blaze of Hades roared from his eyes, branding her as his own in a way buying her never could.

Smoothing her tongue across her bottom lip, she pushed the dress down the length of her legs and removed her shoes. Cool sand infiltrated the soft stockings, tickling her feet. She looked at him with a hot, steady gaze.

Palm leaves directly above swayed with the wind as the captain drew her chemise above her head with an impatient yank. The thin garment joined his shirt, castaways to their passion.

She stood, clad in no more than her stockings. A cool breeze rippled against her heated flesh. His gaze followed, a tangible touch, caressing her breasts, stroking the curve of her waist, fondling the pale, damp thatch between her thighs.

Christina reached for him, to somehow affect him as he had her. Every instinct within her wanted to return the depth of pleasure she felt.

He groaned. "I'm dying to taste every inch of you."

Christina hesitated, watching him. Under the moon's pale glow, he devoured her with his gaze, waiting...waiting for her next move.

Smiling, she dragged her fingertips across the heated skin of his chest, traced the rigid planes of his abdomen, brushing lower against the hard length of his cock.

The captain shot her a gaze that sparked with silent promise. He was going to make her scream in pleasure, and Christina shivered just thinking about it.

He bent and flung her scanty red dress across the tropical sand. Without a word, he crushed her against him, fitting her against his erection. As she pressed her lips to his chest in welcome, he lowered her on top of the discarded dress.

Following her to the ground with a grunt, he drew himself on top of her and compelled her mouth open with the sweep of his tongue. She clutched him, reveling in his scent, the smooth silk of his golden skin over the hard ripples of his shoulders, in the shifting sand beneath her, the salty breeze teasing her.

Then he trailed a hand across her belly slowly, making her burn with each moment he grew closer to that moist place that ached for him. Fingers trailed down, down, taunting her with his suddenly slow pace. Of their own volition, her legs restlessly parted as his hand drew oh-so-near. He watched her with burning eyes as she tentatively opened to him.

With a low curse, he ceased toying with her, grabbed both thighs and dragged them wide open. His stare seemed glued to her wet flesh.

Christina started and gasped, a taut yearning suspending her from everything but need.

Then his fingers were on her—in her—stretching, tantalizing, working the little button of nerves her aunt had told her about into a magic tingle, bringing her heaven and hell at once. The ache centered, raged to a fever. Soon, the fever spiked until she neared a hot frenzy.

"Please. Now," she panted, skin damp with need. "I need..."

"Yes," he panted. "Now."

And with another touch, he sent her soaring. Christina cried out, long and low, as blood rushed through her, pleasure converged, clashed, then exploded.

"God, you're beautiful," he whispered hotly. "I shouldn't do this…"

But his voice told Christina that he wasn't going to stop.

The captain backed away from her just long enough to unfasten his breeches and lower them, exposing the full glory of his wide cock to her.

His flesh jutted hard against his belly, bracketed by lean hips and solid thighs. Heavily veined with an angry purple head, the sight fascinated her. Then he took himself in hand. From a little slit at the tip, he leaked fluid as he stroked his hard length with a tight fist. That sight made her belly tumble, her need roar. Her curiosity surged. What would he feel like inside her?

Their gazes met as he lowered himself to her. His heated fingers drifted down her silk-clad thighs to her knees, curling inside. He spread her legs apart yet again, so wide her thighs quivered.

"Sweet Jesus, I want you," he breathed against her cheek. "Time for truth, Lilli. Was your aunt telling the truth or were you? Have you had another lover?"

Her body throbbed, her nipples hard in the tropical breeze. And the captain looked at her with determined eyes. He wasn't going to move without an answer.

"There's been no man."

The captain paused, then steeled himself with a nod. "I'm not a gentle man. For you, I will try."

With his words echoing in her head, he grazed her breast with his lips, then kissed her mouth. His rigid cock probed her opening. With her arms wrapped around the strong column of his neck, Christina held her breath.

He eased inside her, brushing sensitive flesh and liberating a burst of liquid passion. Then he paused. Muttering a curse, he pushed again. She felt something inside her give way to his possession. The pain Aunt Mary had warned her of ripped through her for an excruciating moment as he pushed his way inside. He withdrew and glided back inside, a little deeper. The hurt became discomfort. As he repeated the process, sliding deeper yet, the soreness gave way. Joy and wholeness coexisted with the ache throbbing between her thighs.

Looking into his face, Christina saw taut restraint in his closed eyes, the grit of his teeth. His breath came fast and heavy.

"Did I hurt you?" he asked.

"Right now, it feels wonderful."

He gave her a strained smile as he thrust inside her again, grinding against her, into her, at the bottom of his stroke.

She moved beneath him, rocking to meet his movements, thrilling to the pinpoints of pleasure that wound throughout her body, into a drugging delight she never wanted to end.

Faster, higher, harder, he moved. He groaned, and she gripped his shoulders, kissing his neck, his hard jaw. Then their mouths met in a union that mimicked their bodies as the craving within her built to something untamed, something that dangled her at the precipice of pleasure again.

The captain shifted, fitting his palms beneath her. He stroked into her again. The pleasure her body sought dawned as light and color exploded around her in ecstasy, this time brighter, wilder than before.

"Lilli," he cried, his body tensing, his cock expanding inside her.

He thrust into her once more, twice. His rough groan rent the air as he slowed his stroke, then stopped. He slumped against her, burying his face in her neck, his harsh breathing a remnant of their passion.

As the fragments of her soul drifted back to her, Christina knew a feeling of joy, as if she'd been reborn. Whole, accepted and treasured; the captain had given her all of these in his embrace.

Tears squeezed from the corners of her eyes as she curled closer to him. Musk and salt overran her senses and coupled with her emotions. What they shared had been significant and rare.

Christina rolled with him as he moved to her side and drew her against his chest. Indolent relaxation swelled within her. She closed her eyes, searching for the words to ask him if the experience had affected him with the same profound sense of awe.

She opened her heavy lids to find the captain searching her face. Before her sluggish mind could form a sentence and voice her question, he kissed her forehead.

"Sleep," he urged. "We'll talk later."

Reassured and content, Christina nestled herself against the length of his warm body, at peace as the damp air rushed across her skin and his arms curled around her. She drifted away, lulled by the sounds of surf and the feel of satisfaction.

* * * *

Inching away, Drex stared at Lilli's slumbering form. Relaxed and trusting, she slept, unaware of his turmoil.

How? The one-word litany reverberated in his head, a representative of his chaotic thoughts. How had she been so naive yet unafraid and giving? How had he allowed himself to become intoxicated by her spicy sweetness?

How had such an innocent rocked his body and soul so completely he felt the craving still, stronger than before?

Drex sighed. He would love the oblivion of sleep now, but his mind wouldn't rest. Lilli's alabaster nakedness, exposed to the moon as if she were a sacrificial offering, hardly contributed to a restful state.

Rolling onto his back, he stared at the stars, in search of objectivity. He'd done what he knew he shouldn't, behaved recklessly with Lilli in his arms. Despite her aunt's tutelage, she was ignorant to many of the consequences of their passion. Damn it, he should have walked away, been stronger. Instead, his lust, fueled by anger, had appeared, demanding gratification, along with a taste of her, and damning the repercussions. But this woman thrust past his usual conscientiousness, evoked desire like never before.

Drex rose to his feet and dressed, taking in the smooth perfection of Lilli's face. The defined angles of her delicate cheeks enhanced the cat-like quality of her green eyes, shining with adoration before she drifted into a light slumber. His heart leapt with hope.

Yet Lilli had proven herself to be much like Ryan. He knew them both too well to believe her reverence would last longer than tonight's tide. Any longer than Ryan's devotion to Chantal.

Armed with those realizations, why did he still feel as if he wanted to gather her close and never let go? What he felt, it was insane…complex and undefined. His emotions asked how he could keep her with him for all the days and nights to follow.

His thoughts raced. Tonight hadn't changed the fact he still needed to rescue Ryan. Tomorrow, he must sail.

Drex's gaze traveled Lilli's naked length. He couldn't leave her here, prey to someone like her aunt, or worse. Of course she had to accompany him back to England. At the voyage's end, when Ryan was freed, perhaps she would still care for him. Then he could think about the future. What they had shared tonight was too hot and sweet not to pursue.

Lilli moaned and stretched, opening green eyes with a smile. "I thought I had a most delicious dream. But you're truly here."

He stroked her hair, wondering how soon he could make love to her again without hurting her. God knew, he wanted to right now.

"Lilli, I've got to go back to England tomorrow. I want you to come with me."

She pushed herself onto her elbow, her eyes wide and dilated and frightened. "England? Why th—there?"

Pausing, he wondered how much of the truth he should give her. She deserved more than he could. "I have a...mission I must complete."

"Oh. Can I not stay here to wait for your return?"

"You're not safe," he said. "Not with your aunt nearby."

She conceded the point with a nod. "Can you see to your mission somewhere besides England?"

"No." He savored her mouth for a sweet moment. Her nakedness waylaid his thoughts until he forced his mind back to the conversation. "Why don't you want to go to England?"

"I—I can't go there."

Her hand-wringing statement puzzled him. Didn't she know he would take care of her? "Why not?" He laughed. "You're not running from the law, are you?"

She shook her head. "No. But my grandfather—"

"Ah, so the truth finally emerges," he teased.

Lilli bit her lip. "I—I suppose I should tell you the truth." She winced. "Who I really am."

He stroked her shoulder, then pressed his lips to her damp flesh. She was a changed woman already, offering him the truth. Hmm, perhaps he should have stopped resisting her charms along ago.

"I'm listening."

Lilli reached for him, entreating, "You must understand. I didn't have a choice. If I had been truthful from the start, you would have never taken me with you and I—"

"You're rambling," he baited with a smile. "So who are you? Princess Charlotte? No, she carries a few more pounds than you."

"You must promise not to be angry."

He smiled. "Why should I be? Tell me your little secret."

She squared her shoulders. Her green eyes, half-hidden by thick lashes, lent her a hint of vulnerability that warmed Drex's insides.

"Lillianne is my middle name. My—my name is actually Christina Delafield."

Drex felt as if time had stopped; his blood ceased flowing. His smile faded. His face became stone. The present became a void filled only with Lilli's pleading eyes and his own pounding heart. He staggered before his trembling legs gave way and he fell to the sand.

She swallowed, casting him an apprehensive stare. "My grandfather is—"

"The Duke of Manchester," Drex finished.

Of all the women in London who could have come to his ship, fate had chosen the Duke of Manchester's granddaughter. The one he had plotted to kidnap. The one he needed to obtain Ryan's release. The one he'd just made his lover.

Drex turned his gaze to her, as she clutched her chemise over her bare breasts, and swore. He'd deflowered her, one of society's beloved. The only woman who could end his hellish days in this dangerous masquerade and mend Ryan's broken family.

"Why didn't you tell me sooner?" His soft-spoken words gave no hint of the turmoil roiling inside him.

"I couldn't," she insisted. "If I had, you never would have let me sail with you. I was sure you would ransom me off or trade me for amnesty. I can hardly risk going back to London. Grandfather vowed to send me to a Swiss finishing school and leave me there indefinitely, so—"

"So you ran away and found me." With a shaky sigh, Drex rose to his feet and turned away. He needed to think.

He strode away toward the island's overgrown interior.

"Please, try not to be angry!" she shouted.

An impossibility, he decided. Angry didn't begin to cover the gamut of his emotions, ranging from fury to disbelief to an urge to laugh at the irony.

He said nothing to her, simply continued into the jungle.

"Don't leave. I know this is shocking, but..."

An understatement, if ever she'd made one. Why her? Why him? What a terrible twist of fate!

He trudged forward, focusing on putting one foot in front of the other and escaping Lilli's cries.

"You cannot leave me here."

A necessity, he knew. He needed time to understand, to sort out his feelings and his duties.

Moments later, the tropical vegetation engulfed him, towering above him, almost obliterating the night sky. The rich scents of wet earth and waxy leaves blended with the varied sounds of night creatures. He walked without a destination.

Drex hated fate. Its dooming ways twisted a man's gut. Nothing in his life had proceeded as planned for the last four years. Not his days as a plantation owner earning community respect, not his desperate wish to forget his mother's exploitation, his birth, his past. Nothing.

Damn it, why had Ryan run away from an adoring wife and small son? Drex had never resented his twin for the upheaval in his life more than he did now.

He swore again. Now he had Christina Delafield to deal with. She'd run away, just like Ryan. He should be repelled by her impulsive behavior. Yet she reached inside his chest and tugged. She mattered to him.

And he'd taken her virginity, made love with her.

Drex raked a trembling hand through his hair. He had never hated the mask and masquerade more since he knew what he had to do. Reality dictated the fact that, no matter how deeply Christina Delafield had imprinted herself onto his heart, he must return her to her grandfather in exchange for Ryan's freedom. She needed to be amidst her element, where her grandfather's clout would ensure she could mingle with and marry her own kind.

And to leave her, to convince her that she belonged with England's elite and not the scourge of the seas, he would have to break her pride— and his own heart.

Chapter Eleven

Christina paced the darkened drawing room from end to end, nibbling on a fingernail. Hancock sat in the corner, his watchful eyes set at a glower.

An hour, blast him! An entire hour since the captain disappeared, leaving her naked and confused on the beach. Of course she hadn't expected him to be thrilled with the truth, but anger she could have combated. But desertion she had never imagined. Nor did she accept.

She shook her head and shuffled to the window. Nothing but the silver swish of the tide against the shimmering sand.

Wriggling self-consciously in the dress she had not been able to button completely, Christina felt grains of sand chafe her back. Though she refused to dwell on the missing buttons of her shocking dress, her anger surged anew. Where was that man?

"He'll be back," Hancock said, as if reading her mind.

Christina whirled and demanded, "When?"

The short man shrugged. "Maybe five minutes, maybe two days. The cap'n does things in his own way, in his own time."

If Hancock intended his words as comfort, he obviously hadn't learned how to do the thing correctly. Two days? She closed her eyes, trying to block out her rising nausea.

She crossed the room again, drawn to the dwindling firelight, and fought the urge to scream or cry—or both. The past four days sat upon her shoulders like an unbearable burden. Everything she'd believed about her aunt had been a lie. Her every dream for the future was crushed.

And the one man she'd begun to regard as her ally, believed to be more than a manipulative bully, had used and left her.

Without future or direction now, she was all alone.

Finally, he returned. The night's wind swept into the room with him, as cool as his masked features. His silence gave no hint of his mood.

He turned to Hancock. "Is her valise still in the coach?"

"Aye," the first mate answered.

With a nod, the captain faced her. "Get in the coach."

"Where are you taking me?" She cursed her trembling voice.

He didn't answer. She crossed the room to stand before him, hoping proximity would give her a clue about his thoughts or intentions. No such luck. His expression remained perfectly hollow, without a single hint of anything as messy as emotion.

A muscle ticked in his jaw. "Get in the coach."

Head held high, she considered telling him to take himself off to Hades, but knew his behavior stemmed from the shock of her confession.

Without waiting for her, the Black Dragon spun around and strode through the door, toward the waiting coach.

The damp night air cut across her skin as Christina discovered that the captain had already seated himself in the coach. Hancock assisted her up, then shut the door, leaving them in shared stillness.

As the vehicle rolled away, sharp silence stretched like a thin wire between them. Christina stared at the Black Dragon, awaiting his reaction, preferably an apology. He uttered nothing, training his stare out the window.

Minutes lasted hours. And still, he said not one word. He merely gazed out the window, as if she did not sit directly across from him. As if she did not exist.

"You left me on that beach," she accused, unable to hold her torment in any longer. "I could barely dress myself."

He didn't even spare her a glance. "You managed."

"With difficulty. I realize you're quite unhappy about who I am, but it need not change us."

"There is no 'us,'" he said quietly, sparing her only the briefest of glances. "What gave you the notion there was?"

His words struck her like a slap. Notion? She'd given him everything! Her affection, her body, her innocence. Could he have forgotten their ecstasy so quickly? Had he chosen to pretend their lovemaking meant nothing now that he knew her as the Duke of Manchester's granddaughter?

The tears she'd held back earlier spilled down her cheeks. "You— you miserable knave! How could you say something so terrible?" she sobbed. "You tr-reat me as if I've wronged you, yet I'm guilty of nothing but speaking the truth."

Fists clenched, she waited for his reaction. Tears tracked down her face anew at his taut jaw and chilling silence.

"You—you detestable bastard!" she shouted.

The coach stopped. Craving fresh air and escape, she lunged for the door. The captain wrapped forceful fingers about her arm to stay her.

"You're not going anywhere unless I take you there."

Implacability dominated his voice, brooking no argument. Too bad she was in the mood for a rousing fight.

Christina jerked from his grasp and swiped the tears from her face. "I can go anywhere I please. You *don't* own me, not anymore, now that you've had your pound of flesh."

"Care to return to your aunt?" he taunted.

"If I did, at least I would expect a stranger would treat me like a trollop," she shot back. "Though next time should be easier, now that you've shown me what to expect."

Christina whirled for the door again, seeking only freedom. Plans and safety would come later, though neither would involve her scandalous aunt.

The Black Dragon hooked his arm about her waist. Dragging her against his steely chest, despite her struggles, he whispered, "What else did you expect, fucking a man whose name you don't know and whose face you've never seen?"

She stilled, struck by the ugly truth of his words.

Over the course of the past six weeks, the small detail of his name had ceased to be relevant. She'd even come to accept the mask as part of his daily attire, which he would doff once she revealed herself. Christina thought she'd known him, enough to believe him decent and good, if overzealous and misguided.

Tonight proved she hadn't known him at all.

"Let me go! I will not travel another mile with you."

"I'm afraid, *Lady Christina*, that you don't have a choice."

* * * *

Four miserable weeks later, Christina hugged her knees to her chest, feeling the sway of the ship…and knowing her heart had broken. She hadn't seen the Black Dragon once this voyage. Hancock delivered all her meals. Anything he had to say to her, Hancock acted as his voice.

The captain had even sent his messenger to inquire if she'd had a monthly since their foolish encounter on the beach. She had, thank you, but wasn't about to say so. Why would he care if she carried his bastard? He had certainly proven he no longer wanted her.

She sank down onto his bunk, the embroidered black dragon on his coverlet an ever-present reminder of him. She'd been foolish to trust a criminal like the Black Dragon with her heart, foolish to allow herself to fall in love with a faceless, nameless man.

Yes, love. Christina dropped her aching head in her hands and succumbed to tears.

For a pirate, or privateer as he preferred, he had seemed so intelligent and reliable, so stable yet concerned. He had represented everything she wasn't but needed to be. At times, he had behaved much like Grandfather, but possessed an unexpectedly gentle heart.

How could she have been so wrong in her perceptions to not see the cad lurking beneath?

The key scraped in the door's lock, and she looked up to see Hancock shuffle through the portal with her meal. She hung her head, feeling hot tears scald her eyes.

The first mate set the tray at her feet. Even the thought of food made her stomach turn sickly. She rolled away.

"Leave me." Her voice was muffled by the coverlet.

"Lady Christina, ye must eat," he insisted. "Yer wastin' away to nothing but skin 'n bones, lass."

"Take it!" she sobbed.

"I'll leave it here, in case ye change yer mind. And I'm to tell you that we're making land tomorrow."

Hancock definitely didn't have the comforting knack. At the thought of never seeing the Black Dragon again, she buried her face in her pillow and squeezed fresh tears from her eyes.

Soon, she would be separated from the man she loved, and he

couldn't be bothered to tell her so himself! She might never see him again. Whether she would plead for his affection or scream into his contemptible face if she did, she wasn't sure.

"Best pack yer things, lass. I'll come fetch ye in the morn." With that, Hancock departed, leaving her utterly alone with only misery for company.

* * * *

"Is she better today?" Drex grilled Hancock the moment the short man stepped into the infirmary, where Drex had been making his bed these past weeks.

"The same."

Hancock's frown prompted additional concern. Drex reined in the urge to shake answers from his first mate. "Well, out with it, man. What did she say to the news we've arrived?"

He shook his head. "Nothin', Cap'n. She cried a little more and turned her nose up at 'er food again."

Drex swore, apprehension gnawing at his guts. This should have been simple. He'd only made love to her once. Why the hell wouldn't she leave him to rot in peace, instead of trying to waste away herself and tearing out his heart in the process?

Because she wasn't like other women.

Lilli threw herself into the fire, head first, with her own brand of passion. Her determination and naive charm enthralled all in her path. Even his crew. Though none had dared voice their opinion, even Hancock, Drex knew from their disapproving stares they all thought him a scoundrel of the worst sort.

He had a hard time sleeping, faced with the knowledge that she seemed to grieve the loss of a bond that could never come to fruition. Knowing that a simple word or two, a gentle touch, would make her world right again. Still, passion so easily given would easily pass. Ryan had proven so with Chantal.

Regardless of Lilli's flight of fancy, he ached to restore her peace of mind, share the tangle of yearning and pain in his heart. But she was his twin's ticket to freedom.

His own heart would simply have to break.

* * * *

127

When Christina emerged from the captain's cabin the following morning, it was to the sight of an unfamiliar rocky coastline. Not that it mattered. The sun's glare against gray clouds burned her aching eyes. Her head throbbed, her stomach turned. The Black Dragon was nowhere on deck.

"G'bye, Miss Lilli," Davie rushed to say. "We'll miss ye."

Holding back tears, she clutched his hand. "God be with you." She glanced at the others behind Davie. "All of you."

Hancock took her arm and led her away. He assisted her into a dinghy and rowed for the shore. Water crashed against the craggy bronzed rocks of the coast in a magnificent spray.

"Ever been to Cornwall, lass?" Hancock asked.

She glanced at the diminutive man, then turned her gaze back to the coastline, heart sinking that he had brought her to England after all. She wondered if he'd come to tend to his business or ransom her back to Grandfather. "No."

"A savage sight, ain't it?"

"Hmmm," she murmured her assent absently.

Her stare remained on the damp cliffs, but her mind wandered elsewhere. Had the captain disembarked already? Or perhaps he wasn't coming ashore. Maybe, in his final act of cruelty, he had banished her to land without even saying good-bye.

She refused to cry again today. The captain had chosen to forsake her, and she would accept his decision with dignity.

Once they made dry land, Hancock assisted her from the tiny boat. A bitter wind whipped strands of hair across her face.

"Ye need me coat, lass?" he asked.

In truth, she'd barely noticed the cold. "No."

They walked the length of the dock. Christina observed the curious stares of the sailors around her but didn't care. Other people's opinions no longer mattered now that her heart had shattered into a million pieces.

They climbed a steep path that wound its way through the stony surface of the hillside. At the top, Christina spotted an austere black coach.

The Black Dragon stood beside the vehicle, black clothing whipping about him in the wind as he saddled a horse.

She swallowed the thick lump in her throat and told herself his presence did not matter to her in the least.

Her racing heart and watery vision proved that she lied.

The captain paused in cinching the saddle to glance across the distance at her. He didn't move, didn't speak. Christina felt the effect of his gaze all over her trembling body. Hot and cold quivers raced across her skin, delved into her stomach.

Christina wished she knew what he was thinking. She shifted uncomfortably from one foot to the other. Still, he didn't look away. Did he stare out of latent care and concern or a curiosity to know if she'd survived his cruel desertion?

She, for one, did not plan to stay and find out. Turning away from the blackguard, she tried to ignore the desperate ache swirling with the writhing agony in her stomach.

A moment later, Christina heard the creak of leather and the sound of hoofbeats. She looked up to find the captain riding away in a flourish of dark hair and a black cloak.

She bit the inside of her lip to restrain oncoming tears. At her side, Hancock peered into her face curiously.

"It's fer the best, lass. Ye and the cap'n, ye come from different worlds. He doesn't understand yours, and ye don't belong in his."

She nodded, trying to accept his outlook, and took his arm as they walked to the coach. He handed her up into the empty vehicle and shut the door behind her. Within moments, the gig rolled away toward a future she knew nothing of.

* * * *

Drex pulled on the reins of his horse in a copse of trees in front of the Fox and Hound Inn. The little-known establishment on London's outskirts would suffice for his secrecy. His arrival in the morning's wee hours would make discovery less likely.

But he had to shed his disguise as the Black Dragon.

He unknotted the silk at the back of his head, feeling exposed yet freed at once. The damp summer air kissed the few parts of his face his beard didn't cover, and he gave an unfettered shake of his over-long hair.

If only stripping his heart of Lilli were so easy.

With a sigh, he stabled his horse, then made his way inside the inn. A room awaited in Greg's name, just as he had instructed his friend via missive to arrange. He'd also had them ready another room for

Christina's arrival with Hancock tomorrow.

Mounting the stairs two at a time, Drex headed for his room, wanting nothing more than sleep. He opened the door to find wine, a light repast of bread and cheese—and Greg sitting by the flickering firelight.

The man's cheerful smile indicated clearly that Greg was quite awake. Drex knew his friend well enough to realize he'd want a long talk.

Greg stood. "I feared I'd become an old man before you arrived."

"The rain in Devonshire slowed me." Drex set his cloak and mask on the chair before him, then shut the door.

His friend stuck out his hand, and Drex clasped it tightly.

"Now that we've exchanged pleasantries, would you please tell me what the hell your note means?" Greg demanded.

Drex sighed and drained the wineglass. "Where should I start? I suppose with the fact that no one could find Christina Delafield because she stowed on board my ship."

Greg's blue eyes threatened to pop from their sockets. "What? Are you certain?"

"Now I am." Drex waved a hand through the air in a dramatic sweep. "After I found out she wasn't married, didn't have a dying mother, and wasn't fleeing a jealous lover."

Greg frowned. "I'm afraid I didn't follow all that rubbish. Married? A jealous lover?" He shrugged and scowled. "Her mother died over ten years ago."

Drex smiled bitterly. "Her lies had more holes than a fishing net. I didn't know what to believe."

"So you brought her back to England to ransom her for Ryan?"

Drex closed his eyes, wishing he could see any other way of freeing his brother, but he'd already exhausted all alternate avenues months ago. "Yes."

"Why Cornwall? Manchester will expect you in London."

"Exactly. If he expects me to land in England at all, it's at London's docks. This way, I travel by coach virtually beneath his nose and take him by surprise. I don't plan to give the knave enough time or information to arrange an ambush."

Greg nodded. "Good thinking. Does Lady Christina know what you intend?"

He shook his head. "I haven't spoken a word to her since—"

Drex broke off, realizing what he'd been about to confess. He couldn't tell Greg—or anyone—that he'd made love to Christina, that he would do it again if he didn't have to sacrifice her in this ugly game of politics and prisoners.

"Since…?" Greg prompted.

Drex just shook his head. "Since she told me the truth. We left Grand Bahama the next day."

Greg peered closely, suspicion imprinted into each feature. "You have feelings for the girl. I can see them all over your face."

Gritting his teeth, he replied, "Whatever I feel is irrelevant."

"Did you…" Greg trailed off. "Ah…well, in more delicate terms, did the two of you—"

"Unless you want my fist connecting with your mouth, I don't advise asking that question," Drex cut in, then silenced him with a scowl.

"I'll take that to mean yes." Greg whistled. "I think you've been stricken but good."

"Excuse me?"

"Cupid," Greg clarified. "Your protectiveness, your melancholy. They point to love."

Drex tensed and pushed the possibility aside. "I plead guilty if love and exhaustion are the same. Can you leave me in peace to sleep now? We'll go over the plan to exchange Lilli for Ryan in the morning."

"Lilli?" Greg questioned, brow raised. "A pet name?"

"Another one of her lies," Drex clarified.

But deep inside, he feared that no matter how much time passed or how far he traveled, she would always be his Lilli.

* * * *

The following morning, Drex rose and ate a light breakfast in his room. He stared out the window, searching for signs of Christina's arrival. He hoped to God she had not tried to escape Hancock. He'd instructed his first mate to use force, if necessary. He doubted the man would do it, however. Hancock had grown fond of the girl. His only hope remained that her gloom hindered her from attempting to flee.

A brief knock sounded. He opened the door, knowing Greg stood on the other side.

"Good morning," Greg greeted.

Drex grunted. It might have been good, had he gotten any sleep, if Christina's visage hadn't haunted him all night. "If you say. Let's discuss this exchange of Lady Christina for Ryan."

Greg glanced back at the door with a frown before he crossed the room and helped himself to a chair. "Now?"

"Help me send Manchester a note. I'll sign it, stating that I want Ryan released in exchange for his granddaughter. We'll meet in one week. As for location, I'll have to rely on your knowledge of London."

Greg paused, then nodded. "I know the perfect place. It's sometimes used for illegal duels. You and Manchester can meet at dawn. It's fitting, don't you think?"

Drex rolled his eyes at Greg's flair for drama. "Very well. Give me directions, and I'll take Christina there myself."

"I shall draw you a map tomorrow," his friend said.

"Perfect."

"Now that business is settled, I have a surprise for you."

"A surprise?" Drex scowled. Greg's surprises were always unexpected—and rarely good. "I don't need a surprise."

Greg rose from his seat and crossed the room. "A pity," he said, opening the door. "Come in." He motioned to someone standing in the hallway.

"Are you certain?" the unseen man asked.

"Of course."

Drex took a moment's notice of Greg's impatience—until the man came into view.

He and Drex shared the same height, the same build, the same eyes. A mirror image of his chin, when clean-shaven, met his gaze. The man possessed dark hair, like his own, but sprinkled with gray at the temples. The man raked a hand through his short hair, as Drex himself was wont to do.

The stranger could only be his father.

The ground shifted beneath him, and Drex reached to grip the table beside him for support.

A wave of incredulity and boiling fury washed over him. His gaze wandered the man who had abandoned his mother to prostitution, leaving two young boys on the streets. Why, after all these years, had the man brought his miserable hide here?

"What do you want?" Drex snapped.

The man stepped backward and shot Greg a questioning glance.

"I'm your—"

"I know who you are," he cut in, curling his hands into fists. "You are not welcome here."

The earl's pained frown emanated regret. "Please understand, I learned of your existence years after your birth. I had no idea your mother was pregnant, son. She—"

"Never call me son."

The man reached across the few feet separating them. The distance may as well have been a chasm, for Drex had no wish to connect with the cur who had abandoned a frightened, pregnant woman so he could continue his life of privilege.

"I've waited nearly two decades to meet you," the man implored.

Drex crossed his arms over his chest and looked away from the man's beseeching features. The earl had made his choice years ago, to walk away from his woman and children. Drex refused to give the man any sympathy now.

"I know you've had a terrible time of it," his father went on. "And I know an apology seems paltry, but I am very sorry."

Drex cursed beneath his breath. Why did Greg have to bring the man here now? He had enough to deal with in trying to free Ryan and release Lilli. The upheaval of dealing with the good earl was more than he needed now. And the man's seeming sincerity added another complication he didn't want to deal with.

"Viscount Monroe," his father gestured to Greg, "informed me that your younger brother, your twin, Ryan, was impressed into the Navy."

Drex refused to respond. His father's concern had come twenty-eight years too late.

"Yes," Greg pitched in. "I also told him all of the methods you've used in trying to obtain his release."

"All of them?" Drex felt his blood begin to boil.

"Yes. He—"

"Are you insane?" he hissed. "Why don't you just pay the town crier to shout that I'm the Black Dragon? Maybe that will catch Manchester's attention."

"I'm here to help you, in any way I can," his father interjected. "I shall renew old contacts, see if I can at least learn what ship Ryan is on. But your secret is safe with me."

"How touching." Drex's voice oozed sarcasm.

His father sighed. "I came here today to tell you that I never married and have no children. Should you wish it, I want to make you my heir. My home and family are open to you and your brother, if you simply say the word."

Without waiting for Drex's reaction, the earl exited the room, leaving a wake of troubled silence.

Chapter Twelve

A week later, dawn spread over the misty slopes of an empty London field, signaling the death knell of Drex's hopes for a miracle. Ryan had not magically been released, nor had he escaped. Drex saw no end to this excruciating exchange of one part of his heart for another.

He was going to have to release Lilli.

She stood behind him, glaring daggers at his back. Hancock held her in his grip.

No one said a word, or breathed, it seemed, as they awaited the arrival of Manchester and his men. Greg had volunteered to lead the man to this secret rendezvous point in order to prevent the possibility of an ambush. And true to form, his friend had disguised himself with an absurd plumed hat, atop a powdered face and wig. The French falsetto he mimicked only added to his outrageous Revolution-era fashion debacle.

Drex stole a discreet glance over his shoulder at Lilli's pale, thin features. Her gaze burned with hostility, and she aimed both barrels at him alone. Only the knowledge that her broken heart must be temporary enabled him to push forward with his plan.

Still, he wished he'd had the opportunity to explain this hostage exchange to her. But the less she knew, the better. Her grandfather would doubtless grill her for information.

Drex heard Manchester's entourage arrive before he saw them. Cursing the dense morning fog, he could only hope his nemesis had not had adequate time to hide gunmen in the surrounding brush.

A lone figure approached through the soupy gray mist. Drex walked toward the man and recognized Greg by the multi-colored hat perched atop his towering wig. His chalky face appeared ghostly in the pallid sunlight.

"Ready?" Greg asked.

Drex nodded, forcing himself to focus on the matter before him, not the woman behind him. "Are they armed?"

"Manchester refused to come without weapons."

With a shrug, Drex accepted that fact. He had not come to meet an enemy without guns, either.

"Did you get a good look at Ryan?"

Greg nodded. "I feel certain I saw him behind his beard and bruises when I peeked in the coach."

Relief spiked through Drex, followed closely by anger. Ryan was hurt, perhaps even bleeding or dying.

He swore. "Tell Manchester to bring Ryan to the middle of the field. I'll meet him there with Christina."

Greg nodded and spun away. Drex turned slowly and faced Lilli. Her face was set in tense, angry lines.

His stomach clenched up like a fist as he approached her. He'd only have these few minutes with her before she left his life forever, eclipsing him from her golden light. He wished they could have privacy, that he could tell her he did not want to let her go. That he cared, despite his better judgment.

He stopped directly before her. The cold fury spitting from her green eyes let him know pretty words and the truth would no longer redeem him in her view—a circumstance probably for the better, much as he regretted her pain. They had too little in common. Just an electric desire that defied the laws of logic.

"You're sending me back to Grandfather, aren't you?" The accusation in her voice told him she knew the answer.

He nodded, unable to find his voice, to unearth the words to hide the tangle of his feelings.

"For amnesty?" She raised a sharp blond brow.

"The less you know, the better."

His answer came out in an even, modulated voice. Yet his emotions warred a bloody battle with logic, duty versus desire, responsibility versus yearning.

136

Forcing the dichotomy of his feelings aside, he reached for her arm to lead her away. She jerked from his grasp. "I hardly need your assistance to walk."

Drex steeled himself against the rising need to drag her into his arms. "Follow me."

The trek across the lonely field seemed interminable. Drex surveyed his surroundings for surprise attacks, aware all the while of Lilli behind him. She smelled of scented soap this morning. That light lilac fragrance, combined with the damp morning chill, permeated his very being.

Resisting the urge to turn back and hold her, Drex concentrated on the crunch of brittle grass beneath his boots, on watching for emerging figures in the fog.

Lilli's once-snug dress now fit as if it had been made for another woman. He wondered when she had last eaten. Her fragility only magnified his guilt. Damn it, shutting her out of his life had not been an easy task for him, either. In fact, he ranked the feat blasted near impossible. But he'd done it. So why hadn't she recovered her former fiery self?

In time, she would. She was angry because he'd planned this hostage exchange without her knowledge or consent. Of course, she would hate him for this. Which was fine, since he would come to think of her as a fond memory, someday.

The argument was sound and sensible and should have made him feel better. But he didn't believe it.

Finally, four figures appeared, materializing out of the fog. He recognized Greg's pasty countenance and Manchester's tight one. Two soldiers flanked either side of them.

"You bastard," Manchester growled. "Where is my granddaughter?"

Drex stepped to one side, revealing Lilli. She gasped and sniffled, and he turned to find her gaze focused on her grandfather. Tears floated down her taut, pale cheeks. She took two quick steps toward Manchester. Drex thrust an arm in front of her, blocking her path.

Her impatience to be gone from him shouldn't bother him, Drex knew. But bloody hell, it did.

The old man clenched his large hands into fists. "By God, if you've hurt her—"

"Where is your hostage?" Drex broke in.

"You'll have to retrieve him. He's in the coach, unconscious."

Drex clenched his teeth, vowing he'd exact revenge, particularly if the Admiralty had caused Ryan permanent damage or death. "Point me in the right direction."

At Manchester's side, Greg gave a nearly undetectable shake of his head, then chimed in with his phony falsetto French voice, "Excuse us. *Oui?*"

Drex watched with confusion as Greg approached and took his arm. Grabbing Lilli, he allowed his friend to guide a few steps away from the gathering. "Don't go to the coach. I heard some of Manchester's men arrive just moments ago. I don't doubt they all have guns pointed at that vehicle."

Drex cursed. His mind raced. He could send someone else to the coach, but refused to risk another's life when his own should be at stake. He considered using Christina as a shield, but cast the idea aside. Risking her safety was unthinkable.

Still, the duke's latest tactic gave Drex little choice but to counter with a new plan.

"Follow me," he said to Greg, then strode back to Manchester, holding Christina's wrist in his grip.

Once he reached the older man, Drex commanded, "You will go back to the coach and drive it to this spot." He pointed to the ground before him. "Then I will release your granddaughter."

Manchester paused, then nodded.

"And when I leave this field, no one will follow."

"No one," the duke choked.

He nodded. "Good."

Manchester walked away. Drex stood tensely.

Inside a minute, the coach arrived, with Manchester on the box. The older man stopped the vehicle and dropped down.

Drex peered into the window. Ryan's identity was unmistakable, even relaxed in slumber and covered by welts of purple and black.

Euphoria swirled through Drex. His life would again be his. He could return home, plant his crops in the earth, see his fortune prosper, give up danger and war and treason. Then he spotted Lilli by his side, her face ashen and angry, and wondered if anyone would really win this battle.

"Take him out of the coach," Drex demanded.

Manchester paused. "He's injured and should be moved as little as possible."

Frustration and anxiety gnawed at Drex's stomach. Based on his visual assessment, Manchester was right. He motioned to Greg, who nodded. "Get someone to bring the coach over here."

"Oui," Greg answered in a single high-pitched syllable, then disappeared into the fog.

A long moment of silence fell over the small group. Drex felt Lilli's small wrist in his hand, warm proof of his sacrifice to his brother's damned sense of adventure. A tangible reminder of the woman he feared he would never forget.

As he turned to her, a pool of tears gathered in her huge emerald eyes. Drex used his grip to pull her close. She resisted but proved no match for his strength.

Words eluded him as he stared for an endless moment into her fair features. The wind brushed an errant strand of her golden hair from her upswept style. Drex caught the curl with his fingers and tucked it behind her ear.

Christina opened her mouth. Drex saw the protest coming before she voiced a single word.

"Don't—" she began softly.

He silenced her with a kiss.

Leveling his mouth atop hers, Drex allowed himself to taste her nectar this last time. She stiffened against him, but her silent refusal couldn't dampen his pleasure. He held her closer and feathered his lips over hers again. After a moment's hesitation, she opened to him.

Something inside him exploded with a wild burst of possession as Christina clung to him. Her kiss became a plea as their tongues met. He tasted despair and desperation.

Knowing he could change nothing, Drex tore himself away.

At the click of a gun's hammer, Drex looked up to find Manchester's weapon pointed at his belly. "Keep your bloody hands off of my granddaughter!"

The mottled red of the man's complexion, along with the gun, let Drex know the old man meant business.

He nodded slowly and grabbed Lilli's arm. He wanted to wish her Godspeed and happiness. But the gaze she cast upon him let him know he ranked lower than Lucifer on her list.

"Give her to me now," Manchester demanded as Drex's coach pulled up beside Manchester's. Hancock jumped to the ground. The duke trained the barrel of his weapon at Drex.

The moment had arrived. Knowing his inadequate well wishes would never repair the damage to Lilli's emotions—or his heart—Drex guided her to her grandfather's side. His fingers slid down her arm in a last desperate caress. She yanked from his touch and turned to Manchester.

The emptiness inside him was mirrored on her face. Knowing he could do nothing to ease either of them pained him more.

"Christina," her grandfather instructed, "behind me a coach awaits. Get inside. I've a few words for this fiend."

Christina turned to Drex, cast him one last green-eyed glance full of anger and despair, heartache and confusion. New tears gathered in her eyes. Then she whirled around and sprinted into the fog. Drex watched her disappear, feeling as if someone were squeezing his heart dry of life.

Manchester growled, "If you've planted a bastard in her belly, I vow I will hunt you down. There will not be a hell good enough for you."

"I didn't."

A strong part of him, one that ached, wished she had conceived that night on the beach. She would still be with him.

"I'll get you," Manchester vowed. "Make no mistake. This battle isn't over."

Before he could reply, the duke turned and rushed away. Drex turned to the coaches beside him, where Hancock was attempting to open the door and reach Ryan.

He stepped forward to assist. He would have time later to miss Lilli—a lifetime, in fact. Ryan needed him now.

Gunshots sounded suddenly, a veritable army of them, judging from the retorts echoing across the ghostly field.

Cursing the wily old goat, Drex fell to the ground, as did the men around him. He should have known better than to trust the Lord of the Admiralty.

A bullet ricocheted off the side of Manchester's abandoned coach with his brother inside. Urgency ignited him to action as he rose and threw himself toward the vehicle.

The coach started to move. Drex clung to the side, one hand clutching the top. He looked up to see one of Manchester's men on the box, whipping the horses' backsides.

They rolled faster with every turn of the wheels. Drex yelled for help, but his men had been left behind. Bullets whizzed past him, their blasts a constant retort. He stretched across the coach's door and jerked on the handle.

The door wouldn't budge.

With a rousing curse for Manchester's treachery, Drex renewed his grip on the top of the rolling coach, then sent a fist flying into the window. Glass shattered around him. A sting and gouging of his knuckles later, blood oozed down his hand and ran in rivulets beneath his cuff.

Shaking his abused fist, he reached for the handle inside the coach's door, only to find it missing.

Horror washed over him in an icy hot rush, crashing through his bloodstream. His mind raced for alternatives, ways to free Ryan from the trap of the swaying vehicle.

Cursing, he reached for the gun at his side and aimed at the man atop the box, who was whipping the horses to a perilous gallop. He paused to aim carefully, knowing he'd have one shot.

He curled his finger around the trigger, ready to oust Manchester's man from his seat.

Instead, he felt liquid fire inject into his side.

He cried out, fingers clutching the top of the coach. His side burned. Glancing down, he spotted a stain of red spreading at his side and knew he'd been hit.

Determined to ignore the pain, he raised his gun again. Aiming seemed a Herculean task. His vision blurred. His palms began to sweat. Drex felt his grip on the coach slipping.

Quickly, he fired. And missed.

Pain and despondency racked him as he gripped the side of the vehicle with damp fingers, hanging on for his very life. He felt the blood running down his side in a hot trickle. Dizziness and nausea assailed him at once.

Drex forced his drooping eyelids open and took in the sight of his brother's beaten face before his fingers slid down the side of the coach and he hurtled to the ground.

* * * *

The constant swaying of the ship made Drex's stomach heave again. He stuck his head over the chamber pot, stomach rolling. With all the gentleness of a hurricane, he lost what little breakfast Hancock had forced down his throat.

When his stomach was empty, Drex raised his head and washed the acrid taste from his mouth with another long swallow of rum. Bleary-eyed, he glanced out the small window and judged the time about noon. He was still on his first bottle today and must drink fast to achieve the oblivion he'd lived in for the past two months. Thoughts were beginning to creep in.

Thoughts that reminded him he'd lost everything dear to him: Ryan and Lilli, his way of life, his freedom.

Drex clenched his teeth in an effort to blot out reality. Damn it, he would not think of that morning, despite the ache in his slowly healing side that served as a constant reminder.

He took another deep swallow to block out memory and reason. Of course, he'd known he must give up his attachment to Lilli for Ryan. But to lose them both…

Hancock bustled in moments later bearing another tray of food. Drex's stomach roiled in protest.

"Ye found the damned bottle, I see," Hancock grumbled.

"Right where you hid them," Drex confirmed, then belched.

Hancock grimaced. "Don't ye think it's time ye be soberin' up and gettin' back to the business at hand?"

"I tried to save Ryan," he slurred. "I cut out my heart and served it on a platter to Manchester for my brother's freedom."

"Don't mean the fight is over," Hancock protested, setting the tray of food on his desk. "There must be more than one way to lick that whelp. And if any man can do it, it's you."

Drex scowled and turned away from the aroma of bread and cheese, pondering Hancock's words as the man left. More than one way to beat Manchester and free Ryan? Perhaps, though Lord knew he'd already tried several approaches and failed.

He fantasized that he could find some way to win his brother's emancipation and Lilli's heart with one clean sweep.

The fantasy faded against reality's glare. He was alone, sick and hunted, without a plan, and trapped in a life at sea without end in sight. He couldn't return to Louisiana and Chantal without Ryan. He'd given his sister-in-law his word.

Perhaps he could return to his first plan, abduct Christina and ransom her back for Ryan.

No, he couldn't, he decided, raking a hand through unkempt hair.

The plan was too risky for a variety of reasons. Manchester would have his granddaughter heavily guarded. Even if he were able to capture her, his last hostage exchange had included bullets. If one hit Lilli, he'd never forgive himself. Nor was he certain he could keep his hands off her. The last few weeks of her captivity had sorely tested his willpower. She would never know how many times he had simply watched her sleep on their return voyage—and longed to curl her body against his and love her long into the night. And if he did make love to her again, could he let her go? Probably not. Besides, just returning to London was a dangerous feat in itself.

He laughed grimly and took another swizzle from the rum. Hell, with Manchester vowing to destroy him, he had no way to gain entry into London in order to find Ryan and convince Lilli that he still wanted her. He'd nearly have to be married to the old bugger to open the doors he needed.

Or married to his granddaughter.

Picking himself up off the floor, Drex set his bottle aside. Marry her. Yes. Perfect! But how? He'd have to be someone of importance. He was no duke. Just the son of a prostitute from London's Whitechapel district.

And an earl.

Greg had warned him that Christina would be considered soiled goods by the *ton* now that she was back in London. If Manchester had any intention of marrying her off, the old goat would have to settle for a social climber or fortune hunter for a grandson-in-law. Hopefully, a wealthy earl's illegitimate son would be good enough.

And once married to Lilli, he would find a way to make her happy while demanding Ryan's release. All that he required was a new disguise—and contact with his father. To achieve both his ends, he could put up with the selfish cur for a few months.

Drex changed his soiled shirt for a clean one and donned his mask. In moments, he strode to the deck, eager to find Hancock. He ignored the glare of bright sunlight and the pounding in his head, and focused on the rousing effects of the salty wind in his face.

"Hancock!" he shouted.

"Aye, Cap'n?" His first mate came running, then observed, "Ye be dressed in clean clothes."

Resolve bolstering him, Drex nodded. "Turn the ship about. We're going back to London."

Chapter Thirteen

Drex sneaked into England via Cornwall. The damp wind and biting mist mirrored his emotions. Stormy. Gray. Uncertain.

Success at this scheme was paramount. Ryan, if still alive, wouldn't live long in his condition. Drex had wasted precious time on self-pity, and he regretted it now. And before another man saw how fun and fiery his Lilli was, Drex had to win her, as well. If he failed now, he risked losing them both forever.

After weeks of turbulent travel and sleepless waiting, he stood before his father's St. James Square door on a chilly Tuesday evening, trying to swallow his pride and contempt.

He knocked. A haughty, shriveled man opened the door and looked down his long nose at Drex. "Yes?"

"I'm here to see Ashmont."

The man sniffed. "Do you have an appointment?"

"No," he said between gritted teeth. "But—"

"I'm afraid he's not at home," the butler cut in.

The old man began to shut the door in Drex's face. He lodged a foot inside the portal before it closed.

Drex pushed the door open again. "I think you'll find he's at home for his son."

The butler stilled. "His son, you say?"

He nodded. "Drexell Cain."

Raising a brow, the butler opened the door. "Wait here."

Drex concentrated on the richly carpeted entry hall. A pedestal cupboard stood beside the wall to his right, crowned by a matching urn. A landscape painting hung farther down the wall, looking indolently expensive, a symbol of wealth.

God, he hoped he could fit into this selfish, sanctimonious society for Lilli's sake. Once married to her, he would reveal himself and make his past transgressions up to her, while working toward Ryan's release. Taking in the opulence around him, he wondered if his simple plan was impossible. He'd known squalor and danger his whole life. How would he ever fit in here?

To his left, Drex spotted his father cantering down the stairs minus a coat, cravat askew. His open mouth and wide eyes spoke volumes about his surprise.

"You've come." His father paused at the bottom of the stairs, a burgeoning smile crossing his features.

Drex shuffled his feet and coughed, fighting the ever-present urge to tell the man he'd always viewed as a selfish knave to go to hell. "I have."

"To stay?"

"For the foreseeable future," Drex replied.

The smile that overtook the earl's face transformed him from a distinguished fifty to boyish. "A joyous day, indeed. One I never thought would come. Come and sit. You look tired."

The earl gestured him upstairs, then down a red-carpeted hallway. He threw open the last door to reveal an elegant drawing room with walls of pale pink.

The intricate wealth of the carved ceiling and Sheraton furnishings took Drex aback. If the man had walked away from his responsibility years ago, instead of marrying beneath him, why was he willing to share it all with his by-blow now?

Once seated, his father gestured him to the ivory-fringed chair nearest the fire. "You've given up the…other pursuit?"

"For now, at least."

The earl leaned forward. "You've arranged Ryan's release?"

"No, that's why I've come. I have another plan, which requires your assistance."

His smile grew wider. "By all means, yes."

"This isn't about sentiments," Drex warned. "I need your position within the *ton* and your title, not a father-son rapport. You left a sixteen-

145

year-old girl pregnant with twins. In my estimation, a man cannot behave with less honor than that."

The earl held up his hands to ward off any further barrage. "Drexell, I swear I had no notion Faith had conceived."

He laughed bitterly. "You were bedding her. Certainly, you knew pregnancy was a possibility."

"I'd hoped for it," his father countered, surprising Drex. "I had asked her to marry me, more than once. I thought if she conceived, she would be left with no choice but to wed me. Instead, I returned from an evening at White's to find her gone.

"I searched. For two years! I could find nothing. I knew my family had a hand in keeping us apart, but no amount of cajoling would persuade them to talk. When I voiced my fears that she was pregnant, my father replied that children begotten on such a woman weren't worth having."

Drex drew in a deep breath. The man's explanation sounded plausible, especially since his mother had never offered one, but he wasn't interested in forming a bond with the man.

"I'd prefer to leave the past there," Drex said.

"As would I, now that you've come here. I should like to learn about your brother and your childhood, as well as—"

"Ryan could be dying as we speak, for Christ's sake," he growled. "I only plan to stay long enough to accomplish two things, then I will return to Louisiana."

"You have your mother's directness." The earl sat back in his chair, hands folded, expression restrained. "You said you've come for help and not sentiments. What do you need to accomplish your two tasks?"

Drex braced his elbows on his knees. "A position in society and enough clout to marry Christina Delafield."

The ensuing silence hung over the room like a black pallor. His father's quiet, expressionless response nettled his nerves.

The earl rose and poured two brandies, then gave one to Drex. "Your intention is to secure Ryan once you've wed?"

At Drex's nod, his father asked, "And what of your marriage after Ryan is released? Will you have it annulled and leave us?"

"In my attempts to save Ryan, I besmirched Christina's good name, which makes her my responsibility. *I* am not the sort of man to abandon a woman in need."

The earl sighed. "I suppose I shall never convince you of my good intentions where your mother was concerned."

"If your intentions were so good, why couldn't you keep your pants fastened around her?"

"Greg seems to believe you succumbed to Lady Christina's charms. If that's true, you know about temptation."

The earl's words gave Drex pause. Yes, Lilli had taught him a lot about temptation. He'd always thought himself a man of strong will. She had proven him wrong. Had his father felt the same way about his pretty upstairs maid?

Drex sipped his brandy. "What I did or did not do with Christina is no one's business. If you don't want to help, I'll find another way to marry her, maybe take her to Gretna Green."

"And stain her name with the *ton* more than you have?"

Drex shifted, staring uncomfortably at the swag of blue and rose drapes. The man was right. He had no palatable option but to remain here until he could make his bows into London society.

"I should have married Christina on Grand Bahama," he said.

The earl nodded, his smile benevolent. "We shall remedy the situation posthaste. You'll need to enter little season ahead. My brother's wife, Lady Allyn, will oversee your training—"

"Training? For what?"

His father nodded. "Dance, deportment, dress, manners. Things you must know to be well received."

Drex shook his head, absorbing the information with shock. Could he not simply make an offer for the girl on the basis of being the earl's son? "I had not planned on entering a season. I have no desire to rub shoulders with the *ton*."

"You must if you wish to wed Lady Christina." He shrugged. "Manchester will be soliciting a husband for the girl during the little season, or so whispers indicate, but with his money, he can be somewhat choosy, even though the girl is ruined."

Drex drank in that information—and the realization that his father was right. The man was already proving helpful. Though he did not have to like the earl, Drex knew he would be smart to listen.

* * * *

That evening, Drex sat across from his father in the drawing room. At the earl's summons, Lord Allyn, Drex's uncle, entered the room. He stopped in the threshold, dressed to perfection in biscuit breeches and a green silk vest, and stared.

"George," he said to the earl, dark eyes glued to Drex's overlong hair and dangling earring. "Who is this...man?"

"Come in, Milton." The earl gestured enthusiastically. "Come in. Where's Agnes? I want her here as well."

Lord Allyn looked to the earl, then back to Drex, as if afraid he might attack. "My lady wife is—"

"Right here," broke in a female voice.

A thin woman entered the room, dressed in a watery gray. She stood only five feet, her fragile features almost untouched by time. Her expression was as wan as the shade of her dress.

Drex shifted uncomfortably in his chair, wishing like hell his father would not try to ingrain him in the family.

"Sit down, you two," instructed the earl. "I'll pour drinks. Agnes, a sherry?"

"A word with you, brother," his uncle said, grabbing the earl by the arm. Allyn propelled his brother across the room, to a writing table against the window.

"Who is this...miscreant? My God, man, he's wearing an earring!" Allyn's angry mutter carried to Drex's ears.

The earl shrugged off his brother's touch. "Get hold of yourself, Milton."

As his father strode across the room, Drex tensed. If Lord Allyn didn't like a miscreant in the house, he wasn't likely to want one in the family. More puzzling, however, was his father's behavior. Drex couldn't see why a man with his determination to know his sons would ever have willingly cast his offspring aside.

"Milton, Agnes." He glanced at each. "This is Drexell, one of the sons I began searching for years ago."

Lord Allyn's eyes dilated, turning from brown to black. "Your son? You cannot mean to take this...person in our home and treat him as if—"

"He's flesh and blood?" the earl countered sharply.

"You—you don't intend to make him the next earl, I hope."

"I'm afraid so." The earl turned away from his brother's sputtering and faced the man's wife. "Agnes, I'd like your help. He'll need to be made ready for the little season, and I trust only you to teach him how to get on with the highest sticklers."

"George, even if he has lovely manners, you know his birth will not be excused by some," she pointed out.

The earl nodded. "Give him every other benefit possible, and money will open most doors. We've a very short time to prepare, three weeks, I believe. You'll have to work miracles."

"Indeed," the lady agreed, her face blank.

"You can't mean to have my wife consort with him," Lord Allyn protested. "You know not what manner of person—" He huffed, fists clenched. "Clearly, he is no earl."

Drex watched the exchange, realizing he had displaced his uncle as heir to the earldom. As far as he was concerned, Lord Allyn could have the title. Still, he let the drama play out.

"Watch yourself," the earl warned. "I'm not dead yet."

* * * *

Journal,

I have encountered the most maddening streak of bad luck! Ashmont's by-blow has decided to give up his privateering ways and join the family. Equally disheartening, the earl's health improves more each day, and no matter how I try to rid myself of his misbegotten son, I fail.

I tried to poison the miscreant. At the moment, he lies abed, losing the contents of his stomach on an hourly basis. Yet with every minute that passes, I know he will live.

With the little season approaching, Drexell will be ill-prepared to mingle with the ton. Ashmont won't be embarrassed. He is the earl, after all. But the rest of his family will suffer the slurs, and worse to contemplate, the cuts. I grant that the outlaw hardly resembles the man who first knocked on our door, but he will not do!

I must continue to make plans that will rid me of Drexell forever and allow me the dreams denied by Ashmont's foolish ways.

* * * *

At Drex's request, Greg arrived at the earl's town house an hour before the little season's first major social event. Drex ceased pacing, pulled on the snug white waistcoat about his middle and turned to face his long-time friend.

Greg stopped halfway across the room. "Is that really you?"

The stupefied expression Greg wore heartened Drex that Lilli wouldn't recognize him. "None other."

Greg's mouth hung open. "I would not have recognized you had you not owned up to your identity," he said.

"I look different, then?"

"I should say. Short hair, no earring or mask. You're dressed in garments much better than serviceable clothing and boots. Your skin is no longer brown." He laughed. "You look much like any London gentleman."

"Truly?" Drex smiled. Perhaps his plan would work.

"Almost. I daresay you cut a better cloth than some of us more idle gentlemen." He patted his rounding stomach. "The ladies will adore you, for both your looks and imminent title."

"I only want one lady. What do you know of Christina?"

"She is set to be at the ball, and all of polite society is aflutter. They think Manchester rather audacious for foisting his soiled granddaughter on them in this desperate husband hunt."

Drex felt resolve thicken, plugging his throat like hemp in a ship's hole. "His desperation should make my job easier."

Greg shrugged. "At my club last night, I heard whispers that other men of greater connection but less wealth will be eager to court Lady Christina."

Drex grabbed his gloves from the table beside him. "Then I shall have to work quickly, won't I?"

As the two men went down and asked for the carriage, Greg said, "I hope your father's health permits him to join us."

"He will meet us there."

Greg nodded. "It will aid your suit to have Manchester see you endorsed completely by your father. The *ton* will whisper less, too. Now remember, your attentions to Christina must not be too marked, else the gossip about her will simply multiply."

"I must see her." Drex toyed with his sleeves, trying to shut out the pounding of his heart. "I know I cannot tell her who I am yet, and I pray she does not guess—"

"Even your speech has an edge of culture now. She could not possibly guess," Greg assured.

"Lady Allyn was quite insistent I rid my vocabulary of most four-letter words," he remarked wryly.

"If anyone could lead you through the *ton's* intricacies in such a short time, despite your unfortunate illness, Lady Allyn could."

Drex groaned. "Don't remind me. My father's physician assured me I knelt at death's door. Perhaps I would have crossed the threshold had my father not looked after me."

"You're less angry with him, then?"

He shrugged. "I cannot divert my mind from my purpose to consider him now. I must win Christina and free Ryan."

"Understood. And what will you do once you've won the fair Lady Christina?"

Drex smiled, envisioning a future of content. "I shall tell her all and hope she forgives me. If she does, no one will separate us."

The carriage stopped and the two men exited to a dark drizzle and a throng of people waiting to enter the town house.

"Remember, you cannot dance with her more than once, perhaps twice, without raising eyebrows."

"Unfortunately, I recall that bit of instruction."

Greg turned for the door. "Good. Let's go inside so you can capture Lady Christina's heart—again."

Chapter Fourteen

Several hours of polite smiles and hand shaking passed before Drex finally spotted Christina across the room, alone. His heart stopped for an instant. Then another.

Her golden hair swung in fat ringlets, unlike the smooth sheen of waves she'd worn at sea. Her narrow shoulders and waist told Drex she had not regained much, if any, weight since their parting.

He scanned her face anxiously, but the distance between them was too great to decipher her expression. Was she still angry? He drew in a deep breath, then walked with purpose toward her.

Greg restrained him with a hand on her shoulder. "Are you mad? You know you must be introduced to her."

Drex swallowed his anticipation and forced his gaze to his friend's face. "I'd forgotten."

"Wait here. I shall find our hostess."

Nodding absently, Drex slid a few paces closer to Lilli. Surreptitiously, he studied her face. The kiss of gold she'd acquired from the sun on their voyage to the Bahamas had faded to proper paleness. He ached upon seeing the listless, gray mood she wore like armor. Yet in the stiff set of her shoulders, she wielded a hint of anger as a warrior would a sword.

Greg arrived with their hostess before he could take another ill-advised step toward Christina.

"Lady Henningston, may I present Drexell Cain-Ashmont, Viscount

Drakethorne," his friend said hurriedly.

The stylish fortyish lady extended her gloved hand. Drex clasped it and bowed.

"Your dear father wrote that you would be attending. I called at his house on Wednesday last, but you were not at home."

Drex forced himself to smile, despite his urgency to be presented to Christina in his new guise. "I am the less fortunate for missing such a beautiful guest."

"La, you have such a flattering tongue." She smiled.

"Not at all," he assured. "I wonder, however, if I could persuade you to introduce me to that lovely creature against the wall." He nodded in Lilli's direction.

Lady Henningston paused, her eyes growing rounder. "I can happily introduce you to many eligible ladies if you are in search of a wife."

Drex gritted his teeth, restraining an urge to throttle the woman for setting down Christina. "Thank you for your kind offer. May we start with her?"

Brows raised, the lady replied, "If that is your wish."

The trio made their way toward the wall. Lilli's eyes widened as they closed in on her.

"Lady Christina, may I present Drexell Cain-Ashmont, Viscount Drakethorne," their tight-lipped hostess murmured.

Heart pounding, Drex waited for her response. He held his breath, palms damp, praying she would extend her hand to him so he could touch her, just once, even through their gloves.

She merely inclined her head, green eyes conveying apathy.

Drex bowed to her. "I'm honored."

"And you know Viscount Monroe," Lady Henningston prodded.

Greg smiled. Christina nodded, adding a murmured "Hello."

"Find me, should you wish to meet other young ladies," their hostess said to Drex, then turned away.

"I should like to meet young ladies," Greg called after Lady Henningston.

With a clap on the arm, Greg left Drex alone with Christina.

He turned to face her, happy to drink in her familiar features. Yet the animation she'd always displayed was absent. Guilt stabbed his gut. Why hadn't she regained her spirit yet?

"I beg your forgiveness, Lady Christina, for the awkward introduction. This is my first social function in London."

She stared without response.

Drex smiled, wondering how much he could say without revealing himself or looking like a fool. "I confess, I've been eager to meet you since I first saw you across the room."

Her gaze zeroed in on his face for an instant. Wariness dominated her features before she focused again on the crowd. "If you have come simply to ascertain if rumors of my scandalous behavior are true, please go."

He laughed. "No, but I appreciate your candor. I simply enjoy a beautiful lady's company." The orchestra, silent for some ten minutes, took the front of the room again. "They're forming a new set. Would you care to dance?"

"No." She refused to look at him.

"Please take pity on a poor fool who's only learned to dance. I cannot tell you how much I require the practice."

She looked at him with wary speculation in her green eyes.

"Besides, once the others see the Earl of Ashmont's long-lost misbegotten son dancing with such a graceful creature, certainly they will direct their silly whispers at me."

To his right, an elderly woman gestured Christina toward the dance floor. She faced the woman.

"Grandmother, I know nothing of—"

"Christina, remember your manners. People are watching."

Jaw tensed, Christina swallowed tightly as he extended his arm to her. With a hesitant stretch, she reached for him, fingers lying tentatively upon his forearm. She cast her glance straight ahead as they made their way to the floor.

They lined up across from one another along a row of dancers, women on one side, men on the other. He bowed; she curtsied. Two women on her left cast her snide, sidelong glances.

Resisting the urge to snap at their small-minded ways, he stepped forward to the music, meeting Christina in the middle. A rush of thrill, a tingle, infused him when their hands clasped.

He had but a few moments, one brief whirl, before the dance dictated he release her.

When they returned to their places in the line, he watched other couples make the same foray into the middle he and Lilli had. He glanced surreptitiously at his partner. She didn't clap, didn't smile. But her little white-slippered foot tapped the floor in rhythm to the music.

Heartened, he smiled. She looked away, her strained posture and tense shoulders reasserting themselves.

The order of dance returned to them, dictating he take her hands and lead her in a dash between the rows. This time, as he took her hands, he gently squeezed.

She tore herself from his grip the moment the figure allowed. He only smiled in return.

When next the dance decreed they join hands, Drex found balled little fists in his palms and a determined glare on Lilli's face.

"You're too lovely to scowl," he whispered above the music.

"I am not interested in your flattery."

He shrugged as they stepped away, then leaned close. "A pity, since I've no desire to turn my attention elsewhere."

They danced apart before Lilli could retort.

The music ended. Drex offered Lilli his arm for escort back to her grandmother. He walked her slowly about the room, standing a hint closer than propriety exactly allowed.

"What is it you seek?" she whispered hotly.

He paused. She was hardly in the mood to talk marriage. "Another dance?"

"Certainly not! You are an audacious cur—"

"Yes." He cocked his head to one side. "And people will talk, no matter how properly either of us behaves. Still, if you wish to decline—"

"I do." She snatched her hand off his sleeve. "Leave me."

Drex paused before the wall from which he had escorted her. Lilli's grandmother still stood to one side, speaking with another group of older ladies.

"Then I shall settle for a smile," he murmured.

She ignored his request with a dismissive sideways glare.

"No?" he questioned. "Then, rest assured, I will collect my smile tomorrow."

With a simple nod, he turned about and left the ball, knowing she stared after him.

* * * *

The following afternoon, Christina sat beside her grandmother as she received callers. Most were her friends, and Christina had known the older women all her life. By their demeanors, she knew they merely tolerated her soiled presence for her grandmother's sake.

She had not one caller of her own, save a pair of unsavory fortune hunters she'd danced with last night. Grandmother had dismissed the two rapscallions in her own subtle but final way, which satisfied Christina. Her only other dance partner, Viscount Drakethorne, had not come. She was pleased, regardless of the irritating twinge of disappointment tugging at her.

Toying with the tips of her gloves, she smiled politely at something Lady Jersey said. Unbidden, her thoughts turned back to the previous night, to Drexell Cain-Ashmont.

He was arrogant and handsome, more so than the average London bachelor. And he'd been bent on charming her into a flirtation.

He was dangerous to her peace of mind.

She'd felt a frightening jolt, a hot spark, run the length of her body when their eyes first met. To deny that he disturbed her as a man, with his candid but urbane brand of charm, would be an utter lie. And if she could help it, she would avoid him, especially since he reminded her of the Bla—

"Christina, haven't you heard me, dear? You have a visitor," said her grandmother.

She plucked herself from her reverie and glanced up to find the very object of her thoughts entering the drawing room. He nodded politely to one starchy matron, flattered a lonely widow, endured an introduction of a countess's horse-faced daughter, then complimented her grandmother for her exquisite taste in furnishings. The man oozed charm.

To her distress, he picked his way across the room, murmuring here and there until he reached her side. By happenstance, or her grandmother's machinations, a seat on the sofa beside her chair became vacant. Predictably, he took it with a wry smile.

He lifted her fingers from the chair's arm and brought her hand to his mouth, his lips lingering longer than proper.

"Lady Christina." He inclined his head.

A spark wound down her spine. The tenor of his voice, even his dark eyes, seemed chillingly like the Black Dragon's. Yet this man had no overlong hair, no earring, no beard, no bronzed skin. He wore only the finest garments. The voice and mannerisms were different. A few similarities couldn't signify. The two men were worlds apart.

This man, though every bit as handsome as the Black Dragon, possessed charm with his looks. She would have to be on guard.

"Lord Drakethorne," she replied.

"I do hope you're not suffering sore toes and dirty slippers from my neophyte attempts at dancing."

"My toes and slippers remain unscathed, my lord," she answered, conscious of her heart's faster beating. Reminding herself that men did not affect her, she drew in a deep breath.

"Then I may sleep well now, knowing I have learned the rudiments of all the polite dances, unless the waltz comes to England."

"Too shocking, according to most."

He smiled and leaned closer. "Tell me one woman here who doesn't like to be shocked every now and again."

"Lord Drakethorne!"

"Not that any would admit to such scandal," he hurried to add. "Still, who doesn't long for excitement in their life?"

Christina's palms turned damp beneath her gloves. She secretly yearned for the carefree excitement of her days aboard *The Dragon's Lair*, even while she despised its captain.

"I'm sure I wouldn't know about such a thing."

He shot her a sideways smile, eyes dancing beneath a roguish shag of dark hair. "Come now, I knew the instant I set eyes upon you that you were hardly of the same mealy-mouthed variety as the other London misses."

More likely he'd been listening to rumors. Stiffening, Christina assured, "I strive to behave with complete propriety."

"Are you not bored doing so?"

How did he know her so well? Though she had vowed since her return to behave with perfect decorum, and had so far, she could not deny that reckless streak within her wanted more. Such dangerous thoughts could only lead to further scandal and heartbreak. She pushed them aside.

"The season exists to conduct politics and make marriages. Many in the *ton* find such doings exciting in themselves."

"I asked about you. What do you find exciting?"

Heart pounding, Christina glanced up to find Lady Jersey hanging on their every word. To her left, Grandmother was doing a good imitation of listening to her guests, but Christina knew the woman's attention had strayed.

"I'm sure I have no notion what you mean."

He leaned closer still. His fingers brushed her own in what appeared to be an accidental sweep. Christina knew better. Tingles plagued her body, feelings she remembered all too well from her summer's escapade in the Caribbean.

"I think you've given the notion much thought. Is it shopping or tea with the ladies you find exciting? Perhaps it's a good book or two."

He paused to stroke his square, clean-shaven chin. She watched his fingers with unbidden interest.

"Or do you enjoy being courted?" he whispered.

She clenched her hands in her lap. Had someone asked her two days ago if she found a man's company exciting, her answer would have been no. Today she could only lament that she found Drexell Cain-Ashmont's unwelcome presence stimulating.

Christina opened her mouth, but her visitor stayed her caustic remark with a raised finger. "Pray, do not answer that last question." He stood with a crooked smile that sent Christina's heart into turmoil and her anxiety soaring. "I think I should like to find the answer for myself."

Chapter Fifteen

Drex arrived at his father's house that evening, filled with Christina. Her scent, her voice. She still looked too thin, but he would change that once they were wed. He envisioned her round with his child and his heart swelled with hope.

He no more than crossed the threshold when his father approached. "Good news. Come with me."

They trod upstairs. At the top, Lord and Lady Allyn stood.

"Hello. Fine day, isn't it?" the earl said to both.

"Indeed," Lady Allyn answered with a tight smile.

Her husband shot a glare at Drex, then transferred the scowl to his brother. "Come, Agnes. I need a brandy."

"I'm afraid Milton isn't adjusting well to the family changes," his father said with a sigh and a shake of his head.

"Good for you his wife keeps him in tow."

"Agnes is a godsend," he said as they entered the library.

The earl shut the door behind him quickly. "I received a note today." His father smiled. "I've found Ryan."

Drex felt his stomach jump up to his throat. "Truly? How?"

"I renewed a few contacts from years past and found someone willing to share that many of the impressed Americans who resisted the Admiralty's treatment were brought to Newgate on trumped-up charges. I decided to pay Newgate's goaler a visit, just in case. For a"—he cleared his throat—"small fee, he was willing to let me have five minutes with Ryan."

"Is he well? He looked terrible—"

"His condition should be much improved soon. I paid the goaler to upgrade your brother's accommodations. I couldn't buy his release.

Manchester would hang him for that, but Ryan will have better care until we can think of something else."

Drex stared at his father. Shock and confusion swarmed his system. The earl cared deeply about the well-being of a son he had never met? Comprehension dawned. The man truly did want his sons.

He thrust a hand toward his father. "Thank you."

The earl accepted the clasp, the new offer of a bond, with a smile so reminiscent of elated relief Drex smiled back.

His father asked, "So how is Lady Christina today?"

"Withdrawn. Distrustful of all men, it seems. How can I persuade her to marry me?"

The earl shrugged. "Perhaps you cannot, at least not now. However, other rogues are hovering near. Lady Jersey is already gossiping about two fortune hunters who called before you."

Anxiety tightened Drex's gut. "I must act now. But how?"

"Ask Manchester for her hand, instead. You can bring her round to your way of thinking once the vows are spoken."

Drex turned her father's suggestion about in his head. The plan was good. She could hardly say nay once her grandfather had chosen a man for her. She had nowhere else to run.

But she would be furious as hell with him.

"Manchester is tight with his money," the earl offered. "He will see you more favorably if you refuse her enormous dowry."

"And ask for the release of American sailors in Newgate instead?" Drex smiled.

His father clapped him on the shoulder. "We think alike."

"For which I'm glad…Father."

With a smile, Drex turned and left for Grosvenor Square.

* * * *

Christina shuddered at the feel of Lord Ralston's arm about her. His breath was none too pleasant. The sweat on his palms dampened her dress. And he referenced plans to renovate his country estate, when everyone knew he hadn't the funds.

Apparently, he'd assumed her desperation would cast him as a good candidate as her husband.

Christina grimaced, then said, "Lord Ralston, I am simply parched. Could you fetch me some punch?"

He didn't quite hide his irritation with a tight smile. "Wait here."

The moment the balding man disappeared into the swirl of the shimmering crowd, Christina darted for the balcony. The door had been thrown open to release some of the steam in the ballroom.

Outside, winter nipped at her nose as she walked to the rail. Wrapping her arms about herself, Christina decided she'd gladly freeze to hide here all night if it meant avoiding Lord Ralston.

Suddenly, she felt a large, warm garment blanket her shoulders. She turned to find Drexell Cain-Ashmont standing behind her, minus his coat.

His dark eyes glittered in the golden moonlight. "Better?"

The gesture, like his voice, struck her as intimate. Disturbed, she shrugged his coat off and handed it back to him. "Thank you, but I wasn't cold."

"I don't recall your teeth chattering when we last met," he teased. "I'm not usually so forgetful."

"Gentlemen don't notice such things," she chastised.

"Which is why I've always thought gentlemen to be silly and tedious. Who enjoys the kind of man who paws his dance partner and talks of his hunting dogs more fondly than his children?"

Christina flashed him a sideways glance. A vivid image of Lord Ralston and his expensive, slobbering mutts materialized. She tried to repress the upward curving of her mouth.

He smiled and draped the dark coat over her shoulders again, cocooning her in inviting warmth.

Drat if the thing didn't smell musky, just like him. Even the scent, something strong and male, brought back unwanted memories of her time with the Black Dragon, of the vulnerabilities of her heart. She pushed the recollections away.

"Why did you follow me out into the cold?" she asked.

His wide-eyed expression revealed mock horror. "I couldn't run the risk of such a lovely damsel perishing in this chill."

"So you and your coat came to my rescue?"

He nodded, expression wistful. "I only regret I could not find a white horse to complete my picture of knighthood."

Christina found herself smiling as Lord Ralston returned.

"There you are," he said, scowl upon his perspiring face. "I've come to see you to supper."

Christina's mind raced. Having no wish to consort for the next hour with this damp creature whose smell had become quite unpleasant, she grasped for a way to leave him behind.

"I'm afraid she's already promised me that honor," Lord Drakethorne answered, rescuing her again. He turned to her with a proffered arm. "Shall we?"

Christina conveyed her appreciation with her smile.

"A stroll in the gardens later, perhaps?" Lord Ralston called desperately to her retreating figure.

"Lord Drakethorne has already given me the tour," she lied.

Once inside, she laughed for the first time in months. It felt freeing, refreshing, like spring might soon bloom inside her. She yearned to cling to the feeling, to forget contemptible exploiters like the Black Dragon inhabited this earth.

"Ah, the fair Christina smiles. Where is da Vinci when life's truly memorable moments occur?"

She laughed. "My smile is hardly memorable."

"You must allow me to disagree. Were you to try, I believe your glow could light up the entire night sky."

"You flatter me too much," she chastised, but couldn't quite erase the smile from her face.

"A difficult thing to avoid with someone so lovely."

Lord Drakethorne made her feel beautiful and worthwhile again. Such dangerous feelings. Her heart wasn't invincible. The Black Dragon had proven so. Yet even as she cautioned herself against a burgeoning warmth, she feared that tonight such admonitions were useless.

She sobered. "I am convinced of your charm, my lord. No need to keep wielding it so intently."

"Around you, I cannot seem to stop." Lord Drakethorne paused. "If you're hungry, I will see you to the supper room."

"I'm afraid I am going to cry off and go home."

"Another time?" he queried.

She paused, not certain how to answer. Should she encourage him? Tonight, his demeanor had seemed exemplary of the kind of husband she required, charming but not overbearing.

"Thank you for rescuing me from Lord Ralston," she murmured.

"It was this knight's pleasure, my lady. Until we meet again?" he whispered over her hand.

Discreetly, she slid her palm from his grasp and, with her heart pounding, turned away.

Chapter Sixteen

Christina stared out the window at gray drizzle that matched her mood. It seemed appropriate that rain should fall on her wedding day.

Of course she'd known she would marry quickly. She simply had not believed the day would come quite this soon. Still, best to marry someone pleasant now so the gossip would die. Wise to align herself with someone not likely to rip out her heart.

She shrugged. Drexell Cain-Ashmont would do.

True, she found his traditional approach in asking her grandfather for her hand irritating. After all, she would have to live with him. Her opinion was important, and Christina meant to make certain he understood that from now on. She would not be tied to a man to whom her wishes were inconsequential.

She turned back toward the fireplace as the Chinese mantel clock chimed. Ten in the morning.

The sounds of shuffling and voices at the front door below heralded the punctual arrival of her betrothed and his family.

A soft knock on the door precipitated her grandmother's voice. "Christina, darling, are you ready? It's time."

She opened the door, and her grandmother folded her arms about her like a warm, sun-dried quilt.

"You look wonderful, child." Her faded lips turned up in a smile. "I've a feeling Lord Drakethorne will make you happy."

Christina frowned. "He married me to free Americans from Newgate and add credence to his position in the *ton*."

"Perhaps, but I believe he is taken with you. If you'll forget the past, contentment will be yours."

163

Forget the past? Though Drexell Cain-Ashmont was gentler, he had yet to prove he was something more than a manipulative cad, any different from Grandfather and the Black Dragon.

Christina pasted on the façade of a smile and followed her grandmother down the hall. Inside the drawing room, the groom and his family waited. Their minister stood in the corner.

Lord Drakethorne sat in a high-backed chair of creamy velvet, fidgeting with the timepiece in his hand. At her entrance, he looked up. Relief loosened his features, and their gazes met. Warmth sprouted in her belly. She'd forgotten his brilliant smile, the one that made her feel desired and female again.

As his gaze lingered, making a discreet sweep of her body, the room receded in her vision. The other occupants seemed to disappear. The heat enveloping her chest dipped lower, to her nether regions, reminding her of her wanton nature. Reminding her that he would expect to share her bed tonight.

She dropped her gaze to the floor as he approached her.

"You look beautiful," he whispered.

Gazing up at him, no response came to mind. He frightened her; she couldn't remain unaffected by him.

Her grandfather saved her from the awkward pause in conversation. He cast a jaundiced gaze at Lord Drakethorne as her grandmother busily seated everyone. The minister motioned Christina and her groom to the front of the room, positioned them by the kneeling mats and began to read from his Bible.

At her side, Lord Drakethorne stood close, smelling of musk and man, as always. A sideways glance proved he looked better than sin in biscuit breeches, a crisp ivory vest and a burgundy coat. He smiled nicely enough, but she knew better than to allow him to penetrate the armor around her heart, no matter how manageable he seemed. She would not survive another broken heart.

Christina heard the minister murmur her name. She returned her attention to him and made the appropriate responses. Lord Drakethorne did the same, then took her hand in his warm, callused one. He slid a cool band of gold down her third finger, and the minister pronounced them man and wife. Lord Drakethorne clutched her hand, wearing a triumphant smile.

As the day crept by and shadows lengthened, Christina grew more nervous. Her new husband did not seem the kind of man easily dissuaded on his wedding night with a simple no. Could she bare her body to him without exposing her heart and soul?

Drat! How could she escape the dangerous possibilities her wedding night—and every other wedded night—would bring? Fingers pressed to her temples, she shook her head. Somehow, she would survive her fate with dignity—and her heart unscathed.

The groom's family departed after the evening's brandy and cigars. Scowling, Grandfather retired to his study. Christina resisted seclusion with her new husband by lingering over a glass of sherry, while her grandmother rose to leave, looking as if she wanted to impart advice about the coming intimacies. Christina looked away, hoping to avoid such a speech. The old woman left.

"Your grandmother seems to think I'm likely to chop you into little pieces and eat you for dessert," her new husband remarked.

With an awkward shrug, Christina rose, resisting the urge to flee. She knew what Lord Drakethorne would want tonight. But the thought of sharing herself with him made her tremble. At moments he reminded Christina of the Black Dragon. At other times, he was a virtual stranger. She knew next to nothing of her husband.

Beside her, he also rose, then reached for her hands. Christina allowed him to clasp her trembling fingers. Looking into the captivating sparkle of his dark eyes, she felt a stirring of feelings she'd believed dead.

"You need not be afraid of me." He gave her hand a reassuring squeeze. "I want only to make you happy."

The fact her happiness mattered to him on any level filled Christina with wary hope. If she could ever forget the past and remember her quest for a pleasant, scandal-free future, she might survive this night.

He squeezed her hands again before releasing them, his expression conveying disappointment at her silence. "I need to have a word with your grandfather."

Did his departure mean he was not interested in pursuing their marriage bed, or was he simply giving her a moment's privacy before he planned to invade her body?

She studied his retreating back. The confident stride hardly looked indicative of a man not interested in a woman's charms.

After his exit, Christina made her way to her room. He would come to her tonight, want to explore and possess her.

God help her.

* * * *

Ten minutes later, Drex knocked on Lilli's bedroom door. Their wedding night had come—a night he had looked forward to for interminable weeks. After long days of dance and deportment lessons, Drex had lain awake in his father's house fantasizing of the night he could strip away Lilli's clothes and restraint and make love to her again. Afterward, she would realize she cared for him. He would reveal himself to her, and together, they would greet a free Ryan. The plan seemed perfect.

She cracked the door, her once expressive face closed. Taut shoulders and stiff posture dominated her bearing. The woman before him, she wasn't the careless, carefree Lilli he remembered from their days together aboard the *Lair*. This tense, careful woman was Christina—a woman he did not know well. A woman he would have to tread carefully with if he wanted his Lilli back.

Endless moments stretched between them as they stood frozen, him waiting for admittance, her unwilling to grant it. His whirling thoughts grew as he took in the agitated rise and fall of her chest, the slight pursing of her full mouth. They stood tantalizingly close. He inhaled her breath, her scent, so achingly floral and familiar.

His eyes made a quick scan of her thinly clad body. A spark of anticipation cut through him, igniting his desire. Christina grabbed a wrapper and struggled into the white garment. As she yanked it closed, she stared at him with angry green eyes.

He cleared his throat. "Shall we talk for a while?"

"Talk?" she challenged. A bitter laugh followed. The cynical sound surprised him.

She was afraid, he realized. A new man, a new life. It seemed logical that such adjustments would breed anxiety.

He nudged through the door, then shut it behind him with a click. "Christina, you are my wife. I cannot deny that I want you."

The honesty of his soft words hung in the air between them. Christina touched a shaking hand to her chest and looked away.

Drawing in a sharp breath, she crossed to the other side of the room. "Before we commence with the distasteful business of marriage, perhaps we should talk after all."

The acidic tone of her voice raised Drex's brow. He strode across the room and seated himself on the stool at her dressing table. The early evening moonlight gleamed with pale vigor through the window, giving her an ethereal glow. Silver light swirled about her. He swallowed against the rise of awareness.

"I am no simpering miss, I assure you," she snapped.

Drex had to smile. "About that, there could be no mistake."

She raised her chin, preparing for a fight. "I intend to further the cause of women in society, and you cannot stop me."

He cocked his head in thought and scanned. Why had she chosen this particular subject tonight? "As you please."

Her delicate hands balled into fists. "I'll read what I want, think what I want and do what I want."

Drex wondered exactly what scheme she was planning, but decided he'd do well to play her game. He nodded.

Instead of placating her, his accord drew her taut-faced fury. "You do not own me. No man does!"

He said nothing, taking in her squared shoulders and gritted teeth, along with her earthy beauty. She wanted a fight he wasn't eager to give. But he knew her enough to believe she wouldn't give up until he pursued her path.

"Do you understand?" she asked, breath harsh.

Drex let silence fill the air for a moment. "I understand. You like adventure and things you know you shouldn't."

Her eyes widened as she gasped. "That is not what I said."

Drex rose and approached her, flashing her a shark's smile when she stood her ground. "Of course it is. You like being where you shouldn't, behaving in ways you know you shouldn't."

Christina's bowed mouth dropped open. Her fists clenched. "Whatever you've heard, I am a lady."

"Yes. And ten times the woman of any other in London. That is the reason I made you my wife."

Christina drew in a ragged breath, momentarily silenced.

"You are beautiful," he murmured.

Her eyes turned wary and wide as she retreated a step.

"I know what you want." Her voice shook.

"Good. There shouldn't be any confusion between us."

He moved closer, closer. Christina stepped back once, then again. The third time, her back hit the wall. Drex followed, trapping her against the hard surface.

"I've longed to taste your sweet mouth," he whispered as his gaze delved hers.

She opened her mouth, probably to deliver a stinging retort. But he leaned closer, mere inches from her. He could have touched her easily, in a multitude of places. He didn't. Instead, he stood so close a whisper of air passed between them.

He found his breath trapped in his chest, his heart racing. The pulsing at her neck echoed his heartbeat. He planned to put his lips there first.

Her shallow breath caressed him like a feather, tantalizing. It transported him back in time. He could almost feel tangy Bahamian air on his skin and sweet Lilli moaning in his arms.

Finally, he touched her. She gasped as he caressed her shoulder. His fingers glided their way to the bare skin behind her neck. She exhaled on shaky breath.

Drex held in a groan. He slid his hand up to her face, then to her hair. One by one, he pulled the pins free as she stood, silent, staring with those wide green eyes he couldn't forget and trembling. "I've waited forever to kiss you."

Though he wanted to devour her, Drex forced himself to brush her lips with his own. A gentle feathering, as if taking the sugar from atop a cookie. She stiffened. He tasted her again, rediscovering the flavor and texture of her lips. Christina's behavior might be different, but somewhere under that starch was his Lilli.

He pulled away, trailing the pad of his thumb across her mouth before he covered her lips once more. This time, he penetrated her mouth and wrapped her stiff form in his embrace. His tongue swirled and played with hers, mated and beguiled.

Slowly, Christina relaxed in his arms. He encouraged her, kissing her neck, nibbling on her lobe, testing the fluttering pulse at her throat. He knew her breathy gasps, and the sounds filled him with triumph.

Slowly, her arms wound about his neck. Drex felt his blood pump through his veins in icy hot streams. His belly tightened. His cock hardened. He devoured her lips with a searing kiss.

Without warning, without reason, Christina wrenched from his grasp and turned her profile to him. Her tense bearing had returned, warning him away. But with golden hair streaming down her back in an angel's cloud and golden light bathing her in warmth, Drex succumbed to his yearning to touch her again.

As he caressed her shoulder, she turned her face to him, her expression flat. Stung, he dropped his hand to his side.

"Last summer, I fell in love," she said without inflection.

Drex smiled softly, wonder infusing him like brilliant sunlight after a long winter. She hadn't forgotten him. She truly had loved him. Perhaps she still did. Elation filled him. He reached for her again.

"He was a criminal by society's standards, a pirate to most. I came to trust him, with both my heart and my body."

Drex touched his hand to the small of her back and tried to nudge her closer. "I know all that. Christina, darling—"

She twisted away from his touch. "I laid with a masked stranger whose name I never knew. I gave myself freely to a bastard who cut my heart out and left me to bleed. It won't happen again."

Drex let his hand fall away, stunned by her bitterness. He frowned as Christina walked past him to the center of the room. Immersed in gilded light, she discarded her wrapper, then her night rail.

Naked, she faced him. Moonlit shadows clung like a phantom lover to the swells and hollows of her body. Pouty breasts and shimmering pink nipples beckoned. The sweet curve of her waist, accentuated by shades of gray, lengthened into a flat stomach and long legs.

Drex lost his breath, his mind, as he stared at the temptation she offered. God, he'd waited forever, it seemed.

Then his stare made its way up again. He took in her squared shoulders and taut cheeks, her face a beautiful fortress guarding her tattered heart.

Drex couldn't move, couldn't speak or comprehend.

Christina cast him another flat stare, then made her way to the bed. Drex's gaze consumed the lithe curve of her waist, the graceful slope of her spine as it dipped to her pale, round buttocks and slender thighs. The ability to breathe left him.

She was angry, he realized through the haze of his desire. The sharp whip of her wrist as she pulled back the bed sheets told him so. With all the regal bearing of a princess, she climbed onto the bed and lay passively across its surface.

"Take me if you want," she offered tonelessly. "It means nothing to me."

Drex absorbed her verbal blow like a punch. He wanted her, had thought of nothing else all day. She wanted no part of him or this side of their marriage.

Across the room, Christina directed her unblinking stare at the ceiling, her naked body tense and unmoving.

Had he really hurt her that much last summer?

He cleared his throat. "Christina, not like this."

She didn't look at him. "This is all I have to offer, all I will ever give you."

The steely pitch of her monotone voice told Drex she meant every word. If he caressed and kissed her, she would try her damnedest to merely endure his touch. If she did respond to him, he suspected she would never forgive him.

If he told her his identity now, she would hate him forever.

Damn it, what a tangle! He'd made the right decision to ransom her, given his situation, but had no idea how to reverse the damages. He would simply have to start over, court her again. Find a way to make her fall in love with him once more.

Drex strode for the door and flung it open, his scowl an unyielding challenge. "I don't want a martyr. I want a wife."

* * * *

Two long weeks later, Christina rose from her seat during the chasm of awkward silence immediately following dinner. Pressing at her temples to lend credence to her headache, she fled from her husband's omnipresent stare.

She paused before exiting, her gaze falling on Lord Drakethorne's now familiar features. A mistake. The man couldn't look anything but powerful, she concluded. Her palms turned damp beneath her gloves just looking at him.

After racing to her room in Ashmont's town house, she shut the door and stood in the dark. She should have called for her maid but didn't. Instead, she pondered her new husband.

Lord Drakethorne and his magnetism would be easy to succumb to—too easy. He seemed content to maintain his distance without demand. He'd left flowers on her breakfast plate last week. The volume of Byron's poetry two days ago had been a surprise, as well. Not because he'd given her a gift but because he seemed to ask nothing in return. At least, not yet.

But she knew what he wanted. Worse, she feared he could make her want it, too.

Christina drifted to the window and parted the sheer curtains. Unless she controlled her emotions, Lord Drakethorne could win her over, placate her with his charm—and control her for the rest of her life. Then again, he might simply choose to use and abandon her, taking mistress after mistress after he'd tired of her. Christina couldn't bear that pain and humiliation. Being abandoned once had been enough.

But his exit on their wedding night… She had never expected the reprieve. Would he really wait until she was ready to give more than the shell of her body to him? Such an idea confounded her, as much as his abstinence the past two weeks. He could take her. The law gave him that right. Why, then, did it matter to him that she wasn't willing to give him more than mere sex?

A knock sounded moments later. His knock, she knew. Funny, she'd already memorized its cadence and volume. Her heart pounded as she straightened the bodice of her dress and her shaking voice bade him to enter.

He didn't hesitate. The door came open, and he strode to the center of the room. Long moments passed. He did nothing more than stare. His intensity spoke volumes on his mood.

"Go away. I have a headache," she said.

"I won't stay."

He walked to the window. The full moon cast a beam of pale light on his features. The jut of his chin, the angle of his nose and those eyes—all resembled the Black Dragon. So much it hurt. Yet she knew no matter how haunting the similarities, reality was much different. No matter how much she wanted to blame Lord Drakethorne for her pain, she could not.

Yet she refused to let him into her thoughts, where he could cause more anguish.

"Christina, I understand that you've been hurt. The man who hurt you surely knows his actions were wrong. I can only say that his reasons must have been good to give you up willingly."

"You're defending him? The knave who took your wife's maidenhood?" she challenged, mouth open in incredulity.

Her husband closed his eyes and reached out to grasp the windowsill. "I think we should forget the past. Both of us."

Christina turned her back to him. "I offered you my body, quite freely."

He closed the distance between them and touched her shoulders.

171

"Not freely. Reluctantly. I want all of you."

The gentle yet provocative timbre of his voice made her tremble. He meant what he said. Every word. God help her.

Tears stung her eyes. "I have nothing more to give."

"You have a heart," he whispered in her ear.

A tremor whisked down her spine, all the way to her toes. She twisted free from his grasp, then stepped away, smoothing a shaking hand down her dress.

"Christina, I will not hurt you. I give you my word."

"Words mean very little to me, my lord."

His footsteps ate up the ground between them. Christina wasn't surprised to feel his hand wrap about her arm. He turned her around to face him.

"It's Drexell," he urged. "Can you not even say my name?"

"Such informality between us does not suit me."

He released her. "This isn't over. I will make you my wife in every way, by your choice, in your time. Not before."

Chapter Seventeen

Another two weeks slid by. Still, Drexell demanded nothing of her.

Christina pushed the surprise from her mind and wandered about the library, lamenting that she'd most likely waste this crisp winter sun indoors, alone. She missed people around her and longed for the days when dresses and matching slippers consumed her afternoons before glittering evenings of dance.

Though she could not fathom why, she missed her husband. Turning away from the bookshelves, she walked to the hearth and sat on the blue settee with a sigh. In the first few weeks of their marriage, she'd found his distance relieving, a godsend even. Recently, something had changed.

The sound of rapid footsteps outside the door brought Christina's gaze around. Drexell paused, scanning the room.

"Good morning. Have you seen my father?" he asked.

She'd never known a man so patient. Why did he behave so?

She gave him a halting smile. "I—he left earlier."

Remembrance burst across his face as he snapped his fingers. "I'd forgotten. He had an appointment this morning."

After a precise pivot, her husband left. Christina exhaled, realizing she'd been holding her breath during his brief visit.

She stared at the vacant doorway. Lonely and empty described her mood. Her grandmother suggested she was punishing Drexell for the Black Dragon's deeds. Perhaps it was true.

No, this had nothing to do with Drexell. She was just restless. Confining herself to the house had never appealed.

Suppressing a sprouting smile, Christina dashed to change her dress, then strode to the stables. If Drexell planned an outing, it seemed a likely place to find him.

Inside the stable, the scents of hay and beast blended with wet earth from a recent rain. She spotted Drexell atop a huge bay, crooning to the skittish animal. The shadows enhanced the dark intensity of his eyes, the chiseled angles of his face.

She fiddled with her riding habit, unsure of her welcome. "Where are you going?"

"For a ride." He patted the horse's head. "She's been favoring her hind leg. My father wanted to test her, see if she has improved." He paused, his smile uncertain. "Would you, ah... Are you interested in coming along?"

Christina glanced outside. The sun's golden light seemed to sweeten the chorus of the birds' song in the air.

"I should like that."

In minutes, a groom saddled another horse and they departed.

Through the morning chill, they drifted without direction, without words. Christina peeked at Drexell, wondering at his thoughts. Did he ever think of her, still want her?

"How is her leg?" she asked, to fill the silence.

He shrugged. "There's no limp. I daresay, she's not likely to win at Ascot anytime soon, but she's healing."

Christina had never been at a loss for conversation in her life. Today, with Drexell, she couldn't think of a thing to say.

Soon they reached Hyde Park, the center of the *ton's* afternoon bustle. This morning, they found it nearly empty, a multi-hued wilderness cultivated for the eye's pleasure.

"Lovely, isn't it?" Drexell said quietly.

She looked around. Buckingham stood in the distance, a stony sentinel. Grass, trying to unearth the first of spring green, stretched up to the banks of the Serpentine. Crocuses and snowdrops would soon douse the park with their sweet scent. The spindly branches of trees crisscrossed the cloudless winter sky.

"Beautiful," she murmured. "I never really noticed it. Mostly, I traversed Rotten Row, seeing others and being seen."

He laughed. "When I was young, my mother told me that Oliver

Cromwell was nearly killed here in this park when he fell from his carriage and was dragged behind it."

"No." She tried not to grin. "You must be teasing."

"It's truth. And worse, his gun went off in his pocket."

Christina laughed until her sides hurt. She couldn't picture the stuffy Cromwell suffering such indignity well.

Drexell turned his face to her, his dark eyes contemplative. "You should smile more. It's lovely."

She bit her bottom lip. "Did you grow up in London?"

His faraway gaze matched his nod. "In Whitechapel."

She knew nothing of his past, of him. To learn he'd been raised in the Whitechapel squalor stunned her. "How did you find your father?"

He hesitated. "He found me."

Drexell pulled on the bay's reins and brought her to a halt. "She's favoring her leg again somewhat."

Christina watched as he dismounted. She stopped her own horse. "How will you get her home?"

He shrugged. "Walk her, I suppose."

Though Drexell seemed perfectly capable of such a trip, it seemed petty to trouble him. "My mount will carry us both."

He paused, his dark eyes captivating hers with an enigma of a stare. "Thank you."

She smiled shyly. Christina knew she had never been demure, yet the emotion seemed appropriate, a reflection of her hopeful uncertainty. Should their marriage be more than a hollow shell? He didn't seem an unworthy man, unlike—

Christina broke off the thought when he flashed her a warm smile that vaporized her composure. She drew in a shaky breath. A seductive husband who seemed to understand her yet demanded nothing? She could have married worse men, much worse.

Drexell tied the injured bay to her mare, then pulled himself up behind her. The hot breadth of his chest enveloped her back. His warm exhalations played at her neck.

"Comfortable?" he asked.

Other than the fact she could hardly breathe because she felt his presence acutely with every nerve in her body? "Perfectly."

His hands came around either side of her and grabbed the reins. She'd been expecting it, but the sight of his calloused and tapered fingers inches from her waist washed her with a wave of heated awareness. Goodness, what was the matter with her?

"Ready?" he asked.

A note, some sort of suggestion, lay in the undertone of his question. The intimation should have worried or angered her. But the spike of excitement piercing Christina, the sliver of thrill, made her turn. She glanced at Drexell over her shoulder. Their eyes met, his face inches away. His dark gaze dropped to her mouth.

Time stopped. The rhythm of her breathing, her heart, increased, as if she'd been dancing one country reel after another. Yet she'd hardly moved a muscle.

He wanted her. Badly. He made no attempt to alter the strained set of his jaw or hide the flare of passion in his eyes.

Desire, pure and undeniable, raced through her blood. She wanted him, wanted to trust him, when he inched closer, his mouth hovering deliciously close to her own.

He paused a mere breath away and stopped.

Christina felt his breath on her cheek, felt the sensuality of his gaze like a tangible touch. Her insides quivered.

He remained motionless.

Suddenly, she knew he would not kiss her until she raised her mouth that last inch to his.

Her heart began to beat wildly. Powerful longing warred with cautious self-doubt. At that moment, she trusted him more than she trusted herself.

Perspiration broke out on her brow, despite the cool air.

"Christina?" he urged.

She drew in a mind-clearing breath but couldn't stop the thought that his mouth would be a firm, erotic heaven, a balm to her soul.

But once she had surrendered, would he remain her good knight? Or become a controlling autocrat? Or simply leave her?

Christina looked away. "I—I think we should go now."

* * * *

Greg dropped in the following afternoon without warning. When the dandified viscount loosened his cravat from his neck, pulling it askew, Drex knew something was wrong.

"Has Manchester contacted you yet?" Greg asked.

Drex rose from his chair by the fire and set his coffee aside with a clink. "Should he?"

"He released the American sailors from Newgate today."

Faster than a bolt of lightning, Drex crossed the room to Greg's side. "Ryan is free?" He laughed. "It worked. I knew it! Where is he? Are they being held somewhere temporarily?"

Greg paused. "Manchester released everyone but Ryan."

The words sank in slowly. Drex felt the air leave his body, felt himself struggling for breath, like a drowning man.

"Manchester refused to release Ryan until the Black Dragon is caught or killed."

The familiar tones of Greg's voice brought Drex back from his numbness. Confusion wrinkled his brow. "Bastard! What the hell should I do now? This marriage was my last hope."

Greg laid a hand on his shoulder. "I don't know."

"God's teeth, I must either give myself into the hangman's care or die now." Drex whirled away. "Why can't something work out according to plan, just once?"

"I wish I had the answer," Greg said from across the room. His usually buoyant pale features matched the gray of his coat.

"I'm not in the mood to die, damn it." He paced.

Long strides took him across the room again, and he raked a hand through his short hair. His fingers sought his left lobe for the earring he wore, then he remembered he'd doffed it weeks ago. Christ, nothing was familiar to him now, not this land, not his family or their society. Not his clothes, his speech or manners. Especially not his emotions for his beautiful but stubborn wife.

"Death does seem drastic," Greg conceded.

"If only I could convince Manchester the Black Dragon is no more..." Drex sighed. An inkling of an idea wound into his thoughts. He smiled.

"Oh, no. Now what trick have you tucked up your sleeve?"

"What if," Drex began, holding up a dramatic finger, "we led everyone to believe the Black Dragon had indeed died?"

Greg's blond brows folded in a frown. "Feign your death?"

"Exactly." His smile widened. "I'll tell Hancock to fetch my clothing tomorrow night, then have him arrange a drowning. All they'll find of me is a scrap of my shirt, a boot, and just so there's no question of my identity, my mask. The body will have drifted down the river Thames, into the ocean."

Greg paused as if in thought. "By George, it might work."

"I will make it work." Drex clapped his friend on the back.

But before he killed his alter ego forever, Drex decided he would pay his wife a visit—in costume. The sentiment she harbored for the masked privateer appeared so deep, she still fancied herself in love with him.

He had to let the Black Dragon help him to win her affections again and turn them to favor her ever-patient husband.

"Greg, did I hear you say your latest mistress is an actress?" Drex asked. At his friend's nod, he asked, "How would she like to help me with a small transformation?"

* * * *

Christina rolled over in her cold bed and opened one eye. Had she really heard a thud at her door or had she been dreaming?

Her chamber looked the same, a bedside stand and a book, a cluttered dressing table, a velvet settee in sunny yellow. The door connecting her room to Drexell's remained closed.

Thump. Christina whirled around and scanned the other side of the room. Her white-curtained window let in muted moonlight—and illuminated a familiar silhouette.

Dark hair fell to his shoulders, glittering gold looped through his ear, a white shirt hung open to his waist and a glittering dagger rested at his thigh.

The Black Dragon.

Christina rubbed her eyes, certain she must be dreaming. When she looked up again, he still stood beside her window.

He looked as imposing as ever, menacing in shadow, like some phantom of the night. Her pulse quickened, along with her anger.

"Oh my… You!" She yanked the covers to her chin. "How did you get in?"

"Your windows are easy to pry open, Lilli. You should have someone look into that."

"My window is not at ground level," she protested, then realized she should be shouting a thousand other words.

"A minor detail." He waved her argument away. "You're looking well. Very well, in fact."

"How dare you come here! My husband could walk in—"

"Husband?" He laughed. "I see you missed me a great deal."

"I shall scream," she warned. "I shall bring every man and woman in this house running."

"Wait." He held up a large hand. "I merely popped in to ask you a question. You can't want to see me die for it."

She drew in shallow breaths for long moments. He deserved torture and death. But why give the hangman all the pleasure?

"Ask quickly. In five minutes, I vow I will scream."

He nodded. "Your grandfather continues to thwart me." He stepped closer. "Since I never received the hostage I sought, I must abduct you and ransom you again. How quickly can you be ready to leave?"

Christina felt her mouth drop open. "You will have to kill me first! You took my innocence, you bastard, and led me to believe I could rely on you. I will not be used again."

"I could have left you on Grand Bahama."

"It hardly matters," she hissed. "The outcome would have been the same."

He stepped forward and grabbed her arm. "My mission is not about your feelings. I have a task to accomplish. You seemed to enjoy the previous adventure. We'll simply have another one. If your husband didn't mind sharing you once…perhaps he won't mind again."

She twisted away from his touch and jumped to her feet. "He will mind, as will I. I am married now. Happily, to a man who is both patient and kind. I will not accompany a cur like you anywhere."

"Kind?" He laughed. "Lilli, kindness won't curl your toes on a cold winter night. A kind milquetoast of a husband can't possibly make you feel the kind of passion we shared."

Christina advanced on the Black Dragon, feeling as if her anger had become a simmering volcano. "Drexell is twice the man you could ever hope to be. And four minutes of your five have passed. I suggest you run now." She leaned forward, chest thrust forward, chin up. "Do not ever dare to come back."

Chapter Eighteen

An hour later, night shadows cast their murky tones on the dockside streets Drex traversed to *The Dragon's Lair*. Unarmed, he felt naked and heartily wished secrecy had not prevented him from bringing his own vehicle. But too many sticky questions would arise if anyone connected him with the Black Dragon's crew.

Drunken revelry abounded, blending with the smells of salt and sewage. A man in the distance lurched toward a lightskirt, singing a bawdy ballad at the top of his lungs.

All seemed normal. No reason for hesitation.

Yet Drex felt eyes upon him, from everywhere, it seemed, despite the fact he spied no one but the drunken songster.

He passed a darkened alehouse and rounded the corner. Drex saw a dark blur of movement and a flash of metal. He turned and found a burly man pulling away from the uneven Tudor wall—and coming at him.

Drex's blood pounded. His heart beat double time as the man grabbed his shoulder and pulled him forward, trying to impale Drex on the blade thrust at his abdomen.

He had no time to think before he swerved away from the oncoming blade, dodged a swipe of the man's fist and grabbed his attacker's hair. He yanked on the greasy strands, satisfied at the man's howl of pain. He pinned the man in place with a knee at his testicles.

"What the hell do you want?" he growled.

The knave only grunted and twisted from his grasp. He kicked out at Drex, connecting with his shin. The blade in his assailant's hand arced toward him. Drex turned and dodged, then retaliated with a biting uppercut. The man's head shot back.

Drex seized the opportunity to slam the man against the splintery wall and pin him there with a hard forearm to his neck. Shadows hid most of the man's face. Dirt and hair hid the rest as Drex grabbed the man's wrist and ripped the knife from it. He held the blade right to the man's gut.

"What the hell do you want?" he asked again.

"Shut yer bleedin' arse," the man bellowed.

The voice sounded familiar, the voice of a man who had reason to hate him.

Talbot.

His attacker lunged again. Before Drex could move, the sailor jabbed Drex's chin with a fierce right-handed punch. As he tried to follow with a left to the stomach, Drex blocked the blow, then gouged Talbot in the nose. Blood and curses flowed.

"What the hell are you doing here?"

Talbot glared at him in acrimony. "I've come to kill ye. Hired right proper to do a deed I would've anyway."

A sudden grunt ripped through the night, precipitating the man's lunge. Fingers bared in a menacing arch, the assailant reached for Drex's throat. He dodged the attack with fast feet but did not see Talbot's kick until it connected with his abdomen.

The air left Drex's lungs in a painful whoosh. He clutched his belly with one hand and gripped the knife with the other.

Supporting his injured nose with one bloody hand, Talbot staggered toward Drex, preparing to attack again. At the last moment, Drex raised the knife, thrusting the sharp silver blade into the cad's belly.

Talbot's expression showed shock below his thatch of red hair. He lurched away, clutching his stomach, glaring at Drex with accusing eyes. Then he crumbled to the ground.

* * * *

With Talbot's corpse slung over his shoulder, Drex boarded *The Dragon's Lair*, which had been brought to London and disguised to resemble a merchant ship called *Lady Christina*.

Hancock greeted him first with a gasp. "Blimey, Cap'n. Who ye got

181

there?"

Drex lowered the body to the deck. Hancock lifted his lantern over the corpse.

"Talbot?" Hancock looked to him in confusion. "We left him in Grand Bahama."

Drex nodded. "He came here and attacked me in an alley. He told me someone hired him to kill me."

Hancock's eyes grew rounder. "Who?"

With a shrug, Drex answered, "I have a guess or two, but nothing solid."

"What will you do with him?"

Drex paused, considering. "I have an idea."

"Your ideas always frighten me," Greg called from the gangplank.

"You're late," Drex pointed out.

"Fashionably." Greg merely grinned. "What is your idea?"

Drex rubbed his clean-shaven chin. "Perhaps my death would be more convincing with a body. And since Talbot…volunteered to provide one when he attacked me, I thought he would do."

"Manchester isn't a thick one," reminded Hancock. "If ye give him Talbot, wouldn't he notice the difference?"

Greg looked up again with a frown. "I know he has at least a vague description of you."

Drex shrugged. "The basics? Or more?"

"At least the basics. Remember, Manchester has been pursuing you with single-minded vengeance these last two years. And your tattoo— everyone knows. Since the old goat has your description, that must be included."

"Even drunk, it hurt like hell to have it done. It also required someone with a lot of skill to create it." Drex paused. "Any chance Manchester has decided such a tattoo is pure fancy?"

"That is possible," Greg conceded. "At this point, I daresay anything is. Just in case, I will suggest that very point to him."

"The ploy might work, at least long enough to free Ryan," Drex said.

Greg grinned. "Let's dress the old chap up, shall we?"

* * * *

Later the following night, Drex sat in the library, pretending to read the *Times*. Christina had retired to her room without dinner. Again. And he worried.

Had she been more affected by the Black Dragon's presence than she had acted? Anger had brought the vitality back to her cheeks, the color and spark back to her eyes. How he'd wanted her there, across her lacy bed bathed in silvery moonlight. But he wanted her as her husband, not as her former lover, especially since she'd claimed to harbor some affection and respect for the man she had wed.

Drex frowned. How would she react once she learned the Black Dragon was "dead"?

Greg burst in a moment later, unannounced. He came bearing toward Drex with a single-minded stride.

"Your visit must be urgent, indeed, for you to have so little care for the seams of your tight breeches," Drex teased.

Greg reached his side, chest rising and falling rapidly beneath an azure coat. "Then you haven't heard?"

"What?" Drex said, folding his paper and setting it aside.

"Manchester has fallen for our ruse."

Drex smiled.

Greg whispered, "I overheard Manchester bragging at Boodle's that he caught a man red-handed with all the appropriate garb, right down to the mask."

"I planned to go with my father to the Lord Admiral's office once the body was discovered and recommend Ryan's release. He refused to let me accompany him, saying Manchester might become suspicious of me, a man with a questionable past, demanding the release of the very man the Black Dragon had sought."

"Can't disagree with that logic," Greg said.

"Traitor," Drex teased. "Let's find my father and celebrate."

"Not yet. Manchester sent a page to dispatch a note to his granddaughter. You must know what it says."

"Christina," he whispered, then focused on his friend. "Of course. Go. Talk to my father. I will find you later."

After Greg departed, Drex walked the length of the hall buoyed by happiness. After the Black Dragon's appearance last night and his odious request, Christina wouldn't mourn the man.

He knocked on her door. She did not answer. Drex knocked again. Still no reply.

He pressed his ear to the cool wood. A series of sniffles, nearly silent, reached his ears.

Lifting the latch with a frown, Drex entered to find her sitting on the edge of her bed. Her head shot up at his approach.

Misty green eyes, drowning in a pool of anger and sorrow, overshadowed the rest of her pale face. In one hand, she clutched a missive. In the other, a handkerchief.

She grieved the Black Dragon, without artifice. Her stark, torn expression told him that. Drex tried to stifle his surprise. She had truly loved him. And he had let her go.

Telling her the truth had become infinitely more complicated. God, what a tangle.

"He—he's dead," she pronounced between tears.

Drex strode the rest of the distance to her and knelt by her side. "I know."

To his surprise, she reached out for him. Drex took her hand and squeezed. Sitting beside her, he gathered Christina's huddled form into the shelter of his arms. She felt so small, so uncertain and cold. Trembling pervaded her body as she raised questioning eyes to his, as if to ask why or how. He could hardly provide her the answers she sought, or confess his alter-identity. Not until he felt certain she loved him enough to deal with the knowledge. Not until she was less fragile.

"Do you still love him?" he asked, the anticipation of her answer making him ache. Though he liked the idea that she had fallen in love with him, as a husband, he found himself jealous.

A moment of silence stretched between them as Christina studied his face. Finally, she shrugged. "When I first met you, I saw shades of him each time I looked at you. Similar eyes, similar noses and chins. Even similar voices. Maybe because I was distraught or that's what I wished to see in you. I've no notion why." She hung her head. "Now when I look at you, I see the kind of man the Black Dragon could have become, had he given up crime and his selfish ways. I see a better man."

Drex stared at the top of her pale head, feeling his heart in his mouth. He wanted to tell her everything—now, before the charade became any more deceitful.

Christina glanced up at him again, this time with dry, determined eyes. "But I refuse to love a man who thinks of no one's wishes but his own."

With his wife harboring such sentiments, his confessions would have to come later, once she had accepted him as her husband completely.

He stroked the crown of her head, thankful she did not pull away. "Someone I knew once taught me that refusing to love another is difficult, even when you know their faults. You can only stop pining for someone when you've reconciled with the past and are ready to accept a new future. Concentrate on that."

Christina's green gaze rose to his face. A frown creased her delicate brow as she studied him, as if solving a visual puzzle. Moments later, her brow smoothed. Clarity lit her eyes.

She sniffled, then smiled. "Thank you."

Drex's reply stuck in his throat when his wife threw her arms about him. Her face rested inches from his. Their breaths mingled and merged. Her lips parted, filling his vision. The ticking pulse at her throat beat in rhythm with his own heart.

The desire he had held in check since reciting their vows leaked beneath the barrier of his will. Clutching her shoulders, Drex closed his eyes and dipped his head toward her.

His lips met the feathery soft skin of her cheek. He lingered there, wanting so much more but trying to content himself by drawing in her powdery, floral scent. Another kiss, this one a heartbeat from the temptation of her cherry mouth, reacquainted him with the downy texture of her skin.

Drex pulled away. Their gazes met. Christina opened her mouth, to say what, he was not certain. At the moment, he ached too badly to hear a refusal.

He covered her lips with his, extinguishing the sound of her gasp with his mouth.

Warm surprise submerged him in joy. Instead of resistance in her embrace, he felt her welcome. Rather than opposition in her kiss, he felt yielding. He stroked her hair, held her tight and kissed her with the oblivion of passion he yearned to share.

His tongue swirled to meet hers, and he tasted her with a groan. Their breaths mated as he held her close, fantasizing of the union of their flesh, their hearts.

And he kissed her once more.

Christina felt his nearness, his touch, through every nerve in her body. Her blood simmered with a longing she'd never thought to feel again. Breath rushed through her lungs in short gasps as she tried to sort the tangle of her thoughts.

Touching him now would not be wise. But he was her husband, a good man, not the Black Dragon.

The rays of the lamplight seemed not to extend beyond the two of them, creating the illusion that no world beyond existed. She paused, frozen by an ache, a sensation she could not put logic to. Pure desire.

Christina felt her teeth sink into her bottom lip as Drexell reached for her again. His hand touched her wrist, then slid down to take possession of her fingers.

A spark zinged through her body, igniting dormant senses.

"Your hands are cold," he whispered.

Christina met his stare in mute reply. She had believed from the time they'd spoken vows that her promise to love and cherish had been a lie, a fantasy she did not believe.

So why could she not erase the realization that she should have tried, at least a little, to care for him without judging him on the merits of another man? She only now realized that she had failed him, failed them both, in their marriage. Her preoccupation with the Black Dragon and the pain he'd brought had kept her from realizing that, despite their physical similarities, they were profoundly different men.

Tears stung her eyes. She wiped them away, reminding herself she was tired and overwrought. The Black Dragon's death had taken her by surprise, though not overmuch, if she were honest with herself. The way he'd lived his life ensured that he signed his own execution order long ago.

Maybe the bigger surprise was her husband. Patient, giving, compassionate, tender. He alone seemed to understand the loss she had endured, her fear to hope in the future. A warm tear slid down her cheek.

He rose and wrapped his arms about her. "Don't cry, sweetheart."

Christina buried her face in the crook of his shoulder, reveling in his familiar musky scent, part sandalwood, part pure man. Though she had fought him at every turn, Drexell had somehow become her anchor. He had not demanded intimacy when he could have, had not commanded her life as if God gave him the right.

Wrapping her arms about his neck, Christina held tighter. Drexell gave a reassuring squeeze in return and whispered soothing sounds in her ear as she spent her tears.

When the storm had passed, she raised her head and gave him an apologetic grimace. "I'm sorry."

"Don't mourn him. He didn't deserve you."

He brushed the wetness from her cheek with his thumb. His dark gaze probed her face, leaving no curve or angle untouched.

"You're staring," she said, looking like a little girl lost.

"You are my wife." He leaned closer, focused on her mouth.

Heat rose in Christina's cheeks as her heart picked up its pace. "You see me every day, my lord."

"It's Drexell," he corrected, leaning closer until a mere whisper passed between their mouths. "And I've waited weeks to hold you this closely."

She swallowed, clutching the kerchief in her hands tightly. "I'm sorry."

Drexell's body seemed to tense around her, envelop her as they sat thigh to thigh, chest to chest, nearly mouth to mouth.

"Shh," he murmured, lifting his large hands to cup her face. "If I kiss you again, will you push me away?"

Her heart leapt into her throat and beat a triple-time rhythm that roared in her head. "No."

Christina felt his groan melt her insides as he covered her lips with his own. His kiss fused their mouths and breaths, arms and wants. It was a brush of heaven.

She parted her lips to invite him in. He accepted the invitation and clutched her against him. He pulled her onto his lap, and she felt his hardness against her belly.

Drexell carried the light taste of ale on his tongue. Christina returned every nuance of the kiss. Her body tingled with anticipation as he pulled her further into his embrace, slanted his lips across hers again and took total possession of her mouth, her mind. The wet kerchief fell from her limp fingers.

He robbed her of breath before he finally lifted his head. She clutched his shoulders to prevent swaying in a dizzied frenzy of pleasure.

Drexell gulped in air. He stared at her, dark gaze greedy as it slid over her burning face and her shoulders. The scrutiny traveled down to her tingling breasts and their joined torsos before he lifted his hot, carnal stare back to her eyes.

"If I wanted to make love to you now, would you lie passively in our bed?" he asked, dark gaze probing all the way to her very soul.

"No," she said into the dark shadows enveloping them.

His fingers tightened about her arms. "Say so. Tell me you want me, no one else."

Christina closed her eyes. A rush of certainty opened them again. "I want *you* to make love to me. No one else."

"God, how I want to," he groaned, then covered her mouth with his again. Flashing lights danced beneath her eyelids as his lips enacted a sensual fantasy that created her short-breathed response. She wanted to draw him into her, sink every inch of his body within her own. Merge completely.

Drexell slid her wrapper from her shoulders, his fingers following the fabric down her arms in a feathery caress. Her skin came alive beneath his touch, as if infused with electricity. He followed the sensual torture with a trail of kisses down the column of her neck, butterfly-light.

As her wrapper fell to her feet at the floor, he guided her to the bed. She lifted herself up willingly, and Drexell followed her to the mattress.

She took nary a breath before he claimed her mouth with a swirling passion that made her head spin. He lay siege to her night rail as his mouth drugged her mind. With a tug and a roll, the garment fell free, and the night air caressed her skin, along with the scent of man and the heat of anticipation.

A moan escaped her throat as his hand enveloped her breast and his thumb brushed her nipple to rigid attention. He repeated the action with the other breast, producing the same sizzling result. Bending to her, he took one in his mouth, squeezed the other, and the bite of desire slashed through her body.

With a sweep of his fiery hand across her abdomen, she caught her breath. His touch roamed across her hips, her thighs, then torturously skimmed the damp ache between her thighs.

He lingered there, his touch light, raising her need…but never satisfying it.

"Open for me," he whispered.

She complied shyly, watching him. Did he like what he saw? Did he want to touch her more?

Drexell more than answered those questions when he stared at her damp folds with hunger, then fitted his hands between her knees and pushed her thighs wider.

"What—"

"Shh," he broke in. "I want to touch you."

Certainly he didn't mean… But an instant later, when his fingers brushed over a sensitive spot that had her gasping, she realized he meant exactly what he said. And more. He pressed there softly, mercilessly until she gripped the coverlet in her hands and closed her eyes.

"Look at me," he demanded, breathing harsh.

It took a few moments for his words to penetrate her aroused senses, but her lashes fluttered open, and she fixed her unfocused gaze on him as he continued his wicked, soul-stealing touch.

"Good," he murmured. "What's my name?"

Before she could answer, he pressed into that bundle of nerves again, and pleasure zoomed closer. So achingly close…

"My name," he prompted.

"Drex!"

He laid a hot kiss on her neck, her shoulder. "Perfect. Look at me, sweetheart. Don't look away."

She raised her gaze to his, then stared in awe. Christina wondered if it wouldn't be wise to hide her desire. To give him her body, she must trust him with her emotions, too. But Drex gave her no quarter, and she didn't want to hold back anymore.

Blindly, Christina reached for the buttons of his shirt. They fell open at the touch of her fingers, revealing the solid muscle that comprised his chest.

Her husband eased her back on the bed and covered her smaller body beneath the power of his own. "Don't be nervous."

She met him halfway as he fused their mouths together in a searing kiss. Suddenly, she felt his bare thighs between hers. Christina did not know when he had doffed his pants but was heartily glad he had when he loomed closer to her core, one breath nearer.

She clutched his shoulders, feeling the cloth of his shirt instead of his skin. No. She wanted to feel him, taste him, encompass him, as he did her.

With a grunt, she tugged at the offending shirt. He ground the hard ridge of his cock against her, ending her furtive movements in a flurry of staccato gasps and a burst of sensation.

"Leave it," he said, his whisper gruff. "We have the rest of our lives."

Before Christina replied, he touched his lips to her chin, then nibbled his way to her mouth. He caressed her breasts, his fingers surrounding the flesh, lifting, cupping, loving. Arousing her again as he brushed and squeezed her nipples, demonstrating that he had the power to make her ache repeatedly.

In one thrust, his kiss possessed her the way his body did—deeply. She felt no pain at the smooth slide of his entry, only fullness and wholeness. He sank into the depths of her body, stealing into her mind, her heart. Then with one strong push after another, he brought her to the brink, even as the damp slide of their skin and their mouths made her feel cared for. He sealed her in the circle of their union.

Once more, he plunged deep inside her, and pleasure splintered Christina, body and soul, leaving her with the knowledge that she belonged with him. A certainty that she would be in his arms and by his side forever washed her with a warm glow of peace she had never known.

Chapter Nineteen

Drex paced the entry hall the following morning. Every turn of a carriage's wheel, every squeak of a door, made him jump.

Damn, his father had left to await Ryan's release over three hours ago. What could be taking so long?

A scrape of boots and a whine of hinges made Drex whirl again. In the door stood his father, wearing a distinguished gray coat and a wide smile. Ryan stood beside him.

A disbelieving smile burst through Drex's shock as he zeroed in on his slightly younger brother. The beard, tattered clothing and bruises he'd worn at the hostage exchange had been replaced by a haircut mirroring his own. The breeches and coat Drex vaguely recognized as garments from his closet.

"Ryan!" Drex said, his tight throat. "You look...healthy, and a damn good sight."

"Newgate's goalers can be amazingly accommodating, under the right circumstances," their father cut in. "Manchester's reluctant nod and my coin lent enough weight."

Drex stepped toward the pair and clapped his father on the back in thanks as he took the remaining steps toward Ryan.

Finally, after four hellish years, the two embraced, a hearty display of backslapping and a manly reining in of tears.

"Thank you for finding me. And risking your neck to do it."

"Father told you?" Drex asked.

"Yes. Father." Ryan laughed, then released Drex. "Seems odd to say that word and know the face."

"Indeed." Drex smiled.

Life couldn't be better. Ryan was free, they had gained a father, and Christina had accepted him as her husband.

The only dark spot was the truth. He'd been withholding it from Christina and would have to confess. Not today. Maybe not even tomorrow. But soon. When he felt certain she could understand he had lied out of love, not spite.

"Chantal and Rory? Are they well?" Ryan's voice trembled.

"Very well. I received a letter just last week saying they were packed to travel as soon as I advised them you were free."

"And she's willing to come?" Ryan asked.

Drex peered at his brother. He never remembered a time when Ryan had been anything but self-assured, as if the world owed him happiness. Had the last four years taught him better?

"She loves you," he finally answered.

"Imagine that." Ryan shuffled his feet. "You've taken care of her and Rory in my absence. I can't thank you enough."

Drex shook his brother's hand. "Yes, you can. Don't seek adventure at their expense again."

Ryan laughed. "I learned better, brother. Adventure is a momentary rush. Love lasts forever. It only took me a few months of heaving my guts out in the North Sea to learn that."

"Good man." Drex smiled.

Ryan shook his head. "You're the best. Chantal would have been better off with you."

"That's not true," Drex contradicted. "I don't love her."

"Ah, yes. I hear you have a wife now. A very lovely wife."

"A very capricious one." He smiled wryly. "Let me find Christina. I want you two to meet."

Ryan nodded. "I've waited years to meet the woman who could cage my older brother's heart of steel."

"I shall fetch your aunt and uncle as well," Ashmont put in.

Drex and the earl rushed up the stairs in search of the others. As they disappeared to the top of the stairs, Drex spied Christina emerging through the front door. She looked stunning in an amaranthus pink riding habit. As she smiled, she withdrew her gloves and smiled at Ryan, who stood ten paces away. Drex ducked into the upstairs shadows to watch the drama unfold.

"Good morning." She ducked her head shyly, then flashed Ryan a coquette's gaze. "When I didn't find you at breakfast this morning, I'd rather hoped we would meet in Hyde Park."

Ryan opened his mouth to reply, then closed it again.

Christina stepped closer. "Drexell, say something. Are you unhappy? Perhaps we should have talked more last night instead of…" She cleared her throat, color heating her cheeks.

Drex restrained a chuckle as she placed a concerned hand on his brother's arm. Suddenly, she stepped back. Her face drew together in a curious, then bewildered frown.

She gasped. "You look like Drexell and dress like him. But you are not him."

Ryan cleared his throat. "No. I'm his brother. His twin."

Her mouth hung open. "He has a twin? I had no idea."

Ryan frowned. "He didn't tell you that he saved me by—"

"Christina, I see you've met my brother. Ryan," Drex cut in on the confessional, then jockeyed his way beside them. "Ryan, this is my wife."

The earl came down the stairs, Lord and Lady Allyn in tow.

"Milton, Agnes," their father said to the pair, "this is my younger son, Ryan."

Ryan kissed Lady Allyn's gloved hand after a polite murmur. Her face remained as tight as the knot of hair at her nape.

Ryan extended a hand to Lord Allyn. He refused to take it.

The man cast a withering glare at his older brother. "Another of your by-blows, George? Really, how indiscreet."

"They're twins, Milton. And if you cannot take a better tone with me, I will ask you to go to the country."

Agnes stepped in. "Milton, they were children born under unfortunate circumstances. Where are your manners? "

A red-faced Lord Allyn whirled on his wife. "Agnes! How dare you criticize me in front of others. Your meddling in private is already too much to bear."

Lady Allyn cleared her throat uncomfortably, then addressed everyone. "I shall adjourn upstairs."

After she whirled away and mounted the stairs, Lord Allyn was left standing among a crowd of enemies and quickly departed.

"I'm sorry," Ryan said. "I can leave for New Orleans as soon as I find a ship."

"I'll hear of no such thing," Ashmont insisted. "You two are family as well. Milton must accept that."

* * * *

The next morning, Christina lounged abed next to Drexell's warmth. He placed an arm about her shoulder, the soft cloth of his shirt rubbing her sensitized skin, and drew her near.

"How are you this morning?" she asked, grinning.

"I feel abused. If we have too many nights like the last one, I daresay I won't live to see thirty," he teased.

She laughed, an unfettered curtain of peace enveloping her. "I hardly forced you."

Drex peeked beneath the sheet at her bare body. "I beg to differ. At the very least, you compelled me."

"You're a wicked man."

He nodded. "Married to the most deliciously wicked woman."

"So when will I see you without that dratted shirt?"

He paused. "When we're not in such a hurry to find the bed."

As he gathered a giggling Christina against him, their lips met. She gave freely, reveling in the joy they shared.

"Thank you for helping me through the difficult first days of our marriage," she whispered. "Your patience and understanding was everything I needed."

He peered down at her, his expression guarded. "My pleasure."

Christina frowned. "I resisted you, not because I disliked you but because you reminded me so much of him. I know you're a much different man—"

The smile fell from his face. His expression turned grave in the span of a heartbeat.

"What is it? What troubles you, that I compared you to him?" She touched an apologetic hand to his. "I'm sorry."

He rolled away and sat up, looking pensive.

"Drexell, please. What is wrong?"

Finally, he heaved a great sigh and faced her. "Remember when I suggested that the Black Dragon brought you back to England and gave you back to your grandfather for a good reason?"

"Yes, but I had no intention of bringing the man into our bed," she insisted. "I shall not again."

He clasped her wrists. "That's not possible. He'll always be between us because—"

"No. He's gone. I've put him out of my heart, and you helped me."

Drex shook his head. "If you put him out of your heart, you put me out as well. I am—"

"You mustn't say that! My feelings for you are different."

Drex would like to have explored her feelings but knew the time for truth had come. "Christina, listen. I am—"

A pounding on the portal drew their startled gazes.

"Drakethorne!" A deep voice on the other side of Drex's door boomed. "Open this door and release my granddaughter."

Christina gasped. "Grandfather? What are you doing here?"

"Come out to the hall this instant, girl!"

She leapt from bed, threw on her wrapper and flashed Drex a confused frown.

Drex sat motionless. He looked stricken…and terrified. What was going on?

"Christina, sweetheart, don't go to him yet," Drex entreated. "Listen to me. I'm trying to tell you that—"

"Come out, you criminal," her grandfather bellowed. "Don't fill her head with any more of your lies."

She whirled to face Drex. "Lies?"

"Christina." Drex scrambled to his feet and gripped her hands. "Please don't open the door yet. I need to tell you—"

The door splintered open with a crash. Grandfather glared at Drex, blue eyes bulging red over his ruddy face. Behind him, four armed officers stood, guns drawn.

"You are under arrest." Grandfather's voice was a thin hiss.

Christina stared in confusion as her grandfather glared at Drex. Her husband returned the grim gaze. He didn't look shocked in the least.

"What is this about?" she asked.

The old man snaked his stare toward her. "He's guilty of smuggling, treason and murder. Not to mention duplicity." His eyes narrowed as he trained his stare on Drex. "Isn't that so?"

Drex didn't deny the accusations.

She whirled to face her husband, fists clenched. Dread coated her stomach; confusion pounded in her chest, throbbing in her temples. "Tell him he's mistaken. He *is* mistaken, is he not?"

Drex cast his gaze to the floor. "Christina—"

"Seize him," her grandfather directed two of the soldiers. Silently, Drex allowed them to grab and bind his wrists together.

"This is mad," she screeched. "Release him!"

"Release the Black Dragon?" her grandfather parried. "I think not."

"The Black Dragon is dead. You said so yourself."

"I thought so. This should prove us right. Men," her grandfather prompted, nodding to his soldiers.

"Christina!" Drex called as one of the men grabbed the back of his shirt and jerked down.

A tattoo of a fire-breathing dragon covered her husband's back, tail winding about his arm in a green coil. The searing red of its eyes throttled her with its gaze, mocking her trust. That tattoo could only belong to one man.

The Black Dragon.

Shock chilled her. Suddenly, she couldn't breathe. Drex and the Black Dragon...the same man? No! But obviously yes. Why would he pretend to be an earl's son and marry her? Why...?

Did it matter? She had trusted him as two different men. Heaven above! In both instances, Drex had spit in her face. He had deceived her. Again. Earned her trust and destroyed it. Again.

Shock waned, replaced by fury that breathed fire in her system. Blood roared in her ears.

Drexell wrenched free from the men and darted to her side. "Christina, sweetheart. This is not the way it appears. Let me explain..."

Christina slapped his face with all the power she could muster. "How dare you! How could you? Did you enjoy deceiving me twice? Did you laugh at me all the while?"

"No. I'm sorry. I can explain everything." The two soldiers grabbed Drex's arms. He struggled and stared at Christina, pleading in his desperate gaze. "I love you."

She raised a pale brow, along with her chin, and fixed him with an icy glare. "This morning, I would have believed you. I'm thankful I know the truth about your lies now."

Christina darted out of the hall, to her room. The sound of Drexell's voice calling her name as the soldiers dragged him from the house rang in her head. She covered her ears with trembling hands and made her way to her chamber.

She scarcely shut the door before bitter tears of fury and pain enveloped her, helping to foster a new hate for her Black Dragon husband—a hate she vowed would never die.

* * * *

Drexell stood against the wall in the taproom at Newgate prison, trying to down the quart of ale for which he'd paid four pence. He shuddered as another draught slid down his throat, the slime seemingly contaminated with the stench of filth and disease abundant here in Newgate. Still, oblivion would be welcome, if only for a few hours.

He drifted back to thoughts of Lilli lying goldenly naked on a Bahamian beach, of his wife teasing him with her coquette's smile in their London bed.

He'd known from the moment Manchester had arrested him that he would likely hang. Somehow, he had hoped Christina would realize his love for her was genuine, despite his deceptions.

Such a fantasy would never come to pass. Ryan, Greg and his father had visited nearly every day of his week's confinement. Christina had not graced him with her presence once.

"Yer lordship," one of the jailers called, voice mocking. "Ye've got a visitor, I'm told. Yer to meet 'em in yer new room in the Press Yard. Second floor."

Drex nodded. His father had arrived and obviously paid the five-hundred-pound entry fee for such lofty quarters. Regret tinged him when he thought of the wasted years of ignorance and hatred he'd directed at the man. But better to have known his father for a short time than not at all.

He arrived to find other prisoners hovering about his door, near the pins comprising their abandoned game of skittles.

"I haven't seen one like that anywhere," remarked another prisoner, clearly educated. "Inside or out of this hell."

A chorus of guffaws echoed within the long, dim room.

He shouldered his way through the small crowd to the door.

"Are ye the infamous pirate?" one thin man asked.

He scowled his answer. "Move. I have a visitor."

The men parted to let him pass, and he supposed his bad attitude preceded him.

Drex reached for the latch on his door; a fellow prisoner dressed in perfectly polished Hessians chuckled. "An understatement, my good man. A very substantial one."

Puzzled, Drex opened the door, not certain who to expect.

The last visitor he anticipated was Christina.

His legs carried him to her side, his arms rising to hold her. She stood with a regal grace she had never displayed before, chin high, skin flawless.

Drex dropped his hands and grappled to find the words to tell her he loved her, to beg her forgiveness. Anything to remove the indifferent expression from her gilded beauty.

"Your father sent some books. I've placed them on the table." She gestured to the furniture in question, then walked to the oblong tiny window, which showed the orange hues of the setting sun. "Do you need more clothing?"

"No. Christina, darling—"

"I hope you enjoy your new quarters."

"Did you arrange them?" he asked hopefully.

She laughed. "Me? No. It was your father's doing. You're probably going to burn in hell. Why pay a small fortune to make your last living days pleasant?"

Drex seized her hand. "Because I don't want to die a miserable man."

"You *are* a miserable man!" She whirled, blasting him with the full force of her anger. "You weren't content to use and discard me once. No, you felt so guilty about the first occurrence, you repeated it."

"Christina, I'm so damn sorry. I love you." He clutched her hand tighter when she would have jerked away. "Believe me, I had no choice. Your grandfather had Ryan imprisoned. I'd been trying to free my brother for the last four years! I had no idea who you were when you boarded the *Lair*. After we made love on the beach, only then did I know the truth, and only then because you told me." He sighed, straining for the right words to convince her of his sincerity. "Ransoming you back to Manchester tore my guts out. But I could not let my brother die, not to spare your heart or mine."

She drew in a breath. "Ryan told me as much. But that does not change the fact you lied to me again when you married me. You lied when you made love to me—"

"No, that's not true."

She whipped her gaze back to his. "Yes. And you lied when you said you loved me. You trusted in the strength of my love so little you withheld your true identity and duped me into marriage. I loved you." Her fists clenched at her sides. "If you had told me the truth, your circumstances... If you had cared for me at all..." Her breath caught on a sob. "Instead, *you* decided everything and controlled me every moment we spent together. You never once thought about what I might want in life. Just like Grandfather, you assume you have all the answers. Well, no more."

Drex struggled to digest the fervor of her speech. He'd never meant to control her, just...just love her.

Pain knifed through his chest. "Christina, you're wrong. Tell me how I can prove my love to you. I'll do it."

"And give you another chance to control me and lie to me?" She shook her head. "Good-bye."

She brushed past him. For the first time since childhood, Drex felt helpless to stop his own destruction.

With her departure, his heart shattered into a million pieces.

* * * *

Ashmont, Viscount Monroe and Ryan all entered the town house late in the evening a week later. Their downcast eyes and deep frowns told Christina the trial had ended with dreadful results.

Christina set down the handkerchief she'd been kneading and swallowed. She looked at the trio expectantly. All looked away.

"It's death," Ashmont mumbled, placing his hat atop a hall table with excruciating precision. "At noon in three days."

Christina's stomach sank to her knees. Though a part of her argued it mirrored the emotional punishment he'd banished her to when he'd crushed her heart, she didn't want him to die. Maybe he deserved to, but she would have preferred to kill him herself.

The thought of a world without Drexell lumped her throat with emotion. Her eyes filled with tears.

Over the past days, her weepy bouts had combined with her fury in the worst sort of despair. The contradiction of her sentiments puzzled her deeply. Why, in the face of everything he'd done, did she still love him?

"What now?" she asked.

Ryan slammed his fist against the hall table, rattling the ceramic vase on top. "I feel so damned helpless."

"But what can we do?" Greg piped in. "In the last three bloody days, we've been over every nuance of the case, every possible escape. We've all offered our entire fortunes to Newgate's goalers to let him escape. They all said money was of no use to them from the grave."

"We must be missing something," Ryan insisted. "Some way to prove they've got the wrong man."

"There's no way to prove something that is not true."

"But my brother hardly deserves to die for trying to free me. God, I wish I'd never left home…"

The loyalty the brothers felt for one another was nearly tangible. Christina had witnessed it in the short time they had all spent under this roof. She understood their love. Commended it, even. She didn't blame Drex for the lengths he'd gone to in order to save his brother. She simply wished he hadn't saved Ryan at her expense with his deceptions.

But in his place, would she have done anything differently?

"Half the crimes they attributed to Drex he would never commit. Raping nuns? Allowing his crew to kill a merchant's family while he watched? No. He would never do such things."

"Never," Greg agreed.

Christina agreed with their assessment. He'd maintained shipboard discipline by punishing her, but he'd never broken her. He'd certainly never hurt her or threatened her with death. He might be controlling but not blood-thirsty. Not a monster.

Not a man she could stop loving.

And if she did not want to watch him die, she was going to have to save him.

Silence ensued. Christina's thoughts raced, weighing risks, calculating facts, until an idea gelled.

She smiled. "Greg, have you any idea if Hancock is still aboard *The Dragon's Lair*?"

"Yesterday he was. I suppose today should be no different."

"Splendid. Gentlemen, gather round. I have a plan."

Chapter Twenty

The noontime sun beat unmercifully hot for a still March day. Rivulets of sweat trailed down Drex's back as he scanned the Tyburn Fair crowd for the golden face he longed to see. The scents of unwashed bodies hung in the damp air. In the distance, an odd boom, almost like cannon fire, rose above the crowd's din.

"A good day for a hanging, don't you think?" Reverend Brownlow Ford said beside him. "Any last words, a confession?"

Drex glared at Newgate's Ordinary. "You'll have to create a tale to embellish your broadsheet. I won't give you anything."

"St. Sepulchre's bell has been rung, my condemned friend, and confession is good for the soul."

"As well as your purse."

The distant boom blared again, but Drex did not spare energy worrying about the sound. The sea of faces swelled to new numbers around the scaffold, all of whom had come to watch the spectacle of his execution, rotten tomatoes and eggs in hand.

Drex dreaded this with every grain of his body. He wasn't ready to die. Damn it, he had only taken the actions duty and responsibility required. The Black Dragon had been his response when more civilized methods had failed.

Manchester shouldered his way through the crowd, glancing over his shoulder at faraway gunfire and black smoke. The red-faced old goat turned and fixed Drex with a sneer of triumph. "I've waited years for this day, you bastard. Watching you swing will give me unparalleled pleasure."

"And what of Christina?"

He paused. "It would seem that in twenty minutes, she will be my concern once more. Were I you, I'd wonder about my lengthening neck," he jibbed before pivoting away and climbing the scaffold.

His father stood behind the Lord Admiral. He, too, glanced at the increasing sounds of the melee a few miles away, then turned back to place soothing arms about him. "Do not despair."

The brief whisper puzzled Drex. Was he supposed to be pleased death would claim him this day?

"Where is Ryan? I want to say good-bye."

"He could not bear to watch," Ashmont said, then turned away.

Could not bear? Disappointment permeated his every nerve. Granted, he would have been in no great hurry to witness his brother's execution, but he would have bid his twin farewell.

Lady Allyn followed his father, acknowledging him with a simple nod, her expression as severe as ever.

Lord Allyn trailed his wife, wearing a smug sneer. "My brother may be mourning. Rest assured, I will celebrate over your grave."

Drex turned his face away, jaw clenched.

Greg filed past next, looking surprisingly unruffled in a China blue coat. "Do not lose faith, my friend."

Drex had no time to examine Greg's whisper before Christina emerged through the crowd, filling his vision. Dressed in a sedate gray, she approached him without expression. She looked tired, her eyes circled and purple-smudged with sleeplessness.

"I had hoped to see you again," he murmured.

She bowed her head. "I did not come to watch you die."

He frowned. "Then why?"

She shrugged, refusing to elaborate. The outlying boom sounded again, louder now. What was that noise?

"I've always loved you," he said. "I want you to know that, and someday, I hope you will forgive me."

"I've no intention of hating a dead man."

With his hands bound behind his back, Drex was powerless to stop Christina from turning away and walking out of his life. And maybe he shouldn't. Only a fool would tie her to a man who was all but dead. And after her impassioned speech in Newgate, only a dolt would believe his wife did not know what she wanted and deserved.

William Brunskill, the hangman, approached without expression. "I can make this painless, for the right price. Though the crowd does love to watch the condemned slowly choke."

Drex closed his eyes, feeling as if the noose resting against his chest were tightening. "I will die either way. I hardly see where the manner in which I die makes a difference."

Another boom was precipitated by a shrill whine. He cast a glance toward the noise, startled by the thick cloud of black smoke that hung over the harbor. Was someone attacking?

The hangman shrugged off the sight. "As you like. The undersheriff will drive the cart out from beneath your feet and you will be left swinging from this beam of Triple Tree." He pointed to the solid wooden length above him, which linked three trees together with three beams to form a triangle.

The executioner stepped on the scaffolding and gestured for the crowd's attention. "Gentlemen and fair ladies," he shouted, "I give you the man convicted of being one of England's most notorious nemeses on the seas, the Black Dragon."

The crowd booed its collective sentiment.

"He will hang by the neck until dead," shouted Brunskill.

The blast of gunfire resounded above the noise of Tyburn Fair, almost silencing the crowd's cheers.

Frowning, Drex searched the scaffold until he caught sight of Manchester. The man's pale eyes thinned with confusion as he looked south to the disturbance.

Brunskill turned back to the matter at hand. "Reverend Ford, have you last words to say upon this condemned man?"

"You in that condemned hold do lie, prepare you, for today you shall die!" the berobed man began the ageless chant. "Watch all, and pray. The hour draws near that you before the Almighty must appear. Examine well yourself, in time repent, that you may not the eternal flames be sent. Now that St. Sepulchre's bell has tolled, the Lord above have mercy on your soul."

Brunskill tightened the noose about his neck. The crowd cheered. Drex refused to hang in head in shame. England was not his country. If he died upholding his beliefs, he would die, not happily, but honorably.

He sought Christina with his gaze. She stood beside her grandfather, head bowed. The angelic cloud of her golden hair framed her pale features. Though he had destroyed her trust, he wished that, before he died, he could prove to her that he'd never meant to hurt her.

But time had run out.

The hangman turned to the undersheriff to give the signal that would pull the cart from beneath him. Drex's gut tightened like a fist. Sweat drizzled down his forehead, stinging into his eyes. He gave a last desperate yank on the rope binding his wrists behind his back. The knot refused to budge.

Suddenly, another shrill whine rent the still. A boom followed, this time so powerful the ground shook.

Women gasped and clutched their children tighter. The horses hitched to Drex's cart pawed the earth nervously.

"What the devil is going on?" Manchester shouted.

A naval officer on horseback galloped through the crowd, which parted like pouring water over a rock. He reached the scaffolding, dismounted, then saluted Manchester.

"My Lord Admiral, the harbor is under attack."

"Damn French!" Christina's grandfather swore. "Forever making war. Gather more men to fight them, Captain."

"Not the French, your grace. The Black Dragon."

Shock stung Drex. The Black Dragon? He jerked his gaze to the scaffold. His father hid a smile with a handkerchief.

Manchester advanced on the officer. "Impossible! The man is about to be hanged. It can't possibly be the Black Dragon."

"*The Dragon's Lair* sailed into harbor about an hour ago and sent one of his crew, Hancock, over with a message."

"What did he say, man?" Manchester barked.

The officer cleared his throat. "The Black Dragon's message said, 'Hang an innocent man if doing so will make you feel the hero, but you will not be rid of me.'"

Manchester cursed beneath his breath. Christina moved to stand beside her grandfather.

The old man paused. Christina placed her small hand on her grandfather's sleeve and, stepping up on tiptoe, whispered something in his ear.

Manchester addressed the executioner. "I shall investigate this attack for its authenticity. Do nothing until I return."

As the crowd roared its displeasure, Drex stared at his wife. Had they all cooked up some scheme to save him? He could hardly believe she had any reason to want his life spared. He urged her to return his glance, willing her to look his way.

She did. Her green eyes burned with mystery, her expression regal, unsmiling. Then she turned away with her grandfather.

As Manchester and Christina disappeared through the hissing crowd, Drex prayed she was involved with this plan. If so, she might still have at least a shred of feeling for him.

* * * *

"Christina, what is this about?" her grandfather barked once ensconced inside his coach.

The vehicle jerked forward in its departure, saving her from an immediate response. "What do you mean?"

"This attack on the harbor, girl! What else could I mean?" His silver brows slashed downward like two polished swords.

"I—I've no notion why the Black Dragon would attack the harbor, Grandfather. Nor do I care. I simply want you to spare my husband's life."

The old man shifted in the swaying coach and turned to face her. "Do you try to convince me that I've arrested the wrong man?"

"Have I not been telling you so for the past two days?" she shouted above the din of cannon fire they drew ever closer to.

"You've been intimate with both, have you not?" he spat ruthlessly. "Can you not tell if they are one and the same?"

"They are not," she lied, folding her damp palms together. "I said as much repeatedly."

"So you slapped your husband upon his arrest for no reason at all." He turned a skeptical scowl in her direction. "Do you truly expect me to believe such rubbish?"

"You've never believed in me at all. I shouldn't think you would start now."

Grandfather swore at the jarring ride and narrowed rheumy blue eyes at her. "Meaning what? That I should have allowed you to become a stage trollop?"

Christina raised her chin. "If I chose. My life is my own," she argued. "As yours belongs to you."

"I make plans and decisions because I care for you, because you know too little of the real world to make them yourself."

She clenched her teeth. "I must learn, as we all must. If you truly care, let me lead my life, whether I succeed or fail."

Grandfather turned a shoulder to her. Though hardly an acceptance, the fact he did not bark a refusal in her face seemed a victory of sorts. "I want the truth, Christina, not an answer designed to protect your husband. Is Drexell the Black Dragon?"

She paused, waiting out the mewl of more cannon fire. "Think about this. You've convicted a man to die with what evidence? An anonymous note containing somebody's theory and the fact Drexell has a tattoo. Neither proves he is the Black Dragon."

"Perhaps," he conceded. "However, do you not think the coincidence is quite suspicious?"

"You said the word yourself: coincidence. One can never tell. *If* Drexell is indeed the Black Dragon, would you truly wish the father of your possible great-grandchild to die a traitor? And if he is the Black Dragon, how do you describe this attack on the harbor while Drexell is shackled at Tyburn?"

Grandfather's thin mouth turned down in thought, the man clearly at a loss for an answer.

Moments later, they arrived at the docks and emerged from the vehicle. Smoke dusted the sky an ominous charcoal and hung pungent with the scent of gunpowder. Another cannonball shot through the air. A tiny boat of soldiers rowing toward *The Dragon's Lair* jumped from the dinghy seconds before it shattered into pieces with a crash. Christina winced at the blast.

"Get back in the coach," Grandfather barked.

"Like hell," she called, running for the nearest dinghy. Three soldiers sat in it, waiting for others.

"Get out," Christina barked.

"Oh, no, me lady. We could not let you row into that battle," one wide-eyed boy replied.

"Christina, get out of there!" Grandfather roared.

"Don't you understand yet? The Black Dragon will not let your sailors near his ship. He will, however, see me."

Manchester hesitated before barking to the sailors. "You," he pointed to a burly sailor. "Row us to that ship."

The man swallowed. "He'll blow us to bits, yer grace."

Christina turned to the sailor. "He won't fire, not once. I give you my word."

At her grandfather's nod, the dinghy set off for *The Dragon's Lair*. True to her promise, not a single shot was fired in their direction. Sending a silent prayer up for Davie in the crow's nest, she waited with a pounding heart until they pulled beside the familiar frigate. A ladder was lowered to them and, one by one, each made their way on deck.

An imposing figure stood at the top, waiting. The black beard and black mask were exactly as she remembered, as were the golden earring and lean lines of his body. The gun he leveled at her grandfather's chest added to his imposing figure.

"Christina."

"Captain," she greeted in return.

Grandfather stood rigid but silent, bearing his own weapon.

"Have you come to hear reason, old man?" asked the captain, legs akimbo in an arrogant pose.

"That will depend on what you have to say, you defiler of innocent girls."

He laughed. "Had I believed for an instant you would have embraced me as her husband, I would have gladly wed her."

Her grandfather scowled. "What do you seek?"

"To prevent you from hanging her husband, an innocent man, I might add. That could damage family harmony. It *would* be a grave mistake."

"Why should you care?"

"I want Christina well cared for. I perceive that he will see to the task far better than you. But as I said in the note, if hanging an innocent man makes you feel hero... It's nothing to me. If you do, however, I will return for Christina and take care of her myself."

Grandfather gritted his teeth, mouth pinched in fury. "I won't rest until I watch you swing, you son of a bitch."

The Black Dragon shrugged. "I fear you shall wait a long time indeed. I plan to retire, you see, return to the life I led before war and politics called my name. My mask gives me the anonymity to do so."

Christina's palms turned damp as a river as she waited for her grandfather's reaction. He turned first to her and studied her face. She prayed he could not read her thoughts. She prayed their ruse worked.

He faced the Black Dragon again. "If you ever come within one hundred miles of another of my ships—or my granddaughter—I will personally hang every brigand on the seas until I find you."

The Black Dragon nodded. "Agreed."

With a curt nod, her grandfather turned and signaled to the dinghy below.

"Thank you," she mouthed to the masked man.

"What are brothers for?" Ryan whispered, then turned away.

* * * *

When Christina and her grandfather arrived back at Tyburn, the crowd had thinned, now suspecting there would be no hanging today. The lord mayor and the magistrate both waited on the scaffold, as Grandfather had sent them notes requesting.

Drexell remained standing on the cart, rope looped about his neck. Sweat drizzled down his forehead. Someone had removed his coat down to his bound wrists, torn away his cravat and unfastened the top two buttons of his shirt.

Several women stood around him, calling out invitations. Christina could understand why. But in spite of his good looks and his good reasons, Drexell had lied, deceived, controlled and manipulated.

Why, then, did she still ache for him? Love him? She understood his motives—no sense in lying—but could she ever trust him again?

Her feelings were irrelevant. If this charade freed Drexell, their marriage could not continue. Christina doubted he would ever understand her, never love her enough to respect her autonomy. Certainly, all of his patience and "understanding" during the early days of their marriage had been a ruse to win her over, earn her trust. She could never accept his emotional shackles again.

He lifted his dark, wolf-like gaze to her. A hungry mixture of pain, pleading and predatory desire filled his eyes. She lifted a cold chin and glanced away but trembled inside.

He would not let her go easily.

Drawing in a deep breath, Christina turned to find her grandfather, the lord mayor and the magistrate conferring. The lord mayor, William Domville, shrugged and nodded. The magistrate shook his head, his vehement argument evident in his wild hand gestures. She climbed the scaffolding and walked to its far edge, glad to put distance between her and Drexell.

As Christina approached the trio, her grandfather snapped a reply to the magistrate. "I saw the miscreant myself. He spoke to me and my granddaughter. He wore the Black Dragon's garb and commanded the

Black Dragon's ship. What else can one think but that Drexell Cain-Ashmont was falsely convicted?"

"You're certain?" the magistrate pressed.

"Quite. He fits the description given in the anonymous letter perfectly—height, facial characteristics, hair color."

"But Lord Drakethorne's tattoo," the magistrate insisted. "It is very distinct, would you not agree?"

Christina held her breath, hoping Grandfather handled this point with the utmost caution.

Grandfather nodded, then added, "A tattoo alone proves nothing. Any man can mark his skin in most any Asian port."

The magistrate shook his head in denial. "I will not turn this man free. You merely attempt to save your family from further scandal. Justice cannot be perverted in this way!"

Christina winced and bit her tongue.

"The perversion of justice would be to hang an innocent man," the lord mayor jumped in. "A search of Drakethorne's belongings found none of the accompaniments of an infamous privateer. As Manchester points out, a tattoo proves little except that the man was probably a drunken fool at one point in his life. I could say the same of you on several occasions, Gerald." Domville chuckled. "That leaves us with nothing, except an anonymous letter from someone who may hate Lord Drakethorne enough to disgrace him into death."

Manchester shrugged. "We can wait until the next Quarter Session, of course. But based on my testimony and with the lord mayor's backing, I believe the Assizes will reverse your verdict, which will leave you an unpopular man for wasting their time."

"I do not like this sudden method of justice!" the magistrate hissed. "Such matters should be carefully considered—"

"Cain-Ashmont was convicted in twenty-five minutes based on circumstance," Manchester pointed out.

The lord mayor said, "Call off the execution and reverse his conviction, Gerald. Manchester is right. If you want to keep your post at Old Bailey, you cannot afford to have the others dislike your methods."

With a resigned grunt, the magistrate conceded, "Fine, but our security for the seas will fall on your conscience."

Grandfather smiled icily. "As it always does."

The lord mayor made the announcement to the last of the crowd, who booed and hissed before exiting the Tyburn Fair in a trample and a cloud of dust.

The undersheriff cut Drex down. Christina watched her husband tear away his coat and roll the stiffness from his broad shoulders.

She released a sigh of relief. He was free.

And so was she.

But she couldn't take her eyes off Drexell. Powerful, sleek. Utter masculine beauty personified. Their marriage, if not legally, was over in substance. When they separated, she would largely have the advantages of widowhood to set up her own house, lead her own life. She planned independence, no matter that he would fight her.

"No!" a woman screeched above the din.

Christina turned to find Lady Allyn advancing toward her grandfather. She frowned with confusion.

"Have you all become daft, to release the Black Dragon?" Lady Allyn screamed. "He is your man, I tell you. This miscreant destroyed your ships and brought fear to the greatest Navy on earth, and you set him free?"

Lord Allyn rushed to her side. "Agnes, what are you doing? They've released him. There is nothing further we can do."

Lady Allyn shook off her husband's restraining touch and pulled a gun from her reticule. Christina's heart stopped when she pointed the barrel at Drexell.

The players on the scaffolding gasped collectively.

"You've done nothing but sneer petty insults at your nephews," Lady Allyn went on. "Did you really believe that would send them packing so you could become the next earl?" Her laugh mocked him. "You never were bright, Milton."

She turned to Drex, thrusting her weapon closer to his heart. "You're not fit to become Ashmont's next earl. I tried to remove you from your father's path, but you refused to leave and you refused to die, no matter how I attempted."

"*You* tried to have me killed?"

She stepped closer, a vicious gleam in her small gray eyes. "I informed Manchester of your activities anonymously, yes."

"You hired others to kill me, as well."

"More than one person, including a fool named Talbot, who managed to get himself stabbed and tossed into the Thames instead," she hissed. "After twenty-one years of marriage to a man I neither like nor respect, I will not allow you to inherit the earldom, or to make your whorish wife a countess. *I* was born to be countess. A grand hostess, you baseborn menace."

Behind her, Lord Allyn grabbed her arms. Agnes struggled and shrieked, "What are you doing, Milton? I will rid us of this albatross if you will let me pull the trigger."

Her husband struggled to control her. "Did you plan to kill Ryan as well?"

"Somebody must if you're to become earl. Do you have the stomach for such a deed?" she panted, twisting against his hold. Her hand, still clutching the gun, flailed in the air.

"And what of Ryan's son, Rory?" the earl asked. "Were you planning to murder a five-year-old?"

She jerked from her husband. "One does what one must."

The lady pointed the weapon at Drex again. Christina felt numb, as if the scenario were being played out in slow motion. Lady Allyn's finger moved. A loud retort sounded in the air.

The bang shook Christina from her lethargy. She dashed to Drex's side, expecting to see his blood spill across his chest. God, would he writhe in agony and die at her feet?

Instead, Lady Allyn collapsed, clutching her shoulder.

Christina looked up in a daze to find her grandfather holding a smoking gun. She stared in open-mouthed shock.

Lord Allyn ripped his wife's weapon from her fingers. "I may dislike George's boys, but I won't have them murdered, Agnes. Think of the scandal!"

At the magistrate's urging, the undersheriff claimed Lady Allyn and hauled her away.

"There is your anonymous letter writer," Manchester said to the magistrate. "A bitter, greedy woman if ever I saw one."

With a resigned sigh, the magistrate turned away.

Christina cast a last glance across the scaffolding at Drex. He stared back. She loved him and she hated him. But she refused to be his wife, to live under the tyranny of his oppressive thumb until whatever affection she'd once held for him made her bitter.

Biting her lip to hold in her tears of resignation, she watched him. He accepted hugs from his father and Greg. Even Lord Allyn shook his hand and apologized for his wife.

Finally, he looked back at her, his glance spearing her façade of self-control. Before she gave in, before she gave him one more chance…

She gave him a chilly nod and turned away.

* * * *

The following evening, Christina sat listlessly on the sofa. Her grandparents had gone out for the evening, leaving her alone with disillusionment and fury. Both gnawed at her like acid.

They had responded with both sympathy and surprise when she'd announced her separation from Drexell. In answer to their questions why, she had replied something vague about differences and his desire to live in Louisiana.

True, a part of her still yearned for him. Yet had she not walked away from him on the scaffolding, she might have fallen for whatever rubbish he spewed next, if only to be near him again.

He would be back, she knew. Legally, he could force her to resume her role as his wife. And she fully expected him to do just that. He would tell her and himself that it was for her own good, but it would be yet another sham to gain his way.

Christina reclined on the sofa to stare at the carved ceiling. A click of the drawing room's door made her pause.

Drexell stood inside the room, her dim reading light polishing him with shadows. "Hello, Christina."

"So you've come," she snapped. "I will not return. I have no plans to be your wife in the—"

"I know. I hardly blame you. I wish…" he said softly, then shook his head. "It doesn't matter anymore. I came only to say good-bye."

"Good-bye?" Wasn't he going to force her back to his side? Attempt to manipulate his way back into her bed?

He shuffled his feet, scanning the carpet, before raising his gaze to her face again. "I know I can never apologize enough. Neither do I expect you to forgive me." He shrugged. "I had endless hours to think in Newgate after you visited. I truly tried to think as you might and realized you were right. I did act as if I knew best. I didn't trust you with the truth and tell you my identity before we married, or why I had to marry you, as I should have. I didn't tell you I loved you on Grand Bahama or that it killed me to let you go after our journey back to England. So many regrets… I was a fool."

"Thank you," she said stiffly. "Now kindly go. I intend to stay here, with my grandfather, until I can establish a residence of my own. I would also appreciate it very much if you would not attend the *ton's* gatherings for a time so that I may—"

"I'm leaving England with the morning tide. I have a plantation outside of New Orleans. I won't ask you to come with me. I'm freeing you to live your life as you see fit."

Christina gasped. Shock set in, vibrating within her aching chest. He was leaving the country? She drew in a deep breath. She wanted this, she reminded herself.

Then why did her heart feel as if he'd ripped it out?

His sigh filled the air, low and sad. "I ask that you promise me two things, however. First, should a child result from our intimacy, tell me. I grew up without a father and would not wish that kind of emptiness on my son or daughter."

Put that way, denying him the chance to see his child, did she conceive, seemed petty indeed.

"I will," she said.

He drew in a deep breath, crossed the room and reached for her hands. His warm fingers enveloped hers in a familiar caress. Despair tangled with painful yearning in her chest.

Drex cast a searing glance at her, packed with supplication and passion. "If you ever decide that you love me, even half as much as I love you, please come to me." He dropped his gaze. "If that day never comes, then this will be our final good-bye."

He took her face between his hands and lowered his mouth to hers. A barrage of sensations hit her as their lips met. Warmth, familiarity, musk, desperation and longing all combined to become an ache.

Before she could protest, he ended the kiss and left.

Chapter Twenty-One

Drex rose from the blue damask méridienne when he heard the doorbell ring. He prayed this visitor was his father, due to arrive any day. He did not need another nosy neighbor eager to add to his misery with their curiosity about his or Ryan's long absences. He groaned. Or worse, another mama, determined to parade her marriageable daughter before a real viscount, despite the fact he'd informed them repeatedly he had a wife in London.

Christina. Her name rang through his mind, her memory as sharp as the scent of fresh-cut orchids on the table beside him.

God, how he had ached for her since kissing her good-bye three miserable months ago.

The morning he'd left London, he had foolishly hoped she would meet him at the *Lair* and accompany him back to Louisiana. She had not. His next wish had been that she would follow close behind, perhaps make him wait a few weeks to teach him a lesson. That dream had not come to fruition, either. He'd even hoped for a brief time that she would be with child and come to him for the babe's sake. A note he received mere weeks ago crushed that hope.

He had well and truly lost her.

In his attempts to guide her to safety and free his brother, he had used and controlled her, rather than accepted her as a partner. Drex sighed, raking a stiff-fingered hand through his hair. What a dolt. Somewhere during his life in England, she had taught him about true love, which meant giving another the room to make their own choices, even if painful.

Unfortunately, he had realized that too late. The ever-present ache inside him swelled again. Could he possibly wake up one day and find that memories of her smile, her laughter, the shade of her crying eyes no longer haunted him? He doubted it. Christina had imprinted herself onto his heart forever.

A servant opened the door, snapping Drex out of his reverie. His father stood in the open portal, valise in hand. The two embraced.

"Drex." His father held him close. "I've missed you."

"I missed you, too." The two broke apart, and Drex asked, "How is Ryan adjusting to London life?"

"Well, indeed. He's liked by the *ton*. Even Milton is coming to accept him."

"And Lady Allyn?"

The earl shook his head. "After her wound healed, Milton placed her in Bedlam. The magistrate agreed it would serve her better than a term in Newgate, given her mental state." He forced a smile. "Now what about you? You look entirely too gaunt, son. Are you not eating nor sleeping properly?"

Drex shrugged. "When I need to. I have much to do here." *And Christina keeps me from concentrating. God, I miss her.* He pushed the thought aside. "Tell me of Chantal and Rory's arrival in London. Do they enjoy their new home?"

The earl's disapproving frown disappeared for the moment. "Rory loves having a bevy of devoted admirers about. And Chantal is so very happy to be reunited with her husband she is already in the family way."

Drex smiled wistfully. He couldn't be happier for his brother, yet…he wished, yearned for, Christina and a child borne of their love.

He cleared his throat, wishing he could stop the pain engulfing his heart. "Splendid. Rory will need a sibling to keep him out of trouble, I perceive, especially someday when he becomes earl."

His father frowned. "You're the elder twin, Drex. The earldom will pass through your children."

He cast a pained glance to the floor, staring at the high gloss of his black boots. "Unless Christina changes her mind and returns to me, I will not have any children."

"Hmmm," came the earl's response. "We'll see."

Drex raised his gaze, unable to hold back the question in his heart any longer. "How is she? Happy?"

"I suggest you ask her yourself."

His father stepped aside. Christina stood in the doorway.

The world tilted crazily around him. Drex reached out to the mahogany table by his side for support.

"Hello," she murmured, looking fresh and tanned and smiling.

"Lilli," he breathed.

She stood in his house! Hope soared within him as he drank in the sight of her in a soft twill traveling dress of lilac that clung to her familiar curves, much as he longed to. A shaky smile graced her lush pink mouth. Drex didn't know what to say.

"Well, I'll have your manservant show me to another room," his father announced.

Drex nodded absently, staring at his wife as the earl quit the room. Had she come to stay?

"You looked surprised to see me," she said.

"Shocked." He took a step toward her, and her familiar floral scent assailed him with an urge to hold her and never let go.

"I was angry with you," she conceded.

"You had a right to be."

"I did. But...I realized before you left England that, in your position, I might have made many of the same choices. You had no reason to trust me when I stowed away on your ship. Or after my recklessness forced you to pay a thousand pounds in gold to rescue me from my aunt. Thank you for that, by the way."

"I wasn't about to let another man have you, no matter what it cost me."

She smiled uncertainly, then bit her lip. Drex had never wanted to hold her more, but he stood frozen, uncertain.

"Tell me one thing," she demanded softly. "Did you marry me for any other reason than to free your brother?"

"God, yes. I know I didn't tell you that I loved you until it was too late. By then, you had little reason to believe me. If freeing Ryan had been my only goal and I cared nothing for you, I would have simply abducted you after returning you to your grandfather. Or found some other way to use you. I was desperate to have my brother back. But I also ached to be with you. Live with you. Love with you. So I chose marriage. I know now that I should have been honest and enlisted your help in gaining Ryan's release. I truly did mean to tell you the truth. I kept waiting for the right time to tell you. It didn't come soon enough."

"Thank you."

"Come in. Sit. I—"

"I need to say something first." She clasped her hands together, looking nervous. "The first month after you left, I prayed you would stay as heartbroken as you looked the day we said good-bye. I hoped you would drown in unhappiness, so you could understand how I felt."

Had she traveled all this way to complete some scheme of revenge? "I'm intimately familiar with misery, Christina. Believe me."

"That first month, I was thrilled you had finally listened to my wishes and left me alone. Then, some insidious little emotion within me surfaced...and I missed you. I found myself lying abed at night remembering you." She bit her lip again. "Th—the way you rescued me from the ratlines on *The Dragon's Lair*, the chilly night you gave me your coat on the Worthingtons' terrace and—and saved me from Lord Ralston's attention." She cleared her throat and whispered, "The first time we made love. The last time... No matter where I went, something reminded me of you—a gesture, a piece of music, a sunset. I recalled how handsome you looked on our wedding day, how patiently you waited for me after. Revenge was not nearly so satisfying then."

"And now?" he whispered, daring to hope. Sweat beaded his brow, streaked his chest. The familiar ache to hold her assailed him. His heart beat in triple time as he waited for her answer.

"Now I realize that you stayed away and put our future in my hands, despite the pain it cost you. You really *listened* to me. No one else has ever done so. I had to reconsider the assumptions I made about you ruthlessly controlling me." She smiled. "After you left, I expected to see you crawl through my window again, demanding I follow you to the ends of the earth. That you didn't proves you care."

"I love you," he told her, his voice honest, his gaze unflinching. "I have for longer than I wanted to admit."

"Then perhaps you will help me. I have a dilemma."

She took a step closer. The sounds of swishing cotton and her shallow breathing swept across his taut nerves.

"I have no notion what to do with my life," she said.

Drex curled his hands into fists, restraining the urge to tell her to stay. "I can't answer that for you. Nothing has changed since I left London. Our marriage rests in your hands."

She took another step toward him, eyes glassy with moisture. "But

I've no notion how to tell you that I need you and I want to be with you always." She sniffled, her mouth twisting down with the onslaught of tears. "Or that I love you, too."

Drex closed the remaining distance between them, kicked her valise from his path, then swept Christina into his arms. Her delicate arms clutched him, and she sobbed into his shoulder.

He smoothed her golden hair with a gentle hand and soothed her cries with a whisper. "You don't have to say anything else. Just stay with me."

She lifted her head and met his gaze, her eyes as brilliant as cut emeralds. Drex smiled.

"Forever. I'll never let you leave me again."

Her words warmed the depths of his heart. He kissed her hands. "I won't ever give you a reason to ask me to go."

The smile that lit her shining oval face warmed Drex's heart. He reached for her. She met him halfway for a kiss of welcome and promise for the future.

She broke away, laughing. "When will you take me to a swamp?"

The change in subject took Drex aback. He grappled for an answer. "A swamp? Christina, it's not the place for a lady to venture. People can be hurt, even die—"

"Trust me to look after myself, to make my own mistakes."

Drex sighed. "How about tomorrow, you curious little minx?"

She threw her arms about him with a saucy smile. "Maybe the day after. I suspect we will be more than busy until then."

He laughed. "God, I hope so. I've missed you so much."

"You'll never have to miss me again."

Drex claimed her lips for another sweet kiss. She sighed. The *ton* might whisper that the Duke of Manchester's only granddaughter was nothing short of reckless. But now that she had tamed her dragon, Christina much preferred to think of herself as happy.

About the Author

Shayla Black (aka Shelley Bradley) is the New York Times and USA Today bestselling author of over forty sizzling contemporary, erotic, paranormal, and historical romances produced via traditional, small press, independent, and audio publishing. She lives in Texas with her husband, munchkin, and one very spoiled cat. In her "free" time, she enjoys reality TV, reading and listening to an eclectic blend of music.

Shayla's books have been translated in about a dozen languages. She has been nominated for career achievement in erotic romance by RT Bookclub, as well as twice nominated for Best Erotic Romance of the year. Additionally, she's either won or been nominated for the Passionate Plume, the Holt Medallion, Colorado Romance Writers Award of Excellence, and the National Reader's Choice Awards.

A writing risk-taker, Shayla enjoys tackling writing challenges with every new book.

Connect with me online:

Facebook: https://www.facebook.com/ShaylaBlackAuthor
Twitter: http://twitter.com/Shayla_Black
Website: http://shaylablack.com/

Visit Shayla's website to join her newsletter!

If you enjoyed this book, I would appreciate your help so others can enjoy it, too. You can:

Recommend it. Please help other readers find this book by recommending it to friends, readers' groups, and discussion boards.

Review it. Please tell other readers why you liked this book by reviewing it wherever you purchased your book or on Goodreads. If you do write a review, please send me an e-mail at interact @ shaylablack.com so I can thank you with a personal e-mail.

Shayla's Bookshelf By Series

EROTIC ROMANCE

The Wicked Lovers
Wicked Ties
Decadent
Delicious
Surrender To Me
Belong To Me
"Wicked to Love" (e-novella)
Mine To Hold
"Wicked All The Way" (e-novella)
Ours To Love
"Wicked All Night" - Wicked And Dangerous Anthology
"Forever Wicked" (e-novella)
Theirs To Cherish
Coming Soon:
His To Take (March 2015)
Pure Wicked (e-novella, September 2015)

Sexy Capers
Bound And Determined
Strip Search
"Arresting Desire" – Hot In Handcuffs Anthology

Masters Of Ménage (by Shayla Black and Lexi Blake)
Their Virgin Captive
Their Virgin's Secret
Their Virgin Concubine
Their Virgin Princess
Their Virgin Hostage
Their Virgin Secretary
Coming Soon:
Their Virgin Mistress (April 2015)

Doms Of Her Life (by Shayla Black, Jenna Jacob, and Isabella LaPearl)
One Dom To Love
The Young And The Submissive
Coming Soon:
The Bold And The Dominant (February 2015)

Stand Alone Titles
Naughty Little Secret (as Shelley Bradley)
"Watch Me" (as Shelley Bradley)
Dangerous Boys And Their Toy
"Her Fantasy Men" – Four Play Anthology

HISTORICAL ROMANCE (as Shelley Bradley)

The Lady And The Dragon
One Wicked Night
Strictly Seduction
Strictly Forbidden

Brothers in Arms
His Lady Bride, Brothers in Arms (Book 1)
His Stolen Bride, Brothers in Arms (Book 2)
His Rebel Bride, Brothers in Arms (Book 3)

CONTEMPORARY ROMANCE (as Shelley Bradley)

A Perfect Match

PARANORMAL ROMANCE

The Doomsday Brethren
Tempt Me With Darkness
"Fated" (e-novella)
Seduce Me In Shadow
Possess Me At Midnight
"Mated" – Haunted By Your Touch Anthology
Entice Me At Twilight
Embrace Me At Dawn

His To Take
A Wicked Lovers Novel
By Shayla Black
Coming March 3, 2015

Racing against time, NSA Agent Joaquin Muñoz is searching for a little girl who vanished twenty years ago with a dangerous secret. Since Bailey Benson fits the profile, Joaquin abducts the beauty and whisks her to the safety of Club Dominion—before anyone can silence her for good.

At first, Bailey is terrified, but when her captor demands information about her past, she's stunned. Are her horrific visions actually distant memories that imperil all she holds dear? Confined with Joaquin in a place that echoes with moans and breathes passion, he proves himself a fierce protector, as well as a sensual Master who's slowly crawling deeper in her head...and heart. But giving in to him might be the most delicious danger of all.

Because Bailey soon learns that her past isn't the only mystery. Joaquin has a secret of his own—a burning vengeance in his soul. The exposed truth leaves her vulnerable and wondering how much about the man she loves is a lie, how much more is at risk than her heart. And if she can trust him to protect her long enough to learn the truth.

* * * *

"...What about you? You're with another government agency, so you're here to . . . what? Be my lover? Does Uncle Sam think you need to crawl between my legs in order to watch over me?"

Joaquin ground his jaw. She was hitting low, and the logical part of him understood that she was hurt, so she was lashing out at the messenger because she didn't have anyone else. But that didn't stop his temper from getting swept up in her cyclone of emotion. "I'm not here on anyone's orders. In fact, I'll probably be fired for pursuing this case because Tatiana Aslanov isn't on my boss's radar. When it became obvious the agency intended to do nothing, I couldn't leave you to that horrific death. So here we are. But let me clue you in, baby girl. Uncle Sam doesn't tell me who to fuck. I can't fake an erection, even for the

222

sake of God and country. That kiss we almost shared? That was me wanting you because just being in the same room with you makes me want to strip off everything you're wearing and impale you with every inch I've got."

When he eased closer to Bailey, she squared her shoulders and raised her chin. "Don't come near me."

That defiance made him wish again that he was a spanking kind of guy. He'd really like to melt that starch in her spine. If she wasn't going to let him comfort her, he'd be more than happy to adjust her attitude with a good smack or ten on her ass, then follow it up with a thorough fucking. A nice handful of orgasms would do them both a world of good.

"I am so done with people lying to me," she ground out.

That pissed him off. "You think I'm lying to you? About which part? Your parents being agents? That I'm sorry? Or that my cock is aching to fill your sweet little pussy until you dig your nails into my back and wail out in pleasure?"

Her face turned pink. "You're not sorry about any of this. I'm also not buying your sudden desire bullshit."

"I will be more than happy to prove you wrong right now." He reached for the button of his jeans. "I'm ready if you are."

In some distant corner of his brain, Joaquin realized that combating her hurt with challenge wasn't going over well. On the other hand, something about arguing with her while he'd been imagining her underneath him hadn't just gotten his blood flowing, but boiling. If fucking her would, in any way, prove to her that he wasn't lying, he was beyond down with getting busy. If she let him, he'd give it to her hard and wicked—and repeatedly.

"No!" She managed to look indignant, but her cheeks had gone rosy. The pulse at her neck was pounding. Her nipples poked at her borrowed shirt angrily.

He put his hands on his hips. If she looked down, she'd see his straining zipper. "Do you still think I'm lying?"

"I'm done with this conversation."

"If you're telling yourself you don't want me at all, then you're the one lying."

"Pfft. You might know facts about me on paper, but you don't know me."

"So if I touched your pussy right now, you wouldn't be wet?"

He'd always liked a good challenge. It was probably one of the reasons he loved his job. But facing off with her this way made his blood sing, too.

"No." She shook her head a bit too emphatically. "And you're not touching me to find out. Leave me alone." "You're worried that I'd find you juicy.

You're afraid to admit that I turn you on." He stalked closer, his footfalls heavy, his eyes narrowing in on her.

"Stay back," she warned—but her eyes said something else entirely.

"Tell me you're not attracted to me." He reached out, his strike fast as a snake's, and gripped her arms. He dragged her closer, fitting her lithe little body against him and holding in a groan when she brushed over his cock. "Tell me you want me to stop. Remember, you don't like liars. I don't, either."

She didn't say a word, struggled a bit for show. Mostly, she parted her lips and panted. Her cheeks heated an even deeper rose. Her chest heaved. Never once did she look away from him. "I'm involved with someone else."

"If you think whatever you've got going with Blane is going to stop me . . ." He didn't bother to finish his sentence; he just laughed.

"So you're not listening to me say 'no'? You're not respecting my feelings for another guy?"

"Let's just say I'm proving my sincerity to you." He tightened his grip. When she gasped and her stare fell to his lips, triumph raced through his veins. "I'm also testing you. That pretty mouth of yours might lie to me, but your kisses won't."

Joaquin didn't give her a chance to protest again. Normally, he would have. Women 101 was never to proceed without express consent, but this thick air of tension electrifying his blood and seizing his lungs was something entirely new and intoxicating. Their fight seemed to be helping Bailey forget her shock and sadness, not to mention the fact that it revved her, too. She wasn't immune to him—not by a long shot. Thank fuck.

Thrusting a fist in her hair, he pinned her in place and lowered his head.

The Bold and The Dominant

Doms of Her Life, Book 3
By Shayla Black, Jenna Jacob, and Isabella LaPearl
Coming February 10, 2015

After spending weeks trying to reach Raine Kendall, Dominants Liam O'Neill and Macen Hammerman have finally broken past the walls to their submissive's wounded heart. Before they can enjoy their newfound closeness, Liam's past comes back to haunt him when his ex-wife drops in—with a secret that could tear his world apart. Forced to leave Raine in Hammer's care, Liam is stuck on the outside, stewing in frustration and insecurity…and wondering if Raine no longer needs him or if Hammer alone completes her.

Always the pillar of strength, Hammer tries to help Liam while sheltering their woman. But Raine soon discovers the truth that threatens the trio's chance of a happily-ever-after. Determined to hold them together, the two men cook up a scheme to uncover the ex's secret. When an old nemesis returns and targets Raine, can Liam and Hammer come together to slay the danger and save the woman they both love?